Coming

The neighbor, now scowling, said, "My name is Sam Rayburg. I live two doors down. I represent the neighborhood, and I insist on knowing your intentions."

Kate shrugged, with a twinkle in her eye. "Well, the sign says *Crisis Pregnancy Center*, so I'm just going to take a wild guess here, and say there will probably be some pregnant ladies stopping by from time to time."

Mr. Rayburg frowned and said testily. "You can't do that. This is a residential area, zoned specifically for single-family homes. No commercial property is allowed on the block. Lady, you aren't even allowed to sell Tupperware without the block commissioner's written consent.

Kate smiled sweetly. "Well, that shouldn't be a problem, since I have no intention of selling Tupperware. Besides, this is a non-profit organization. Now if you'll excuse me, I have places to go and things to do."

"But… but," Sam Rayburg stammered.

She slammed the door in his face. Turning to her niece, Kate smiled. "Okay, now all I gotta do is find some pregnant ladies who'd like to visit me."

What They Are Saying About
Coming Home To Mercy Street

"*Coming Home To Mercy Street* is the gripping story of characters so real I wanted to add them to my prayer list. The author weaves an intricate and graceful tale of fear and regret, of hope and courage. Gordon knows that before he and Renn can look to the future, Renn must first, with God's help, deal with a past she'd rather forget. Nancy Arant Williams has written a compelling keeper."

—Teresa Morgan
A Risk Worth Taking May 2003
Satin And Steel, October 2003
http://wings-press.com

"*Coming Home to Mercy Street* is a powerful, inspiring drama, injected with the right amount of humor and goodwill. Nancy Arant Williams has created some very endearing characters who, though not initially driven by God's love, eventually come to embrace it. This is a story any reader could embrace."

—Kathryn Lively, author of
Little FLowers and
Saints Preserve Us

"A story that hooked me from page one, Nancy Arant Williams' *Coming Home to Mercy Street* reveals the author's keen perception of human nature. It is a touching and humorous novel of empathy, self-discovery and resolute love."

—Andee S. Davis

"*Coming Home To Mercy Street* is a zany story. I totally loved it. Ms. Williams did a beautiful job bringing her characters to life. The humor in this book had me laughing and helped to hook my interest. I fell in love with Kate and Renn and felt their desperation. *Coming Home To Mercy Street* is a must for your personal library. I couldn't put it down and hope to see many more books by this talented author."

—Laura Hilton,
The Word on Romance

"Author Nancy Williams tells a fresh story infused with humor and delightful characters in *Coming Home To Mercy Street.* The book reads quickly and is difficult to put down. Be prepared to laugh and be touched by the real life characters. *Coming Home To Mercy Street* is a keeper. I hope to see more books by this talented new author."

—Linda Baldwin
About.com

"From the very first page this novel is off and running. If I was in a theater I'd forget to eat my popcorn. Renn is a great character. She grabbed my interest immediately. I totally loved *Coming Home to Mercy Street.*"

—Barbara Brooks

"This is a wonderfully warm, deliciously delightful read, peopled with believably human characters. Nancy has created a masterful blend of fun, tension, pathos and love into a fast-paced story that kept me turning the pages to the very end. I was truly captivated."

Peggy Phifer Author, Editor,
Wordsmith Shoppe News:
www.wordsmithshoppe.com

Coming Home

To Mercy Street

by

Nancy Arant Williams

A Wings ePress, Inc.

Inspirational Romance Novel

Wings ePress, Inc.

Edited by: Lorraine Stephens
Copy Edited by: Sara V. Olds
Senior Editor: Lorraine Stephens
Executive Editor: Lorraine Stephens
Cover Artist: Crystal Laver

Wings ePress Books
http://www.wings-press.com

Copyright © 2003 by Nancy Arant Williams
ISBN 1-59088-860-X

Published In the United States Of America

May 2003

Wings ePress Inc.
403 Wallace Court
Richmond, KY 40475

Dedication

To my family,

John, Jeremy and Piper,

who persevered with me through the dark times,

until we made it out into the Sonshine.

Prologue

Renn Harper shook her head in disbelief. She had done it again. She had always been a 'rescuer', but this was ridiculous.

It all started when her Aunt Kate called and said, "Sweetie, I know you already have a full plate, but I wonder if you would be willing to move in with me for awhile. At least while the children are here."

Kate's manipulation skills were second to none and her niece recoiled at the thought of being near her for any length of time. Renn would have refused the request immediately but for something in her aunt's voice. That *something* had elicited unfamiliar feelings of compassion in her. It wasn't the first time her compassionate nature had gotten her into trouble.

Renn felt more than shocked to learn that Kate's children wanted to come home. Her son, Berke, a forty-two year old investment banker, from upstate New York, would never make the list of Renn's favorite people. Kate's oldest daughter, Evin Clayborne, two years younger than her brother, spent most of her time among the beautiful people. Divorced, she ran a successful ad agency in a suburb of D.C. Kate's youngest daughter, Brynn Blanchard, at thirty-five, partnered in a prestigious Virginia law firm. Even to Renn's untrained eye, she seemed discontented in her marriage to another attorney.

The children visited infrequently and never twice in one year. But now, not six months after their father's death, they were making an appearance. The question was—why?

Recalling the sound of Kate's troubled voice, Renn was puzzled. What could Kate possibly have to fear?

She could see no apparent reason for her aunt's insecurity. Kate had come into millions upon the death of her husband, Rick Martingale. A research scientist with a large pharmaceutical company, he made his money by wisely investing in company stock, which the firm matched one for one.

From all appearances, their relationship had looked solid. Over the years, Renn watched, enamored of the way Rick kept his wife's manipulating to a minimum by simply holding up his index finger to silence her nagging. It seemed a long-standing and mutually satisfying signal, leaving little room for arguments, and amazingly, no residual resentment.

But it didn't really surprise Renn to learn of strife in the family. In fact, there had been little love lost between Kate and her children. Rick, a gruff absentee father during the children's growing up years, left his children exposed to years of their mother's constant wrangling, until they could scarcely tolerate her presence.

Kate, like Peter Pan, never grew up. Raised as a baby princess, she had simply gone in search of greater kingdoms to rule. And now Renn found herself in what could prove to be a heated battle of the wills. She heaved a sigh and shook her head. *Help Lord*.

One

"What on earth am I doing here, Lord?" The words poured out before she could stop them. After nervously stowing her bag in the guestroom closet, Renn Harper pulled her hairbrush out of the drawer, observing her anxious looking reflection. For the first time it hit her just how stressed she felt.

"Okay, get a grip, girl," she told the woman in the mirror. She had stalled leaving the room for long enough.

Renn mentally squared her shoulders and headed down the hall. She found Kate in the library, searching the desk drawers.

"Knock, knock," Renn announced.

Kate smiled, and said, "Come in, dear. I was just looking for some important papers I might have overlooked."

At age sixty-two, Kate appeared ten years younger. Slight with dark hair, which she kept colored, she looked at the world through deep hazel eyes.

Renn said, "If you want help in your search, tell me what we're looking for and I'll pitch in."

Kate looked hesitant, shaking her head. "Thanks for offering. I'm not certain yet exactly what I'm looking for. When I find it, I think I'll recognize it, but there's not much anyone can do to help."

"Is there anything else I can do for you?" Renn asked,

regretting the words even as she spoke them.

"Well, you can help Martha prepare lunch."

I just knew it. I'll be helping the maid and the gardener if I don't learn to keep my big mouth shut.

With still another hour until lunch, Renn let herself out the back door and began to check out the neighborhood. As she meandered down the lane, she took in the preponderance of Georgian and Renascence structures, with an occasional Romanesque oddity tossed in for good measure. Her aunt lived in one of the oldest and most exclusive suburbs of Kansas City. All the homes were enormous and opulent, unlike the homes in Renn's neighborhood, or the one where she had grown up.

The day was glorious, sunny and warm for the middle of April, with just a slight breeze caressing her cheeks.

Little rain had fallen during the normally wet month of April and it occurred to Renn that a drought might be in the offing. But in this neighborhood, a drought would have little effect. The gardeners already held carte blanche to run sprinklers twenty-four hours a day if necessary. No measure was too extreme to keep the flowerbeds lush and green.

Renn circled the block, noticing the more inviting, smaller homes one street away.

She turned the corner and could see down the alley behind Kate's house, where gardeners usually left their trolleys of spades and shovels. No garden trolleys were visible now. Only Berke and Evin, resting in wire and canvas lawn chairs, soaking up sun, obviously deep in conversation. He picked up a trowel off the ground.

Renn held her position, two doors away, unseen in the shade of a garage, watching. The pair argued loudly, becoming more animated by the minute. Berke flew out of his chair, yelled something unintelligible and heaved the trowel as hard as he could. It landed upright, its tip piercing deep into the ground.

Evin stood and retorted something angry. Too far away, Renn could hear none of their conversation.

Deeply curious now, she silently stole past the far sides of the garages that stood between them. She found a shallow alcove next to the garage door nearest them, where she could watch and listen unnoticed.

Berke said angrily, "You know Dad didn't trust Mother with money, which is exactly why he went to such lengths to keep it out of her reach. She has an extremely fair allowance, but now she wants it all."

What is going on?

Evin cleared her throat, releasing an audible sigh. "So how do you propose we deal with it?"

Berke stood up, retrieving the trowel, and hit it against the palm of his hand, making an ominous *thwack*. "I don't know yet. I'm afraid she'll somehow find a way to get around all of Dad's safeguards and spend the money, or tie it up some way, so there will be none left for us, when she dies."

"How could she possibly do that?"

He flopped back down in his chair. "How does she do anything? She finagles and manipulates until everything is just the way she wants it. I know she'd like to dump the house, get something small and travel, but I don't think she has the means to do it, unless she can find a way around the trusts. But listen to me when I say—I wouldn't put it past her. She's been a conniving manipulator from my earliest memory."

His sister frowned. "I can't argue with that. Just spending five minutes in the same room with her stresses me out. She hasn't a good word for any of us, no matter how well we've turned out."

"Knowing all that, you'd still rather just fly away, and see her ruin everything, leaving us nothing to inherit?"

"Well," said Evin, "it depends on how long I have to stay. I know I can't deal with her for more than a week. I'd die first."

Berke said, "Well, we'd better come up with a plan, and fast, if we're going to derail her. If only we knew exactly what she was thinking. I don't know how to act when she talks to me in those pseudo-sweet tones. It affects me like fingernails raked across a blackboard. I want to scream and tell her to shut up."

"You aren't the only one, brother dear."

Evin rose from her chair and ran her long fingers through her glossy brown hair. "Well, whatever we do, I'm only in this for one week. One week. Then I'm leaving. And in the meantime, I'm staying out of her way as much as possible."

Brynn, the youngest sibling, strode toward them, straight-faced. "Mom said you were out here."

"She knows?" Evin frowned in disbelief.

"Why wouldn't she? She has eyes in the back of her head. We've always known that."

Berke dragged another chair into the circle and Brynn collapsed into it. She crossed her pudgy legs and pulled on her snug slacks. The exact opposite of her slender, sophisticated sister, Brynn wore the demeanor of a bulldog, and had the instincts of a street fighter.

She glared at her brother. "So what's going on? Who pulled your chain, Berke? You look like you could kill someone."

He said nothing, while Evin rolled her eyes. "Mom wants to sell the house and travel. If she figures a way to do that, she'll spend every nickel of our inheritance. In fact, I think she'd take immense pleasure in doing it, just to see that we get nothing."

With a perturbed shake of her head, Brynn said, "How do you know that?"

Berke raised his left eyebrow. "She's made it crystal clear, though not necessarily in words. Why are you so out of the loop on this one?"

"You know she and I have never seen eye to eye. She

doesn't tell me anything unless she has to."

Evin asked, "So what do you think we should do, Brynn? Is there any way we can keep her away from the money?"

"Dad took care of that before he died. He locked everything up in trust. He talked to me about his plans. He made sure she had enough to keep the house and pay the bills. Enough to live in the style to which she is accustomed, but not enough to be dangerous, or blow the whole wad."

"Well," Evin shook her head. "She must've found some way around it, because she's been talking to a realtor about selling the house."

Brynn sprang from her chair, trembling in fury. "What? How is that possible? She can't touch the house."

"I don't know," Evin said, shaking her head, "but I met the realtor myself yesterday."

Brynn stopped pacing just long enough to pull off her three-inch heels. How anyone could walk in those things was beyond Renn. Why anyone would want to—seemed to be one of life's great mysteries.

Berke stood. His striking, dark good looks now distorted by anger, he watched his sister pace. "Will you sit down? You're not helping by getting nuts on us."

Brynn sat, but crossed and uncrossed her legs fretfully. "What about Dad's attorney? Why can't we talk with him and find out what's going on? He would know the limits of Dad's plans. He should be able to tell us if she can sidestep his wishes, shouldn't he?"

Evin huffed, "Come on, let's go to my hotel and call the lawyer. You do know his name, don't you, Brynn?"

"Of course. It's Mathew Cromwell. Dad's old golf buddy."

Brynn glanced at her brother and sister, warily. "So who's going to tell Mom we're not staying at the house?"

Berke shook his head vehemently. "Not me, man. No way."

Evin shrugged. "I'll tell her. Berke, I'll ride with you, so wait for me. I'll be right out. Brynn can follow in her car."

He laid angry rubber as he backed out of the driveway in his new Porsche convertible, and sat, gunning its engine at the curb. Brynn slid into her burgundy Mercedes and Renn could see her fussing with her hair and touching up an already thick layer of lipstick. *Did these people never think of anything but appearances*?

Renn watched, as a few minutes later, Evin joined Berke in the car and they sped away. She wished she could've heard the conversation between Kate and her daughter, but could imagine the short but fiery confrontation. Her aunt never had any other kind.

Renn wandered back down the alley and came up the street, using the sidewalk, just in case anyone was interested.

She slammed the door, and heard Kate call, in a quivering voice, "Renn, dear, is that you? Where are you? I thought you were going to help Martha with lunch."

Renn plastered a smile on her face and strode into the dining room. She hated this room, with its salmon colored stucco walls, its dark-stained table for twelve, and oversized chandelier. Ballrooms were for balls, not family meals.

She seated herself on Kate's right. The table looked lost, abandoned, in the cavernous room, with only two chairs filled. It reminded her of elementary school, when most of the class was out sick with the flu.

Renn herself never got sick. She'd been one of the few students with a perfect attendance record every year. Too bored to stay home, she had found school at least a temporary escape from her mother, a chronic hypochondriac.

Renn's parents weren't able to have more children after she was born, due to her mother's fragile health. But her mother milked the infirmity for all it was worth. While Aunt Kate played the part of the baby princess, in control of a large fiefdom, Jill grabbed sympathy by the throat, refusing to let go for love or money.

Their younger sibling, Meg, had died at the age of three, in a drowning accident. Renn believed that, had she lived, Meg probably would have been as neurotic as her sisters.

Helping herself to Swiss steak and scalloped potatoes, Renn could only wish she were home. Home in her small town apartment, not far from Kansas City. She even found herself missing her tedious job as a proofreader for a small Christian publishing house.

Graduating with twin Bachelor's degrees in journalism and literature, Renn sought work in the newspaper business. In a playing field flooded with intense competitive types, her dream died a slow and painful death. Disillusioned and desperate, she had settled for her present, worse than boring job. Resigned now at thirty-three, she was more or less content with her life, with no regrets.

Overall, Renn felt fortunate. Unlike most of her peers, she owed no one. Her apartment was decent, with reasonably stable rents, and she had begun to pursue her dream of writing. A newly published author of articles for Christian women's periodicals, she secretly thrilled at seeing her name in print.

She thought her life might be complete if she got a cat. *Maybe.* She wasn't sure she wanted to commit—even to a pet. She was still weighing the pros and cons, and so far, had not adopted a cat.

Kate sat silent during the meal. The tension was thick enough to cut with a knife.

"Are you okay, Aunt Kate?"

Her aunt's voice quivered with emotion. "The children promised to stay with me for the few days they're here, and now I find they've booked rooms at the Radisson. They sprang the fact on me just before leaving." After a pause, she added, "I know what they're thinking. They're terrified I'll run off with their inheritance."

Renn laid down her fork, her concern evidenced by a crease between her brows. "Kate, what is going on?"

Her aunt, who had yet to take a single bite of food, shook out her napkin and placed it on her lap. "Well, I've got them in an uproar, because I want to sell the house and move. They are under the impression that I like rattling around in this old mausoleum for months at a time, seeing no one but the gardener." Her lips creased into a tight, straight line. "Well, they are sadly mistaken. I hate this house. It's too big, and drafty. I just want something cozy and easy to care for as I get older. Does that make sense?"

"I guess," Renn said doubtfully.

Kate said, "Why are you looking at me like that?"

Renn swallowed a bite of Swiss steak absently. "I just wondered why you didn't arrange for all this before Rick died."

Kate's brows furrowed in a deep frown. "Hmm... let's just say he wasn't crazy about the idea."

"Well, why not? Why should he want to keep you here if you hate it?"

"He never gave me credit for having a lick of common sense about finances. He thought he was the only one around here capable of managing money."

"So what are you up to?"

A cagey look appeared on the older woman's face. "Well, over the years, I handled the household accounts and tucked away money of my own. I have invested and made good on my choices. Of course, this is just between you and me, dear, but I would do just about anything to get shed of this place. As I grow older, I want to live without worrying about housekeepers, gardeners, and maintenance. I don't mind having nice things, but, in my opinion, this is overindulgence."

"Hmm…"

"What are you thinking, dear?" Kate asked.

"Oh, nothing, really. I thought you enjoyed being well off with a beautiful home."

"Well, I've never been fond of it. But at least while Richard was alive and I had someone to share it with, it was home. He's the one who wanted to live here. It was his dream. But now that he's gone, it's just a sumptuous empty shell, echoing with loneliness. Sometimes I think I'll go crazy staying here by myself."

"Is that why you asked me to come?"

Kate hesitated. "Not exactly, dear. I just didn't want to face the children alone. They can be so tiresome sometimes. So controlling."

Renn's first thought was—they came by it honestly.

Instead she said, "So can you sell the house?"

"Well, I hope so. I haven't seen the trust papers and I can't get the lawyers to give me a straight answer as to whether I can, or not. I did have a realtor out to give me a market analysis the other day. She said it wouldn't be hard to sell. I consulted her in a fit of optimistic, wishful thinking."

"What are your other options?"

"Not many. But I've been thinking it over. I've decided that, if nothing else, maybe I can make life so miserable for those in charge, that they would let me break the trust to be rid of me."

"By doing what?"

Kate smiled, her eyes animated. "Well, there's a very worthy crisis pregnancy center, who would love to have even temporary use of the place. I was thinking of letting them have the first floor during the daytime. I can only hope it will upset the neighbors enough to petition me out of the neighborhood, maybe even force the court to let them buy me out."

Her eyes twinkled. "Can you imagine the neighbors' astonishment when I put up the sign saying, *Crisis Pregnancy Center, Open To The Public*, right over the door?"

"You aren't serious, are you?"

She nodded. "I sure am."

"You'd go to those lengths to get out of this house?"

"Well, can you imagine me rattling around here, up and down those stairs when I'm eighty? No ma'am. I want a single level condo, with one or two bedrooms, a fireplace and a view. Oh, and a first floor laundry room."

"Well, you could put a laundry room in the mud room here, couldn't you?"

"I could. And that would be perfectly acceptable to the trustees. But I don't want to, dear. It's just not home anymore, now that Richard isn't here to share it."

After a brief pause, Renn asked, "Do you miss him, Kate?"

The older woman sighed. "In some ways yes, and in others, no."

"What do you mean?

"Well, you probably never saw this side of Richard, but he could be extremely demanding, almost smothering at times. Not that I didn't love him, but there's something somewhat liberating in being on my own. I hope that doesn't sound heartless.'

"No, not at all… So how did the children hear about your plans to sell?"

"Actually, I told them. At first I thought they might be on my side and see how ridiculous it is for me to live alone in this monstrosity. Unfortunately, they don't agree with me at all. I am going to need live-in household help as I get older, when I can no longer handle the stairs."

"And that's not a problem for the trustees or the children?"

"Oh, no, dear. They've planned for all that. It's written up that when I get so I can't manage getting up and down, they'll put in one of those escalator seats, right on the grand staircase and hire nurses, cooks, or whatever else I need. But no matter what, I still can't sell and get something smaller. At least that's what I've heard. As I said, I have yet to see it in writing. "

Renn frowned in bewilderment. "It seems obvious that the estate would save a bundle on household help and expenses if you were allowed to sell and buy something more practical."

Kate shook her head. "That's not the issue here. Both the children and the attorneys see me as incompetent to handle my own affairs and manage my finances. For some reason, they seem to think I'll go through the rest of Richard's millions in a heartbeat if they let me have a single cent."

"Have you sat down and told them about your investments and how they've turned out?"

Kate grimaced. "They will barely speak to me. And they don't seem to be in a listening frame of mind either."

Renn sighed. "Well, there must be some way around this."

After a short silence, Kate looked at her niece, thoughtful, her hand resting on her chin. "Do you see me as high handed, and domineering?"

Renn was stunned at the sudden change of topic. "What? Who said that?"

"All of my children, at one time or another, have said it, almost verbatim."

Renn was rendered speechless for a minute, but Kate refused to back down, saying firmly, "Well, do you?"

"Do I what?"

Kate said, "Listen, I realize I haven't been the easiest person to get along with. But I want to know, have I alienated you as well as my own children?"

"Do you want me to be honest?"

Kate's voice was soft as she said, "Of course, and don't

worry, you won't hurt my feelings."

Hesitating just long enough to gather her courage, Renn said, "Well, I know it may have seemed like you were encouraging your children when you made suggestions, but sometimes that can feel like control and criticism."

"And that's how it felt to you?"

"Truthfully? Yes. Sometimes I have felt stifled, as if you don't respect my abilities, or your children's. I think it made me want to look elsewhere for approval."

Kate's eyes filled with tears and Renn, illogically, felt responsible.

The older woman sighed. "I never realized I was doing that. I honestly didn't. I felt like I was doing the best I could for all of you."

"I know, and I'm sorry. I didn't mean to hurt your feelings."

The older woman patted Renn's hand. "Don't worry, dear, I'll be fine. I just feel sad that I could have hurt you and not known it. At least I'll be able to deal with the truth, now that I know what it is."

Kate followed her niece into the kitchen where Renn filled a teapot and turned on the burner. "How about a nice cup of tea, Kate?"

"To tell you the truth, I'd love some."

Kate stared, dejected, into the flame flickering under the kettle and turned, saying, "Do you suppose I can ever win back my children's trust?"

"Boy, I don't know. They're pretty set in their ways, aren't they?"

"Well, they learned it from the best of teachers, their father and me. He was as much of a... what do they call it these days... control freak, as I ever was. Maybe more. I think perhaps he just wasn't as obvious about it."

Renn gazed at Kate as if seeing her for the first time. *Who is this woman?*

They took their tea into the comfortable and sumptuous library, where Renn started a fire in the stone fireplace. She tucked her legs under her in the corner of the massive leather couch, pulling an afghan over her. Somehow these rooms always seemed chilly.

The older woman tilted her head, watching Renn. "You feel the draft, too, don't you?"

The younger woman nodded.

Her aunt said, "You know, I've had the furnace replaced and checked, but they always say there's nothing wrong with it. The house is built like a mountain and insulated to the nines. But to me, it always feels cold. Period."

"It's odd, isn't it? You'd think a house this well built would be warm."

"The furnace man said the ceilings were too high to be practical. But if I lowered them, which I've thought about, these huge rooms would look ridiculous. That's one of the reasons I would love to unload it."

Renn said, "The heat bills must be tremendous."

"Do you know, dear, that I have never seen a utility bill? I have absolutely no idea what they run. They've always been taken care of by someone else. And now the trustees pay the bills out of the trusts every month."

"Hmm…"

Kate said, "Renn, there are some of your favorite peanut butter cookies in the cookie jar by the stove if you'd like some with your tea."

Renn couldn't stifle a smile. "You haven't forgotten?"

Her aunt laughed and said, "How could I forget that you ate an entire dozen raw cookies as they sat waiting to go into the oven. What were you… two at the time?"

"I can't really remember, but Mom said I was two. I've

always liked peanut butter cookies. It's a character flaw, I guess."

"I wouldn't go quite that far, dear."

Renn brought the cookie jar into the library. Lifting the lid, she said, "They smell great."

She held it out to Kate. "Oh, no thanks, dear. I had Martha make them for you."

"Oh, oh, I can feel those lost pounds calling my name. Okay, one cookie. I'll have one."

Kate gave her niece an admiring glance. "I wanted to ask how much you've lost."

"Twenty-five pounds." It had taken her six months to get the weight off and there was no way she was going to let it creep back on.

"You look like a million, sweetie. And I really like the way you've highlighted your hair. It lights up those beautiful hazel eyes."

"Thanks, Kate. I've got tons more energy now that the weight is gone."

They said good night after the news, taking mystery books with them. They had *that* in common, at least. They loved reading Robin Cook, Mary Higgins Clark, and Sue Grafton. But no nightmare material ever made it into the stacks of bedtime reading fare. The scarier ones they left until the bright light of day.

Renn gave up and turned out her light at eleven-thirty, wondering what tomorrow would bring.

Two

Renn woke to the sound of birds outside her window. It was a balmy, spring day, with just a sigh of a breeze gently swaying the leaves.

She showered, dressed, and went down to make coffee, scrounging for cold cereal. Kate appeared a few minutes later saying, "I've got a meeting with the crisis pregnancy center in a few minutes. You just make yourself at home, okay? Martha will be in from ten to one, to clean up, do laundry and make lunch. She usually puts supper in the refrigerator as well. If you can think of something you'd particularly enjoy, just let her know and she'll take care of it. See you later, dear."

Renn had scarcely finished cleaning up her dishes, when the door opened to admit the three angry Martingale children.

"Where's Mother?" demanded Berke.

Renn put her chin on her hand and leaned on the counter. She said, "Oh, she said she had a few errands. She won't be back for hours."

Now that had been a stretch of the truth. *Forgive me, Lord.*

Evin looked smug. "So where did she go? What's she up to?

An involuntary sigh escaped Renn's lips. "Sorry, she didn't confide in me as to her *exact* whereabouts."

Brynn's face contorted in anger. "Come on, guys. Let's get

17

out of here. We'll come back later."

Berke looked askance at Renn. "Are you sure you don't know where she is?"

She grinned, shaking her head. "Now why would I lie?"

He frowned, then nodded toward his sisters. "She knows something."

The air vibrated with the slam of the door as they left.

When Martha showed up a few minutes later, Renn was surprised to see that it was already ten o'clock.

"Hi Martha. Long time no see."

The older woman drew her into a warm embrace. "It's been years, hasn't it? My, but you've grown into a beautiful woman."

Leaving Martha to her work, Renn donned her Nikes, grabbed her mystery and went out to the yard, which was filled with the fragrance of myriad flowering plants in vibrant pastels. The spring, so far, had been unusually warm and none of the blooms had frozen, as sometimes happened in April.

Before she realized it, she was comfortably nestled in the covered canvas hammock, deeply immersed in an intense scene. It wasn't long before she realized she wasn't alone. From the porch steps, a young man in white coveralls and tee shirt sat watching her.

She jumped a foot, seeing him there. "Oh, sorry, I didn't see you there. May I help you?"

"Sorry," he said with a grin. "Didn't mean to scare you."

With tiny crow's feet at the corners of his blue eyes, and smile wrinkles at the edges of his lips, he was older than her first impression led her to believe. His thick brown hair reminded her of a thatched roof, topping his sturdily built frame, as if he lifted heavy things for a living.

He said, "Hi, I'm Gordy. The gardener."

She laughed, unable to help herself. "Gordy the gardener?"

"Yeah, pretty pathetic, huh? What are you reading that has you so spellbound?"

"Oh, just a good mystery, nothing very literary. Nothing important."

He sighed and nodded in understanding. "Just a lose-yourself-until-tomorrow kind of thing, huh?"

"So you like mysteries, too?"

"I'm a hopeless mysterian."

She rolled her eyes. "A what?"

He looked thoughtful for a few seconds before he explained. "Well, you know how people call themselves hopeless romantics? Well, we mystery buffs need a great word that describes us, and I made that up just for the occasion."

"Works for me, Gordy the gardener."

He studied her with interest. "So what's your name?"

"Renn Harper."

"Nice to meet you, Renn Harper. Cool name. Is it short for something else?"

"No, it's just always been Renn. My mother had a thing for unusual names. Oh, am I in your way, you know, hindering your gardening efforts?"

"Well, I was going to turn on the sprinkler system. I haven't put it on timer yet, but I hate to impose on your reading niche."

"Oh, that's no problem. I can read anywhere."

He asked, "So where are you from?"

"I live in Stafford. A little bedroom community. A suburb of K.C. Do you know it?"

His lips turned up at the ends as his eyes widened. "I sure do. I have an aunt who lives there. Actually, she's no relation, but I've called her aunt for as long as I can remember."

"What's her name?"

"Ellie Mayhew."

"Oh, I know Ellie. She's adorable. And isn't it a small

world?"

He asked, squinting, "So how do you know Ellie?"

"Well, she doesn't get out much, and I take her meals on wheels sometimes."

"Oh, I see. You're her 'wheels' lady."

"Nearly every Saturday."

"She's mentioned you a time or so."

"I hope it was good."

He said, "If I recall, she seemed crazy about you, but she isn't wild about the food you deliver."

She sighed and shrugged. "I know. I wish I could do something to change that, but it's all government regulated, with prescribed amounts of salt and seasonings. Mostly none, from what I hear. It's a shame, isn't it, that these dear elderly folks have to eat tasteless food."

"Say, how'd you like to take a walk to the park after I get through trimming the hedges for your aunt?"

She hesitated briefly, before she agreed. "Sure, I guess. Don't you have other work you have to do?"

"Not really. This is my slow day. Most days I have at least two lawns to care for, but today I only have one. I do four others on this block. I work on your aunt's yard twice a week, so in three days, I'll be back to mow and trim for her. Until then, I just play catch-up, weeding, and mulching and occasionally planting something."

Just then, the sprinklers sprang into action, catching them both off-guard.

"Uh... I'm sorry," he said, flushing in embarrassment, "maybe I did put the sprinklers on timer."

They were drenched by the time they got out of the target area.

He brushed the water from his sturdy arms, as if that would take care of the problem. "I guess I'll have to run home and change. I'll be back in no time. Hey, you won't be gone when I come back, will you?"

"Listen, I live here, at least for right now."

His eyes widened in pleasure. "You do? Great! See you in a few."

His loose overalls made odd whapping sounds as he headed down the block.

Renn changed into dry clothes, hanging the wet ones over the line in the laundry room. Martha noticed, and smiled, "Just toss them in the washer. I'll take care of them."

"Oh Martha, I hate to be any trouble."

"Listen, it's no trouble at all. In fact, your aunt doesn't have half enough to keep me occupied. This is my most boring stop. Why don't you go ahead," she said with a twinkle in her eye, "and mess the place up a little? It'll make me feel like I'm earning my keep around here."

Renn's eyes twinkled in mirth. "I'll do my best to leave you a bathtub ring."

"Thatta girl."

Martha's movements exuded energy, and the laugh lines around her mouth evidenced a genial disposition. She wore her white hair permed, and was casually dressed in jeans and a sweatshirt.

Gordy returned within five minutes, leading Renn to wonder where he lived.

She sat on the porch, reading her mystery, while he dug around in the flowerbeds. Shortly, her backside wearied of the concrete slab. When she could no longer get comfortable, she found a lawn chair cushion and tucked it under her. Every so often, she noticed Gordy glancing in her direction. Her book was so good, however, that she almost forgot about him. But not quite.

In less than an hour, he knocked on the pillar she was

perched against, and said, "Knock—knock. I'm finished. Ready to take that walk?"

Renn picked up her book, marking her place and set it inside the front door. She locked the house, pocketed the key and glanced at him.

"Where are we going?" she asked.

"To the park. Just up ahead."

She looked to where he pointed and realized it was close, less than a block away. She couldn't recall seeing it before and was pleasantly surprised. Like the surrounding neighborhood, it grew lush, with flowering plants and bushes. Renn couldn't help but smile, seeing the abundance of colorful, oversized playground equipment.

The sun chose that moment to recede behind a cloud, making her wish she had grabbed a jacket. She shivered.

"You cold?" he asked with a sidelong glance.

"I hate to admit it, but I'm freezing. I never even thought about grabbing a sweater."

He pulled his long-sleeved sweatshirt over his head, leaving him wearing only a blue pocket tee. "Here, put this on."

She argued, "But then you'll freeze."

"Nah, I never get cold."

He sat down on a swing and she took the one beside him, struggling into the warm sweatshirt that smelled slightly of fabric softener.

He said, "So what do you do?"

"Do?"

"You know," he said with interest, "what kind of work?"

"I'm a proofreader at a small Christian publishing house in town."

"Oh yeah?"

"Yup. I've been there a long time."

"Do you like it?"

She was thoughtful for a few seconds. "Well, it's routine. I mean, it's never been all that exciting, as you can probably imagine. But I love the atmosphere. It's relaxed and the people care about each other."

"So how did you end up working there?"

"I'd have to say by default. My dad wishes I were doing anything else, but there's not much available to someone with journalism and English lit. degrees, without a Master's."

"No kidding. I have a minor in psychology."

"What was your major?"

He laughed, and made a face. "Horticulture. Now wouldn't you just know it?"

Showing off, he jumped out of his swing and began to push hers. He had pleasing features, hair that wouldn't stay put, and laughing blue eyes.

He pushed her really high on the swing and had her squealing as he ran underneath. "Gordy, not so high. Please."

He seemed thrilled to have terrified her. "Hey, where's your sense of adventure?"

Her knuckles were white as she held on for dear life. "I think I left it back in the fifth grade, the last time I sat on a swing."

When she asked about his work, he told her of his love of growing things and she could hear the passion in his voice as he spoke. She wanted to ask him about his psychology degree, but the opportunity never presented itself. In fact, she hardly got a word in.

After a while she said, "I don't know about you, but I'm starved."

"Me, too."

She said, "I can offer you a mean tuna salad sandwich. What do you think?"

"Sold."

23

He raced her the last fifty feet to the front porch, beating her by a mile. They collapsed on the steps, laughing, and catching their breath.

A Tupperware bowl in the fridge contained the tuna mixture. Only minutes later, Renn pulled out the toasted homemade bread, and piled it high with tomato, and lettuce. Absently, she added seasonings to the salad mixture. She filled the plates with grapes, and baby carrots, and began to make a big pitcher of raspberry tea. She suddenly stopped, and looked up.

"Do you like raspberry tea?"

He nodded.

She gave him an appraising glance. "I thought maybe you were one of those macho types who won't drink tea."

"Listen, when it comes to food that I don't have to cook myself, I'm definitely a yes man. I have a well-deserved reputation for eating anything that doesn't eat me first."

She shook her head at his silly turn of phrase.

Gordy took a bite of his sandwich, and said, "Mmm… this is the best tuna sandwich I've ever had."

She looked dubious.

He noticed her look of doubt, and added, "I'm serious. What did you do to it?"

"Nothing special. Just added a few spices and a pinch of sugar, a little gray mustard, and relish. That's about it."

"Well, I hope you won't mind if I ask for the recipe. On my salary, I eat a lot of tuna. And I've gotta tell you, I've never really liked it until now. In fact, it's been hard to look another tuna sandwich in the face at times, knowing it would be so… well… fishy, if you get my drift."

His word picture made her smile. "Sure, let me jot it down for you while I'm thinking about it."

A minute later she handed him the slip of paper, which he

pocketed as if it were diamonds. "I feel like you just gave me a new lease on life. Thanks."

She rolled her eyes, laughing. "You're crazy."

"No, seriously. I eat soup, grilled cheese, tuna, and lots of salads. Not that I couldn't do better if I wanted, but I sort of pride myself on living a simple life."

After lunch, he seemed reluctant to leave. She said, "I had a good time at the park. I can't remember when I've felt so young."

His voice was soft as he asked, "May I call you?"

She shrugged as a shy smile lit her eyes. "I guess. Hey, I don't even know your last name."

"Manning. Gordy Manning, the third."

"Wow, the third. I'm impressed."

"Well, don't be. It's really not worth getting excited about."

"Why is that?"

He lifted his left eyebrow. "That's a story for another day. I will call, though, if you'll let me."

She nodded.

"Of course, I'll probably see you around anyway, since I spend a good part of my working career in this very garden." A twinkle appeared in his eyes. "See you, and may your grass grow tall and fast."

He slammed the door on his way out. Renn frowned; she'd forgotten to ask where he lived.

Just then, Kate popped around the corner of the kitchen and said, "So you met Gordy. What'd you think? Cute, isn't he?"

Renn shrugged. "Well, sort of. He's nice."

A knowing smile lit Kate's eyes. "He's way too intelligent to be a gardener. Did he mention that? I'll bet he didn't."

"No, he just said he held degrees in horticulture and psychology."

"Oh, so you did visit with him?"

Renn said, "He talked me into going to the park to swing. It was fun."

"Well, that's good." She paused before continuing. "Let me fill you in on my little plan. Oh, by the way, the children haven't been by, have they?"

"Yes, actually. They popped in right after you left."

A worried crease etched the older woman's forehead. "You didn't tell them where I was, did you?"

"Are you kidding?"

"Good. Well, listen to this. The crisis pregnancy center is losing their lease, so my timing couldn't be better. Their building sold to the abortionist in town, who's trying desperately to shut them down, and they have to vacate by the first. That gives them a couple of days to get moved in."

"Kate, did you really invite them to move in here?"

"I sure did, kiddo, and we're going to have a ball."

Renn shook her head, wide-eyed.

Her aunt continued, "This has been in the offing for several days. I sprang for one of those canvas signs you hang up. It's four by ten feet. So the world will know that we're open to the public. I had to pay extra to get it on such short notice. I even stopped by the Messenger Office... that's the local paper—and put in an announcement that as of the first, we're open for business."

"You didn't!"

"I'll get out of here one way or the other."

Renn chuckled. "I just bet you will."

She was getting up to clear the table, as Kate said, "How would you like to stick around awhile and help me on my little crusade?"

Ren looked thoughtful. "I'll have to check with my boss and see if he'll be needing me. I'll let you know as soon as I know anything though, all right?"

The phone rang and Kate surprised her by saying, "It's for you, dear."

Puzzled, Renn picked up the phone and heard Gordy's voice. "Hey, I have a chance to get two tickets to see Michael Dempsey in concert and I wondered if you'd like to go."

"I guess I've never heard of him."

"What planet did you say you were from?"

When she didn't respond, he said, "Sorry, that wasn't very nice, but honest, he's a cool contemporary Christian artist. Our age and everything."

"What do you mean our age? How old do you think I am?"

"Middle to late twenties, I'd say. How'd I do?"

She laughed. "You're crazy, do you know that?"

"You already said that. It's not the worst thing I've been called, but what do you say? Do you want to go?"

She said gently, "I guess I'd like to know you a little better before going out. I hope you understand."

"Sure, that's cool. See you around then." She could hear a twinge of disappointment in his voice.

"Thanks for the offer. Really. I appreciate it."

She hung up, feeling ambivalent. She really liked the guy, but didn't know him from Adam. From past miserable experiences, she had learned to go slowly when it came to relationships.

Kate walked in a few hours later, dragging a heavy, folded canvas sign. Just then, Renn recalled that the cousins hadn't shown up a second time as they'd promised.

Dropping the canvas bundle on the floor, Kate waved the corner of the banner and said, "I'm going to call Gordy and ask him to help me mount this thing. I got all the hardware, but I think it's a two-man job. I could sure use *your* help."

Renn's mouth opened involuntarily, taking in the sign as Kate unfurled it. "I can't believe you, girl."

"I know, I've been told I'm a couple of sandwiches short of a picnic, but then a few is better than no sandwiches at all, right?"

A huge pile of laundry was calling her name from the kitchen table, when Gordy rang the bell.

"Hey, your handy-dandy, all-around cordial, fix-it man has arrived."

He was showing off for her benefit and she couldn't help but giggle at his antics. He took one look at the banner and did a double take. "That's the banner you're mounting on the front of your house? Are you crazy?"

Renn shook her head. "Don't look at me. It's Kate's idea."

He looked at Kate quizzically. She said, "What's wrong with it?"

"Well, for one thing, you're living in a single family residential area, not a commercial zone. Whoa, lady, you're going to be in hot water before you can say Peter Pan."

"Do you think so?"

"Listen, I know the neighbors around here, and the one thing about which they do not possess a sense of humor—is their homes. This is going to mean war. I guarantee it."

Kate looked at him sideways. "So does that mean you won't help me mount the sign?"

He stuck out his tongue with a frown. "Do I look like a quitter? Besides, this is probably the most excitement this neighborhood has seen since VE Day."

Kate laughed and shook her head. "You weren't even around for VE Day."

"Well, I can use my imagination, can't I?"

Where did this guy come from?

He dragged a twenty-four foot metal ladder from the garage, making a terrible racket. At this rate, the neighbors would know the score even before the banner was hung. Then he found a rickety wooden extension ladder for Renn. During the next hour and a half, Gordy's witty one-liners kept Renn laughing, causing her to teeter precariously on her perch. Even her longest reach was barely long enough for the job.

He began by drilling holes in the base of the second floor balcony for the mounting brackets. The banner was seriously heavy. A big wind could haul it to kingdom come, if not affixed properly on all four corners, with supports about every two feet, in between.

He shot a wiseacre look down at Renn. "You're a little short for this kind of work, aren't you, shrimp?"

"Hey!" she shouted back, feigning a pout.

The letters on the sign were over a foot tall and printed in bold black script. The neighborhood and the world would discern their mission, in no uncertain terms, with one swift glance in their direction.

Renn felt a little nervous, anticipating the battle to come. Not only the cousins, but also the neighbors, and even the city fathers, could be breathing down their necks in no time at all.

After standing on the ladder, with her arm extended for what seemed like hours, Renn finally said, "Hey, you going to get to my end anytime today? Come on. I'm dyin' over here."

His smile was warm when he said in a sing song voice, "I'm coming. I'm coming."

The sun felt warm, a while later, when Gordy stood admiring his handiwork. "Thanks for the help. I don't think your aunt could've done your part. She's gutsy, but a little over the hill to be on a ladder for such a long time."

Renn shook her head in amusement at the thought. The way he put things was funny, and he wasn't even trying very hard.

~ * ~

They were finishing supper, when the front door slammed and in stomped the cousins. "Mother," yelled Brynn, "what on

God's earth do you think you're doing?"

Kate picked up her napkin, dabbed at her mouth, and smiled. "And hello to you, too, Brynn, dear."

"Mother, have you lost your mind?" Evin shouted from the front door. Kate's usually sophisticated daughter now looked as ordinary as anyone else, glowering in anger.

Berke plopped into a chair across the table from his mother, shaking his head. "How you could do something like this, shaming us all, is something I will never understand."

Kate shrugged. "Children, I want you to listen. I have made a very important decision. I have meddled in your lives for entirely too long, not even realizing I was doing it. But now that I know, I've decided it takes too much energy to meddle at my age. I just want you to know that I will be giving no more advice or suggestions. If you need them, you'll have to write to *Dear Abby*."

Her niece knew Kate had no intention of being humorous, but Renn couldn't stifle a giggle. Unfortunately, she was alone in her humor.

The cousins glared at her in silence.

Brynn said, "Renn, you're helping her in this ridiculous endeavor, aren't you?"

She shrugged. "All I did was hold the sign."

Kate said, "I am getting out of this house, one way or the other. And I am doing it the only way I know how. So, if you will excuse us, Renn and I have some things to discuss in the library over our coffee."

The three children stared after their mother open-mouthed, shaking their heads; a minute later a vibration shook the house as the front door slammed behind them.

Renn shook her head. "Wow, Kate, you're taking your life in your hands, talking to them that way."

Kate sighed and leaned against the counter. "At my age,

honey, it's not much of a risk. It does a body good to live life on the edge. Much better than being emotionally dead and not realizing it until years later."

"Is that what this is? A grab for the brass ring of adventure?"

The older woman gave her niece a rueful glance. "That's not my goal, but I can't say I wouldn't welcome some excitement. If nothing else, I've got the kids' attention. And in a day or so, I'll have the neighbors' and the city's, too, if all goes well." She took a sip of coffee and said seriously, "There's just one thing you need to keep in mind."

"What's that?"

"Don't forget to duck."

The younger woman's eyes lit up in glee. *The metamorphosis is now complete.*

Kate picked up the dishes and headed for the kitchen, leaving her niece still marveling. Her aunt no longer resembled the meddling woman she had moved in with.

As she went to bed that evening, she could only wonder what would happen next.

Three

The sound of the doorbell reverberated through the house at seven-thirty the next morning, and Renn opened it in her pajamas, to find a squad of neighbors on the porch. The spokesman, a distinguished-looking gentleman in his early sixties, stepped to the door, looking grim. He noticed her pajamas and looked her up and down with a frown.

After a short hesitation, he gestured toward the banner. "This is a practical joke, isn't it, young lady?"

Stepping aside, Renn said, "Listen, I think you'd better talk to my aunt."

At that moment, Kate walked down the stairs, looking classy and competent.

"Did I hear someone ask for me?" she queried casually.

The grim-faced man said, "Mrs. Martingale, we must know. Is this is your idea of a practical joke?"

Kate took her time answering, brushing nonexistent lint off her slacks and fussing with her collar.

She finally said, "If it is, it's the most expensive practical joke in history. I'll have you know I paid eight hundred smackers for that banner. Does that sound like a practical joke to you?"

Renn couldn't believe her aunt could be so cavalier. Her own nervous system felt frayed.

The man, now scowling, said, "My name is Sam Rayburg. I live two doors down. We represent the neighborhood and insist on knowing your intentions."

Kate shrugged, with a twinkle in her eye. "Well, the sign says crisis pregnancy center, so I'm just going to take a wild guess here and say there will probably be some pregnant ladies stopping by from time to time."

Mr. Rayburg frowned and said testily, "You can't do that. This is a residential area, zoned specifically for single-family homes. No commercial property is allowed on the block. Lady, you aren't even allowed to sell Tupperware without the block commissioner's written consent."

Kate smiled sweetly. "Well, that shouldn't be a problem, since I have no intention of selling any Tupperware. Besides, this is a non-profit organization. Now if you will excuse me, I have places to go and things to do."

"But… but," Sam Rayburg stammered.

She slammed the door right in his face.

Turning to her niece, Kate said, "Okay… now all I gotta do is find some pregnant women who'd like to visit me."

Renn grinned conspiratorially, and Kate drew her into a big hug.

The younger woman asked, "Do you suppose the neighbors will organize a picket line?"

Kate laughed at the thought. "*That* I gotta see. People in this area value their ability to keep a low profile above all else. In fact, they'd sacrifice just about anything to maintain a dignified persona. So it's highly unlikely that we'll see them carrying picket signs."

"Let's hope you're right."

Renn took time to dress for what she knew would probably be a three-ring circus.

A few minutes later, she answered a knock on the door to find a police officer, followed by the cousins, who stood on the porch.

"Are you Kate Martingale?" he asked. Renn stepped aside as Kate held out her hand.

Her niece watched as the officer handed Kate an envelope, inside of which was an injunction, demanding that she cease and desist operation of the crisis pregnancy center, according to local zoning laws.

The cousins looked particularly smug, when they silently turned to leave.

Renn couldn't help but feel proud of her aunt, who seemed to take the threat of legal action in her stride.

Kate left a while later and returned with several vehicles trailing behind her. They pulled up at the curb, and supplies and lightweight furniture, from the local CPC, nearly flew into the house. Several older woman and even a few pregnant girls of varied ages pitched in to help. Periodically, she noticed that the mothers-to-be stood out on the front walk and stretched. Back pain, was Renn's guess.

Several more cars and a few pickups followed a while later, with men tumbling out, eagerly grabbing things to haul inside.

Kate held the door and supervised the move. Office equipment, supplies, and classy comfortable-looking furniture found a home on the first floor of the mansion after the former pieces were moved aside, or stored in the garage. Several small but inviting sitting areas appeared in the stunning thirty-five by twenty space.

The dining room was quickly transformed into an office/counseling room, with the ugly table banished to the garage, along with its dozen formal chairs. Renn thought Kate looked particularly pleased to see the table depart.

The older woman said, "I've always despised that thing. It's ridiculous for one or two people to eat at a table made for twelve. We're going to eat in the kitchen from now on. What do you think?"

Renn couldn't help but smile. "You've read my mind, Kate. I've never liked that thing either. It's just never lent itself to small, intimate conversations, has it?"

"You got that right. I'd better get busy," said Kate, heading for the door.

Renn wandered into the kitchen, where Martha was working on lunch. The older woman grinned and Renn said, "What's so funny?"

Martha said, "I've been praying, for years, that something would blow Kate out of her spiritual apathy, and I think this will just take care of that little problem."

Renn's eyebrows shot up. "Martha, you're a Christian?"

"I sure am, honey, and I know you are, too. This is going to be fun, isn't it? Waiting to see what the Lord will do next? Almost as exciting as those mysteries you enjoy so much."

Renn said, "You know, I have a feeling this whole thing will either blow up in our faces, or turn out to be the most fun I've had in years."

The older woman nodded. "You're probably right, but one way or another, it won't be dull, will it?"

"I think I can safely agree with you on that. What's for lunch?" Renn asked.

"Salads. Including a giant Caesar, as well as fruit compote and some chicken salad for protein. Takes a lot of energy to move a ministry, you know."

"Mmm…sounds great. Do you need any help?"

"Sure, honey. Just tear up that romaine for me and put the Caesar together."

Martha wielded a sharp knife, deftly chopping celery for the chicken salad.

Renn said, "I feel so bad that Kate can't sell the house and find something more comfortable for her."

Martha lips twisted into a narrow frown. "I've got to say I'm not surprised. It's just like Rick to do something like this. I think he saw her as nothing but an empty-headed female. She'll always be comfortably fixed as long as she lives here, but there is no provision for her to move. At least that's how it looks now."

After a pause, she continued, "I have to brag on her. I know she won't mind if I tell. She saved and invested a good deal of her household money, scrimping where it wouldn't be obvious and has a nice little nest egg to show for it."

"She told me. I think she's amazing." Hesitating only briefly, she added, "She's even changed since I moved in."

"I know," Martha said, with a knowing look. "She's stopped controlling, hasn't she?"

"You noticed it too?"

"Honey, I'm with her everyday. I'd have to be blind as a bat not to notice something like that. She's a lot more fun now, too, isn't she?"

Renn said, "The twinkle is back in her eyes. Or maybe I shouldn't say *back*, since I guess I've never seen it before. Perhaps it's something new."

"I can tell you about that. She had it when she was younger. She and I have been friends ever since I began keeping house for her nearly forty years ago. She exuded spunk and joy in those early years. But Rick's tight control was like an insidious disease and, after a while, it seemed like someone had wrung all the joy right out of her."

"Hmm… That had to be hard to watch."

"Boy, howdy, was it ever."

"Did Uncle Rick claim to be a Christian?" As if to explain, she said, "I never saw much of him."

She chopped chicken breast into tiny cubes and stuck them in a large glass bowl with the diced celery. "He sure talked like one, but I think it's more likely that he memorized the rules and joined the club rather than actually flowing with any fruits of the spirit, if you know what I mean."

"I sure do. He always seemed tough on himself and everyone else, in a gruff, paternal sort of way."

Martha frowned. "Not to speak ill of the dead, but I think he knew just how much power to use to get his way. Those three kids are proof positive of his heavy emotional hand on them. If they aren't three of the most miserable people I know, I don't know who is."

"Can't disagree with that. The irony is that they're so successful. From the world's point of view, they have everything they could possibly want. Did you see Brynn's Mercedes and the Porsche Berke is driving?

"I did. But, merciful heavens, you should've been here to watch them all squeezing into his dinky sports car the other day."

Renn said, "You know, I have a theory that people take up more room when they're mad."

Martha giggled, hugging her. "Oh, honey, it's going to be so much fun having you around."

A crowd of over twenty stood in the living room as Renn walked in. The director, Craig somebody, was asking the blessing on lunch. Kate looked at Renn and asked, "Is lunch ready?"

"It sure is. Everyone come and help yourselves."

Martha set a huge bowl of chips and a vegetable tray next to the beautiful array of salads. A crystal pitcher of lemonade and one of iced tea sat off to the side, with rows of glasses nearby.

Renn made herself useful by pouring drinks and handing out napkins and forks.

Spirits were high, when Craig tapped a knife against his glass and said, "I want to thank our benefactress for her generosity, for however long it lasts. Thanks, Kate."

He grinned at her with a look of affection. *Hmm… I wonder if there's something between them.*

After lunch, the leftovers of which weren't enough to feed the birds, she and Martha cleaned up. She could hear Kate's voice, directing traffic and finalizing furniture placement.

"Martha," Renn asked, "what about Craig? Is he married?"

"He's widowed. His wife, Anne, died of cancer a year ago."

"It looks to me like he's got his eye on Kate."

"It's plumb obvious, isn't it?"

"How did they meet?"

Martha lowered her voice. "She donated to the CPC, then started volunteering there, even before Rick died, because he forbade outside employment."

Renn shook her head. "What a prehistoric way of thinking."

"Well, from where I stand, the issue isn't whether you work outside the home or not. The important thing is to be where God wants you. Some folks He wants in the home and some out. However, it does seem that wherever He wants you, the grass is always greener… if you know what I mean."

Renn said, "So Martha, are you happy now that you're finally earning your keep?"

She grinned. "You'd better believe it!"

"Is she going to feed them like this everyday?"

"Well, probably, but most days only one or two people will man the center. I'll enjoy having something to keep me busy.

And maybe I can even help out in some small way. Who knows what doors the Lord may open?"

After washing dishes, Renn wandered into the living room, now a warm and inviting reception room. Off to the right, a wicker partition stood to hide the office equipment. On it, several classic, framed hunting prints hung, impressively displayed.

At the far end of the room, another wicker screen enclosed Craig's office. In the dining room, now an office/counseling room, a volunteer loaded pamphlets and videos into a walnut bookcase, which earlier had held a collection of Lladro figurines.

The large bathroom now housed a cherry wood highboy, commandeered from an upstairs bedroom, to house necessary pregnancy testing materials.

Renn couldn't help but shake her head and smile. It had all happened so fast. The mausoleum no longer echoed with emptiness. A new atmosphere of expectancy prevailed.

Martha stuck her head around the corner. "I was looking for you. I think I'm going to leave the rest of the cleaning until the move is complete. Will you tell Kate for me that I'll be in early tomorrow to finish up?"

Renn smiled. "Sure thing, girl. See you later."

Martha left with a spring in her step. Just after Renn closed the door, someone knocked.

Gordy's cheerful face grinned at her from across the threshold.

"Hey, it looks like this is where the action is. What's going on?"

"Come in," Renn said, "and see for yourself."

His eyes widened. "Yikes, she really went and did it, didn't she?"

She nodded.

He said, "No flack from the neighborhood folks or those kids of hers?"

"Oh, sure. Plenty of that."

"So tell me, what's happening?"

She sighed and shook her head. "The cousins came by with a police officer, to deliver an injunction, and the neighbors gathered on the porch before eight this morning, to protest, just as you predicted. You seer you."

He laughed, pushing his bushy hair out of his eyes.

"So—what? She's not taking the injunction to heart? It looks like she plans to set up shop here permanently."

She shrugged. "That's the way I read it."

A frown creased his brows. "I wonder what will happen if she refuses to cooperate with the law? She can get into major trouble, if anyone forces the issue."

"Well, I'll bet we find out in a big hurry."

He met her gaze. "So what are you up to?"

"Not much. Just finished helping Martha fix lunch for this mob. Did you eat?"

He looked wistful. "Actually, no. I don't suppose there's anything left?"

"Not a crumb. But I know she has chicken and noodles set aside for supper and she's got a thing for making way too much. We have scads of food left over after every meal."

"Well," he said as a wide smile spread from one ear to the other, "you just might be seeing my face around here more often if that's the case."

"Make yourself at home," Renn said, gesturing him to a barstool at the counter.

She added, "I'll just be a minute, okay? Pour yourself some tea or lemonade. It's in the fridge."

He poured a tall glass of lemonade and sat down, staring at her.

"What?" she said.

"Just wondered when this new endeavor will officially open for business."

"Aunt Kate must have been planning this for several days. She's already put an announcement in the paper. It's opening tomorrow, at nine a.m."

"Wow, that's what I call fast work."

"The CPC lost its lease, and needed to be out before the first. It seems the building was purchased by the local abortionist, who was hoping to shut them down permanently."

"Well, that's one way to get rid of the opposition, isn't it?"

She said, "I heard one of the volunteers say they were praying, and thought they'd be out on the street, until Kate came in and invited them here."

"Well," said Gordy, as he shook his head. "This ought to be very interesting."

"That's an understatement if there ever was one."

"Were the kids mad?"

She rolled her eyes. "Is the pope Catholic?"

"Yes, I believe he is."

She made a face. "The kids were furious. But they looked pretty smug when the officer handed Kate the injunction."

"Doesn't look like they know her very well, does it?"

Renn said thoughtfully, "You know, I've only been here a few days, but Kate's done a one-eighty. I mean, she's a changed woman."

"In what way?"

"Well, you know that she's been a somewhat controlling woman?"

He hesitated before nodding. "I'd have to agree, that sounds like Kate."

She shook her head. "Well, not anymore."

"Really? What happened?"

41

Renn paused, handing him a plate of food, and a napkin. "I'm not sure. She asked me if I thought she was calculating and manipulative, said that's what her children told her."

His eyes were wide, as he took a sip of his drink. "And what on earth did you say?"

"I asked her if she wanted the truth. She did. So I told her that I felt she was holding on too tight, probably not even realizing it. She agreed, saying she thought she had always done the best she could for her family."

"Go on."

"She looked sad and said she had never seen herself as manipulative. I really think that was the turning point. In fact, she told the kids the other night that she didn't intend to make any further suggestions, or give any more advice and that if they wanted it, they'd better write to *Dear Abby*."

"And how did they take that?"

"Well, I don't know exactly. Right after that, she invited them to leave, saying she and I had business to discuss over coffee."

"Whoa, is she living dangerously, toying with those three."

She gave an involuntary sigh. "That's what I said. I think they'll make her life unbearable, given half a chance."

He looked bewildered. "What's all this about anyway? I don't get it."

Renn sat down, and watched him roll his eyes in pleasure as the fork full of chicken and noodles hit his taste buds. "Hey, this is great. I could get used to this kind of cooking." He paused. "Oh, yeah, you were saying?"

"It all started because Rick refused to believe that Kate could handle money. I guess for some reason he saw her as flighty and irresponsible, which she isn't. But he locked everything up in trusts and she only gets money for necessities, enough to be comfortable and keep up the house. He tied up the property, so she can never sell. She hates rattling around in this monstrosity—her words. She wants to get rid of it and find something small and comfortable."

He looked puzzled. "But what does that have to do with what's going on now?"

"Well, since the trustees and the kids won't let her sell, she invited all these people in, to keep her company, to say nothing of being used in their ministry."

He grinned before his eyes widened in awe. "And?"

"She thinks if her behavior is outrageous enough, she'll get either the kids or the neighbors to buy her out or throw her out and let her be on her way."

"But the trust can't be broken, can it?"

"I guess it depends on what kind of trust it is. The trustees aren't really explaining the details, so she's taken matters into her own hands."

"I'll say."

At that moment, Kate strode into the kitchen. "Hi Gordy." She glanced at Renn, "Honey, could you keep the coffeepot going for the gang? They said they could use a jolt of caffeine right about now."

Gordy laughed and tilted his head. "A jolt, huh?"

Kate joined in the laughter. "That's what they said. I think it might be fun hanging about with young folks again."

"It looks like it's rubbing off already," added Gordy.

"Thanks for the help, dear," said Kate, turning to leave the room.

As Renn started another pot of coffee, Gordy shrugged his shoulders. "I see what you mean. That's not the Kate I've always known and loved. No resemblance whatsoever."

"See, I told you."

He swallowed a sip of lemonade, then said, "So how long will you be staying?"

"Well, I talked to my boss last night and he said things are slow. Summer always is. It probably won't really pick up until just before the next school year begins. He offered to let me have the summer off if I want it."

He gazed at her with interest. "So do you? Want the summer off, I mean?"

She shook her head in disbelief. "If you would've asked me that four days ago, I'd have said I wanted out of here ASAP. But things have changed so much now that I think I'll hang around just to see what happens. Kate offered to pay my bills until I go back in August."

His eyes were twinkling as he said, "It's like one of your mysteries, isn't it? You just have to stick around for the ending."

They joined the group in the living room and helped put the finishing touches on the place, before the crowd dispersed. A short time later, Kate excused herself for a much-needed rest, leaving Renn and Gordy to fend for themselves.

Gordy said, "Well, I'd better be on my way."

"What? Things to do and places to go?"

He shrugged. "Not really, just don't want to be making a nuisance of myself."

She frowned. "Did I give you that impression?"

"Well," he sighed, laying his chin in his palm, "you did turn down my invitation to the concert. I didn't know whether to take that as a hint or not."

Renn gave him a rueful smile. "Let me clear up this little misunderstanding. I like having you around. You make me laugh, and I need more of that right now."

He wiggled his eyebrows and flipped an imaginary cigar in a Groucho Marx imitation, saying, "Glad to help, sweet thing."

She giggled at his antics. "See what I mean? Everything that comes out of your mouth makes me laugh. You're a funny guy, Gordy."

"I don't try to be, honest."

"I know. That's why it's so perfect. You don't even know you're doing it."

He gazed at her with interest. "So why wouldn't you go to the concert with me?"

"It's really nothing personal. I've just had some bad experiences with guys. To be honest, I don't feel I know you well enough yet."

He looked serious. "I believe what we have here is a trust issue. Okay, well... what say I remedy that situation right now? What would you like to know?"

She shrugged but said nothing.

He looked thoughtful. "I'll give you the Reader's Digest condensed version of my life. Don't worry, it's not going to put you to sleep."

"I never thought it would."

"Okay. Well, once upon a time, I was a baby."

She tilted her head, wide-eyed, to see if he was serious. He was, so she squelched a giggle that threatened to overflow and listened.

He went on, "My mother died when I was born. Oh, I forgot to say I'm thirty-four." After a pause, he continued, "I was raised by my dad, who still lives in the city. He's a good guy, but very serious, an attorney. By the way, I got two-thirds of the way through law school and decided I could never do what he does. It's a drag. Sorry, that was an aside." He gave her a mischievous smile. "Let me get back on track."

He cleared his throat. "My grandparents cared for me when Dad had to travel, which he did frequently, and they were the best thing that ever happened to me. They loved the Lord and lived their Christian life with enthusiasm and joy. In fact, I've never met anyone else who was quite so adept at living the abundant life. It changed me. My father's influence could have made me hunger after money and prestige, but my grandparents had exactly the opposite effect on me."

"They lived just a block down, on Millstone Road. They left me the house when they died. I was their only heir, besides my father and he had no use for the place. You'll have to come and see it sometime."

She smiled. "I'd love to."

"Where was I? Oh, yeah. I attended law school. And like I said, I liked the idea of pleasing my dad. But not bad enough to do the attorney-in-a-three-piece-suit routine, or charge fortunes from people who could scarcely afford it. At first Dad flipped out when I told him it wasn't for me. There were a couple of years where he barely acknowledged my existence. But I didn't let it bother me. If he wanted me in his life, he knew where to find me."

He continued, "I guess he must've decided he could live with my lifestyle, because now we talk about once a week. It's not like we're terribly close, or anything. But listen, I'm grateful for what I can get at this point. I don't mind being an only child, and I like being by myself, except for holidays, when families have such great times together."

"So you're an only child? So am I."

"Really?" He blinked, tilting his head, stretching back in his stool.

She frowned. "What?"

"I thought for sure you were from a family of four or five well-adjusted kids. I mean you seem so normal."

"I don't know about that."

He said, "So there you have it. Any questions from the peanut gallery?"

She grinned and shook her head. "No sir. No questions." She paused. "Wait, one question. Why did you choose to be a gardener?"

"Because it fills me up and lets me bless the Lord with every touch of my hand. It's fulfilling and relaxing and I love it."

"I'd say you're good at it, too."

He stood up, and bowed at the waist. "Why, thank you, ma'am."

She laughed, rolling her eyes at his crazy antics.

"Okay, your turn."

"For what?"

He said slowly, patiently, "Your turn to tell me your life story."

She felt a hot flush creep up her neck. "It's boring. Really. Not interesting at all."

"Why don't you let me decide?"

"Well… okay. I was born in Kansas City when my parents were very young. I almost wondered if… well, never mind. Anyway, my mother died of heart disease last year. Dad's still around, doing construction work, but he's actually a writer, which is why I took to my chosen field. He had me proofreading as soon as I could read."

"He works in construction and is a writer? That seems like an odd combination."

"You wouldn't think so if you knew him. He's really big— strong, with muscles out to here. He has a hard time sitting still without an outlet for lots of energy. The odd part is that he's got the heart of a writer."

"Sounds like an interesting guy."

"He is."

"Are you close?"

"No, not really. I never quite measured up to his standards."

"Okay, go on," he prompted.

"Well, besides Dad, Aunt Kate is my only surviving relative, unless you count the cousins, which I don't, because they think they're too good for me. But that's okay. I can still love them from afar," she said, rolling her eyes.

"What was your mother like?"

"Oh, she was fragile. She had a heart condition for years, and like Aunt Kate, she milked it for all it was worth. I'm not saying I didn't love her, but she didn't make it easy."

"What does that mean?"

"Having been sick most of her life, she was used to lots of attention, so even when things were going well, she had this way of wringing the sympathy out of everyone who came within twenty yards."

He nodded. "Oh, one of those."

"Yup."

"Well, you seem to be pretty well adjusted."

"You do what you can with that type of person."

"Wow, such insight from one so young."

"I'm not that young."

"What are you, let me guess? Twenty six, am I right?"

"Sorry, no cigar. I'm nearly thirty-four."

"Bummer, I'm usually right on target. I guess it's your baby face that makes you seem so young."

She made a face. "I don't know whether to take that as a compliment or an insult."

He gave her a wide, winning smile. "A compliment, of course."

She said, "Let's go into the library. No need to spend our entire afternoon in the kitchen. Oh, do you like peanut butter cookies?"

"Ooh, lead me to them."

She handed him the cookie jar and said, "Bring them with you, why don't you?"

He sat on the floor just as she had thought he would. He crossed his legs, Indian style, and put the cookie jar in the space in between. "Hey, just give me the high sign if you want a cookie, and I'll toss you one, all right?"

She favored him with a wry smile. "I'll be sure to do that."

He took a bite and slowly chewed it. "Whoa, these are great. In fact, they're superb."

She grimaced at him, shaking her head.

He shrugged. "What?"

"You must be a pretty terrible cook, if everything you've put in your mouth in this house tastes like ambrosia."

He rested his chin in his palm, with his elbow perched on his knee. Meeting her gaze, he admitted, "Guess I've never really thought about it, but I think you may be right."

After a pause, Renn asked, "So what do you do when you're not gardening?"

"Oh, I read a ton. And I write a little."

She grew wide-eyed. "You do? What do you write?"

"I keep a daily journal, then I write whatever stories pop into my head. It's an outlet, just for myself."

"I write too."

"Oh, yeah? What do you write?"

"Magazine articles, essays, stories, devotionals... and the occasional poem."

"Wow, I've got a serious writer on my hands. Published, I assume?"

She smiled, feeling shy, "Yup. And loving every minute of it."

"Hey, that's really great. I can finally say I know a published author."

Just then, a loud crack shattered the silence. Renn jumped up, startled; Gordy hit the floor, running toward the sound.

"What was that?" she asked.

"A gunshot, if I don't miss my guess."

They saw the shattered window at the same time. The entryway sidelight lay in a million shards. Kate came down the stairs as Renn left to get the dustpan and broom.

Kate frowned, looking upset. "What on earth?"

Gordy said, "Apparently, someone isn't wild about your CPC idea. Listen, you call nine-one-one, then if you have a phone book, I'll call a glass replacement source."

When the authorities were on the way, he took the phone and had glass promised by six o'clock.

Renn swept up the mess and gingerly retrieved the bigger pieces of glass, tossing them into the trash.

Shortly, Gordy and his tool pouch covered the hole with plywood, and order was restored.

A single male police officer, named Kevin O'Reilly took a report, dug a twenty-two caliber rifle slug from the stairway wall and said, "I can't imagine your neighbors are thrilled with the idea. In fact, if I were you and didn't want any more trouble, I would remove that sign immediately."

Kate simply shook her head, after which time the officer shrugged, said, "It's your call," and left.

A few minutes later, Gordy confronted Kate, who seemed fretful.

"Now, listen, I told you this would cause trouble. You need to decide whether you're strong enough to deal with it or not."

She looked at him crossly. "It's a shock, that's all. I can gear up for the rest. If you think I'm giving up this fight just because the other side might play hard ball, you're mistaken, young man."

"Well, I'm glad to hear it. There for a minute, I thought you might want to throw in the towel."

"No way. Whatever they can dish out, I can take. In fact, if they tear the house down around me, I'll finally be free of it, won't I, one way or the other?"

It tickled her niece to see Kate's hackles raised in strength.

Gordy said, "Hey, Renn, why don't we go to the park? It's such a beautiful day."

She looked at Kate, who raised her left eyebrow and said, "I'm officially giving you the afternoon off. Now vamoose."

Renn hated to leave, in case another round of assaults erupted. But the confident, even stubborn look on Kate's face reassured her.

Gordy said, "Don't forget your jacket. I don't have a sweatshirt to give you today."

"Thanks for reminding me."

They had stopped at the corner, waiting for traffic to pass, when Renn noticed a silver Porsche rush past. As Gordy beckoned her, she said, "Wait, that was my cousin's car. I have to go back. I can't leave Kate there alone to deal with those jackals."

They ran the half block home and burst through the door, just after the last cousin disappeared inside.

"Mother," Berke yelled. "Where are you?"

"I'll be down in a minute," she called from upstairs.

Gordy and Renn took seats at the kitchen counter, waiting, visiting quietly.

"Well." Berke scowled at Gordy's inquisitive glance, "what are you looking at?"

With a smirk, Gordy said, "Oh, nothing. Nothing at all." He averted his gaze.

Berke turned to his sisters. "Those two are accomplices in this little bit of chicanery. I'd put money on it."

Evin glared at her cousin. "Renn, why don't you just go home? You have one, don't you?"

Gordy stood up as if to protect Renn. She tugged him back into his chair.

She said, "I'm a guest of your mother's, and I will leave when she no longer needs me."

Brynn sneered. "I'll bet Mom's money is an attraction, isn't it, Renn?"

Renn smiled and said softly, "Oh, haven't you heard, she has no money. It's tied up in some kind of *trusts*."

Brynn's mouth clamped shut and a scowl appeared.

Gordy gave Renn a subtle high five behind the breakfast bar and grinned. "Nice one," he commented, under his breath, so only she could hear.

Kate descended the stairs looking cool and calm, as Berke jerked his hand toward the door. "What happened to the window?"

"Somebody shot it out," she said quietly.

Evin shouted, "Mother, can't you see that you're not only endangering your own life here, but devaluing the property, doing this?"

"Now dear, don't worry. The Lord is my protector and I'll be fine."

"Give it a rest, Mom," Brynn remarked caustically.

Berke said sternly, "Why is that banner still up? What is all this office furniture doing in here?" He paused, "Mother, you couldn't have... in spite of the injunction, you moved that despicable organization in here?"

"It's my house and I'll invite whatever guests I see fit. Now, if you'll excuse me I h…"

"We know," said Brynn sarcastically, "places to go and things to do."

Renn looked at Gordy, who stood, as if to emphasize the command to leave.

Hatred flamed in Berke's eyes. "And just who do you think you are, trying to force us out of our own home?"

Gordy grimaced. "Last time I looked, *buddy*, this was your mother's house, not yours."

Berke yanked open the door so hard that it hit the wall behind it with a resounding thud. He followed his sisters through it, without a word, and slammed it behind him, violently rattling the new wood in the window opening.

Renn put her arm around Kate's shoulders. The older woman looked frail as her bravado evaporated. "Are you all right, Kate?"

She sighed and pursed her lips, looking dejected. "I'll be fine. I haven't had this much excitement since old Mr. Dingle, from next door, came home drunk and tried to break in, thinking this was his house."

Four

The next morning, the CPC director and one volunteer arrived at the house at eight-thirty and let themselves in with keys. Renn hurried to dress, realizing her mornings spent wearing pajamas in the kitchen were long past.

The doorbell rang and once again a police officer stood in the doorway. Behind him were at least a half-dozen glum-looking neighbors, with Sam Rayburg heading up the pack. The officer handed the injunction to Kate, who was completely unperturbed. "Thank you, Officer," she said. Closing the door, she laid the paper on the entry table without even looking at it.

Before the hour was up, two girls came in for pregnancy tests, and one teary eyed young man appeared, needing post abortion counseling. His girlfriend had chosen to abort his child, and he seemed overcome by grief.

Martha showed up at her usual time, apologizing, "Sorry to be late, but my car battery must need replacing. I couldn't get the thing to start until my neighbor jumped it for me."

Martha began dusting and running the sweeper between clients, but sensitively stopped when the bell rang again.

At lunchtime, Renn found Martha in the kitchen, preparing the fixings for tacos. "Listen, Martha, it's going to be really frustrating for you to keep house with people coming and going at all hours of the day. Tell you what… if you want to do the cooking, laundry, and kitchen stuff, I'll handle the dusting and vacuuming at least on this floor, after everyone's gone home for the evening. What do you think?"

A radiant smile broke out on the older woman's face. "Oh, honey, you are a godsend. I was wondering how I was going to be able to get it all done. Are you sure you don't mind?"

"Not at all. I don't really have enough to keep me busy around here and a person can only read so many books."

Martha arranged the trays of food on the breakfast bar. "Okay, do you want to let them know that lunch is on the table if they are interested?"

Gordy showed up at the same moment, saying, "I could smell tacos from outside. Got enough for one more?"

Renn couldn't help but smile. "Sure, Gord, come on in. Help yourself."

He ran his hand through his wild hair, and grinned like a little kid. "Your cooking could be habit forming, girl."

"This is one meal for which you'll have to thank Martha."

"I will, thanks."

The noon hour ushered in a lull in activity and the CPC crew of two appreciatively dug into the tacos and fruit laid out on the kitchen counter. Gordy filled a plate for himself and another for Renn. He said, "Come on, we're going to eat in the shade of the garden."

Renn grabbed two sodas, before following Gordy out the back door. She settled herself into a comfortable wicker chair in the dappled shade. The mid-day air was warm.

Gordy popped the tab on his soda. "So what's the latest? Any more skirmishes?"

"No, all's quiet on the home front, except for the cousins' brief appearance last night and you were here for that."

"Well, that's good."

They ate in silence for a while and he asked, "Do you suppose the trustees are going to do anything about this?"

"I haven't got a clue what the trust agreement even says. I wonder if it forbids a public establishment from opening. The cousins think their mother is doing this for the sole purpose of shaming them."

"I know. And I think she's one gutsy lady, standing up to them."

Renn fidgeted and her brow wrinkled, as a new thought occurred to her. "Gord, you don't suppose the kids would try to hurt her over this, do you?"

He frowned. "What made you think of that?"

"I don't know. I just wondered. They've already said they think she's nuts. I hope they're not brazen enough to try to have her committed or anything. I guess I don't trust Berke. He gets so angry."

"Hmm… I never thought of that. I guess we'll have to keep an eye on them."

After depositing their dishes in the sink a while later, Gordy went out and resumed his mulching and mowing, while Renn went to her room, pulled out her laptop and began writing.

She found Kate in the upstairs office a while later and asked, "Kate, you don't suppose Uncle Rick left copies of the trusts here in the house, with his important papers, do you?"

"That's exactly what I've been looking for, but I can't seem to find anything in the desk and I don't know where else to look."

Renn's mouth worked, as she tilted her head thoughtfully. "Did he have a safe?"

"Not that I know of. But then, he never would've told me about it if he had, and I wouldn't know the first thing about where to find it, would you?"

Renn gestured, and said, "Come on, we'll look behind the prints on the walls and knock on the wood. That's what they do in the movies when they're looking for a safe."

A warm smile lit Kate's eyes. "Kind of like a Matlock mystery. One of my favorites." She handed her niece a tiny piece of paper, with transparent tape around its perimeter. In block print, someone had written R29, L68, R12.

Renn glanced up, puzzled. "What's this?"

"I found it stuck under the bottom of his desk drawer. I have no idea what made me put my hand under there."

Renn perused it, and nodded. "There must be a safe somewhere, because this is the combination." Renn tucked the paper in her pocket.

Now even more determined, they pounded on walls and looked behind framed prints, searching for false walls, but found nothing

They were about to give up, discouraged, when Renn's bare foot hit something under the desk. "Ouch. What is that? It hurts, whatever it is."

When she looked, she saw nothing. On her haunches, she slid her hand over the rug's surface, finally grinning up at Kate.

"I think I've found something. Help me move the desk." It was all they could do to scoot the massive mahogany desk a foot to the right.

The heavyweight Turkish carpet, too, consumed all their strength to roll it and move it aside.

As they rolled the carpet back, a small safe revealed itself. Its combination lock was perfectly flush with the floor. Renn sank onto the floor and pushed the hair from her eyes.

"Oh, Kate, this is it. Let's see if we can open it."

They were flushed, overheated and now excited at the discovery.

Her aunt sat down on the floor, with perspiration covering her forehead and upper lip. She wiped her face on her shirt and said, "I think I'm too old for this."

Renn pulled the tiny paper from her pocket and began turning the dial according to the combination. To their great delight, the lock opened on the first try. As the door opened upward, Renn realized she had been anxiously holding her breath.

While Kate stuck her hand inside, her niece fished a flashlight out of the top desk drawer, shining it into the depths. Kate pulled out several leather file folders, all tied with ribbons.

"This is what I've been searching for," Kate breathed, her eyes glistening with tears.

"Oh, Kate, I know everything will be okay."

Her aunt swiped at her eyes. "You're right. I'm just being silly."

Opening the first page of the top folder, Kate read, "Trust account, number three eight six five o, beneficiary—Katherine Martingale." Written in legalese, it might as well have been Greek.

Renn could still hear the mower running in the backyard and said, "Wait here, Kate. I'll be right back."

She scurried down the back stairs and out the door and found Gordy mowing the last corner of the yard. She waved to him, and he signaled he would be finished shortly. She waited for him to turn the mower off before yelling, "Gordy, Kate and I could sure use your advice."

He wandered over, looking bewildered. "Advice? About what?"

"You said you had some law school background, and we need somebody to translate legalese for us."

He stared at her, as she turned to walk inside.

He called after her, "What are you guys up to?"

"You'll see."

She led him to the upstairs office, where Kate had an open folder in her lap as she sat cross-legged on the floor. She smiled at his approach, "I'm glad you are still here, Gordy. We need you to translate for us."

He picked up the top sheaf of papers, reading for a time, before he said, "Well, this first one says that all of Rick's money is bequeathed to Kate upon his death and is invested with Cromwell and Davis, Trust attorneys."

"I already know that. Keep reading," Kate urged.

"Well, the trust provides you a monthly check for household expenses and insurance, an allowance for your personal needs and an advance, should you have an emergency. Each advance can be no more than one thousand dollars and the attorneys must have a written request for the sum, before issuing a check. That's about it for the first folder."

He leafed through the second file and said, "This one discusses his investment holdings and states that the interest and dividends will be placed in a separate account. To be used for the upkeep of the house and the maintenance or purchase of vehicles or any repairs they may need."

Gordy read through the third and final folder, and said, "This is the one concerning the house. It states that the house may not be sold for any reason during Kate's lifetime. It doesn't say, however, that she can't give it away or use it for a CPC."

"Really?" Kate's eyes widened in pleasure. "He thought he had all his bases covered, but I'll bet he never imagined I would do this."

She rose, brushed the wrinkles out of her rayon shirt and headed toward the door. She took the folders with her, studying them as she walked, and left Renn and Gordy to straighten the room. Gordy stood up, pulling Renn to her feet.

They were just pushing the desk back into place a few minutes later, when they noticed the cousins standing at the door.

Berke angrily demanded, "What are you doing in my father's office?"

"Your mother asked for our assistance," Gordy snorted, glaring at the arrogant man.

Berke's face darkened in fury. "What did Mother want in here? And why did it include moving furniture?"

"Why don't you ask her yourself, *Bubba?*"

Berke's eyes flamed. "My name is Berke and don't you forget it, *gardener.*"

With a firm resolve, Gordy strode the four paces toward the door and gently slid his fingertips under the expensive lapels of Berke's jacket, as everyone stood transfixed. Gordy's muscles rippled with barely perceptible rage as he stared Berke down and said, casually, "No problem*, Bubba.*" Gordy dropped his hands after smoothing the lapels.

Kate came out of her room just then, closed the door and said, "Hello, my dears. How are all of you?" She smiled, as if glad to see them.

Brynn asked, "Mother, what were these two doing in Dad's office?"

"Just helping me clean up."

Evin snorted. "Yeah, like we believe that."

Kate smiled pleasantly. "You believe what you will, dear. You always do, don't you?"

Everyone followed Kate downstairs, and the air was thick with tension as she poured tea and lemonade, as if it were a tea party, instead of a knockdown, drag-out.

Berke said, "We've just been to see the attorneys, and they will go to court to fight you on this zoning issue."

Kate said, evenly, "Let them. If they sue, it will simply suck up a good deal of the inheritance you have coming. It's not a problem for me if it doesn't bother you."

Evin stood suddenly. "Mother, this is a beautiful home. I can't, for the life of me, understand why you would want to leave it."

"No," Kate said, "I'm not surprised you don't understand. You never cared to ask how I felt about any of this."

Berke stood to his feet, and put up his fists, like he might hit his mother. Gordy rose to tower several inches over the angry man, daring him to act.

Instead Berke said, "Come on, guys, let's beat it. Mother is acting like a nutcase and nothing we say will sway her lunatic tendencies." He turned to face Kate. "Let me say, Mother, that you'll regret it if you try to change one iota of Dad's wishes."

She shrugged. "Oh, well, I have a lot of regrets. Some far worse than others. I don't suppose one more will make much difference."

Brynn snapped, "What exactly does that mean?"

Her mother shook her head. "You children and the way you turned out—so cold and calculating, is a major regret. I feel somewhat responsible. But I believe your father had a much greater influence on you than I ever did."

Berke sneered. "And a good thing too. At least he had a good head on his shoulders."

"Now, Berke," Evin soothed, "let's not make a bad situation worse. Let's go. We don't want to be late for our meeting."

As the door closed after them, Gordy shrugged. "I wonder what they're cooking up."

Kate said, "Let's don't give it another thought. We have what I've been looking for. At least now I know what the trusts entail."

They could hear confusion at the front door and Kate excused herself. The neighbors, at least ten of them, all talking at once, stood in the doorway.

Sam Rayburg was obviously not a happy camper. He plunged in, shaking his fist at her. "Mrs. Martingale, didn't you read the injunction? You were to have ceased operations and removed this sign before the end of the business day today. You are ignoring a legal document. You can't do that. It's against the law."

Kate's eyes flashed in anger. "This is my home, Mr. Rayburg, and I can have as guests whomever I please. And there is nothing you can do or say to stop me."

He scowled. "We can haul every piece of equipment out to the sidewalk and just let you deal with that."

She said firmly, "Yes, I suppose you can. And I can have you arrested for trespassing. Now if you will excuse me, I have things to do." She turned, and gestured for them to leave, as if dusting lint from her lapels.

Sam hunched his shoulders, glared and said, "You haven't heard the last of this."

"I suppose not," Kate said with a shrug.

After they were gone, Gordy asked, "Anything to eat around here? I'm starved."

Martha handed him a dipper and pointed to a huge pot of chili, clearly another of Gordy's favorites dishes. After supper, he helped Renn clean up the kitchen, as Kate excused herself with a headache.

After she knew Kate was out of range, Renn wondered out loud, "Do you suppose Kate is stressed more than she's letting on?"

He shook his head. "It wouldn't surprise me."

When Gordy left a little later, Renn busied herself on her computer. She had the final draft of a short story completed. The next step would be to figure out where to submit it.

She pulled out an inspirational fiction she had been working on, and after only a few minutes, found herself deeply involved in the plot. She broke her concentration only long enough to go down to the kitchen. She washed a crisp Granny Smith apple that crunched and spurted juice with the first bite. When she finally went to bed, a whole ménage of winning characters flitted around in her head.

Five

When Renn woke the next morning to an overcast sky, tendrils of fog fingered the window ledges, seeking entrance. She hated gray days. A few in a row made her feel disoriented and sluggish.

Looking out the front window, she noticed a few picketers carrying signs saying, *Women for Choice* and *It's a Woman's Right to Choose.*

Oh-oh. The pro-choice demonstrators had finally put in an appearance. They'd been expecting them for days.

Pulling out her Bible, Renn turned to the book of Hebrews, chapter twelve, and verses twelve and thirteen.

She read: "Therefore strengthen your feeble arms and weak knees. Make level paths for your feet, so that the lame may not be disabled, but rather healed. Make every effort to live in peace with all men and be holy; without holiness no one will see the Lord."

For reasons she didn't understand, she felt the words were important.

Ambling down the stairs a little later, she saw that Craig was already sitting at his desk, making notes. He smiled before saying, "Hope we're not imposing. Although how we couldn't be, I can't imagine. Sitting right in the middle of your laps, as we are."

Renn shrugged. "Listen, it's not my house. I'm just a guest and your being here doesn't bother me a bit. In fact, I really like the way the place is coming to life."

He said, "I've made some coffee, if you'd like some. Why don't you come and keep me company?"

She poured her coffee and stirred in her creamer. As she sat down, she glanced at her watch, which read seven-ten and said, "You're awfully early this morning, aren't you?" After a pause, she added, "I assume you saw the picketers out front?"

He sighed, as his brows knit into a straight line. "I saw them. I should have known we wouldn't get away without some flack from them, especially after they thought they had closed the clinic by buying the building." She could see she had interrupted his thoughts.

"You asked if I was early. Sometimes that empty house makes me want to escape to… anywhere else. Know what I mean?"

"I heard you lost your wife. I'm sorry."

"You know, I've never lost anyone before, and I never understood the process of grief. It seems like it's taking forever to recover from it."

"Maybe you're rushing it?"

He looked up, surprised. "Why would you say a thing like that?"

She frowned, embarrassed. "Oh, forgive me, I don't have a clue where that came from."

"I do. Keep talking."

Hesitantly, she ventured, "Well, it just occurred to me that when we're in pain, we might be so desperate to get past it that we fail to learn what the Lord has to teach us in the middle of it. Does that make sense?"

"You're quite perceptive for your age, aren't you?"

She felt herself color. "Well, I don't know about that, but sometimes He gives me these tiny glimpses. That sounds pompous, doesn't it?" she said, with an embarrassed giggle.

"I don't think so."

She continued, "I'm just saying that since I haven't experienced what you're going through, it may sound like advice from Job's friends."

She noticed his intense green eyes fill with tears. At one glance, she could see all the traits of a hard-driving workaholic. Even approaching retirement age, his hands were constantly in motion, fiddling with something. He probably read everything he could get a hold of. And if she didn't miss her guess, CNN News was of constant and compelling interest.

The position of director seemed a poor fit for his personality. Did he have a business degree? She decided it was none of her business.

She stood to her feet. "May I get you more coffee?"

"If you don't mind, I'd appreciate it."

As she handed him the refill and turned toward the kitchen, he said, "Do you have a few more minutes you could just sit with me?"

"Sure, I guess," she said, settling back into the chair. She warmed her hands on the cup, deep in thought before she looked up to meet his gaze.

Fidgeting in his chair, he looked distinctly uncomfortable. He said, "You're wondering how I got this job, aren't you?"

She felt warmth creeping up her neck. "How did you know that?"

He looked grim. "Because I can see in your eyes what is reflected in my own, every time I look in the mirror."

She didn't know how to respond.

He said, "I have a degree in business and a choleric personality. Do you know much about personality types? Well, I'm the hard-driving, hyper one."

He tapped a pencil, even as he talked.

She couldn't help but smile. "Well, going caffeine-free might be a start."

"I can't. It's an addiction. Besides, I'm like this even without caffeine."

She looked thoughtful. "You don't seem very happy here… Are you?"

"No. To be honest, I've never even admitted that to myself. The business degree seemed important to the board, so I took the job. If it weren't for the volunteers who help, I'd be at cross-purposes with the ministry."

"So," Renn asked, "how do you feel when unwed mothers come in?"

He chewed his lip before answering. "Well, I'd have to say the first word that comes to mind is *impatient*."

She asked gently, "Why do you suppose that is?"

"Because they got themselves into the messes they're in."

After a brief pause, she asked, "So, does that mean that they don't deserve mercy and grace?"

He frowned. "My head knows all that stuff, but my heart doesn't countenance it at all."

"You must really hate your job."

He gave his head a slight shake and held out both palms. "Just a little less than my empty house."

Renn crossed her legs, licking her lips. "Do you mind if it ask what your wife thought when you accepted this job?"

"She saw the CPC in the same light as you do. And she thought the Lord could use me here. I guess neither of us really wanted to see that we'd made a mistake. By the time I figured it out, I no longer desired other employment."

There was an uncomfortable pause before she said, "Do you have a statement of faith for the center?"

"Sure. Save the babies in the name of Jesus. That's it in a nutshell."

"Hmm... but what about the mothers?"

He shrugged. "What about them?"

"How do you handle them? What do you say?"

"Well, of course, we try to be loving when we say that they're killing their babies. We try to show that we care about them too. But that's secondary to saving the babies."

Renn sat, looking at her reflection in the remaining coffee in her cup.

Craig said softly, "Please tell me what you're thinking."

Lord, give me the words. She tilted her head, closing her eyes, "Well, I was just wondering what it must feel like to be a young woman who is pregnant and unmarried. I've never had the experience, but I can imagine that it must feel like a death sentence." She was pensive before continuing. "If I were a college student, struggling to make ends meet, with say, two more years of school to go, and I found myself pregnant, I can't imagine that I wouldn't just want a way out. Any way out."

He looked at her aghast. "You can't be serious." After a pause, he said, "Do you really mean that? Even as a Christian, you'd feel that way? The baby would be secondary to the issue of your life?"

She shrugged. "I've heard that the drive for self-preservation is supposed to be the strongest we humans possess."

"Meaning what?"

"If I were that college girl, who has to stay in school to keep her scholarships and grants... to make a decent living at graduation, then that would be the primary goal. Everything else would be secondary. Including a pregnancy and a baby."

He looked like he'd been shot.

She continued, "Look at a mother whose husband is out of work, who already has her hands full with three or more children and no income. What a hardship that baby would be."

"I'm listening," he urged, sitting forward in his chair, and resting his chin in his palm.

"Or if I were a Christian girl who'd been raped and ended up pregnant, I think my first inclination would be to preserve my reputation. It wouldn't be an easy decision to make. Somehow, I just don't feel it would be nearly as cut and dried as we'd all like to think it is."

She added, "Having a baby out of wedlock, even if you decide to give it up, has to be a humiliating experience." After a pause, she continued, "And how often is marriage even feasible? Sometimes the guy turns out to be a jerk and would make lousy husband material. Maybe the timing is totally wrong and he's got eight years of school to finish. What if his parents disapprove and the pressure to walk away is just too great? I don't know… the scenarios are legion."

Craig frowned. "But you're only looking at this from the woman's point of view, not God's."

She was quiet, before she said softly, "Look I'm really not comfortable talking to you like this. It's not my place. I think there's even a scripture about it in first Timothy, if I remember correctly."

"Listen, if I'm okay with it, then you needn't worry about that part of it. Just think of us as two friends, sharing our hearts. Okay?"

She sighed, then hesitated before asking, "Are you sure?"

"Please go on."

She pressed her lips together in deep thought before she said, "Okay, You said I was just looking at this from the woman's point of view and not God's. Well, who's to say what

God's viewpoint is?" She paused to collect her thoughts. "Listen, my favorite book is Psalms, where it says God draws near to the broken hearted and the lowly in heart... I'm sorry. I'm not expressing myself well at all."

He said, "You're doing fine. Please... I think I really need to hear this."

She could see, from the look in his eyes that she had his complete attention. Even his fidgeting hands were now still.

She set her cup on the desk and folded her hands in her lap. "Scripture says God has compassion for the hurting, even if they've caused their own pain. Look at David the psalmist. He's called a man after God's own heart. And yet his choices nearly ruined his life and that of his family." After a pause, she said, "Who of us doesn't cause our own pain at times? Even Christians don't do it right all the time. If He cut us off from His love because of our bad choices, how often would we be left out in the cold? Desperate, and alone, without His compassion?"

He looked down at the blotter on his desk, not moving a muscle.

Tilting her head, she went on. "Haven't you ever made a bad decision, then turned to the Lord, knowing He loved you, and would run to help when you called Him?"

"I suppose," he said with a frown.

"Will you hand me that Bible over there, please? I read something this morning that I knew the Lord wanted me to see, but I didn't understand why until right this second." Her excitement grew when he handed her a parallel study Bible, with four different versions of each verse.

She opened it and said, "I'm reading Hebrews twelve, verses twelve and thirteen, out of the Living version. It says, 'So take a new grip with your tired hands, stand firm on your shaky legs, and mark out a straight, smooth path for your feet, *so that those who follow you, though weak and lame, will not fall and hurt themselves*, but become strong. Try to stay out of all quarrels and seek to live a clean and holy life.'"

She moved her finger across the page. "The NIV says it this way: 'Therefore, strengthen your feeble arms and weak knees. Make level paths for your feet, so that the *lame may not be disabled,* but rather healed. Make every effort to be at peace with all men…'"

He intently studied his hands. She was quiet for a few seconds before she said softly, "Do those verses say anything to you?"

He grimaced and paused. "Don't shoot your own wounded?"

She nodded. "That's the way I read it."

He frowned, with a slight shake of his head. "I've read those verses, but they never said that to me before." His eyes filled with tears, and he covered his face with his hands, shuddering with sobs. "Oh, may God forgive us. We've been trapping and crippling our own wounded."

After he had calmed himself, Renn said, "You know, the apostle Paul held the coats of those who stoned Stephen, but he repented. And just look what the Lord did with his contrite heart."

When he looked doubtful, she said, "We can only live according to the light that's been revealed."

A few minutes later, he stood and reached for her hand, taking it in both of his. "I don't know you very well yet, Renn, but I think you came down here just for me this morning, and I appreciate your willingness to stick your neck out and speak the truth. I'm going to give some thought to what you said."

A volunteer walked through the front door just then, and looked from Renn to Craig, who were just coming into the kitchen for more coffee. "Hi," she said as she smiled. "Everything okay?"

He returned her smile. "I think it will be shortly."

He winked at Renn as she left the room.

The doorbell sounded just then. Renn opened the door to two terrified, young girls, who looked too young to drive. She noticed the picketers were now gone.

Renn's heart went out to the girls. She smiled warmly and said, "Please come in." They looked at each other, questioning, and the shorter girl's eyes filled, as tears ran down her cheeks. Renn put her arm around the girl and drew her into an embrace. "It's going to be okay, sweetie," she said. "May I get you guys something to drink?"

They looked grateful, but declined.

She handed them over to the volunteer, who seemed like a comforting soul.

Kate came down the stairs and picked up the mail the postman had just shoved through the slot in the door. She wandered into the kitchen, sorting through it.

Her worried look, as she opened an envelope, brought Renn to her side. "Kate, are you okay?"

"I don't think so," she said with a sigh.

"What is that?"

"A letter from the court, demanding that I go for psychological testing next Monday at ten. My children are saying I've flipped out."

"Oh, Kate, what are you going to do?"

"I don't know. Do you have any ideas?"

Renn sat down at the kitchen table and rested her chin on her hand, thinking. "What if you were to find a psychologist, someone respected, and have your own testing done? Then you would have your own expert witness if this goes to court."

Kate looked up, frowning. "I can't believe my own children would want to see me labeled incompetent. But I guess when money is involved, I shouldn't be too surprised."

Renn said nothing; she stood, put her arm around her aunt and held her.

"You know, Kate, I am proud of you. I think the way you stood up for yourself and did what you had to do, even inviting the CPC here, is very courageous."

"Well, it wasn't that philanthropic an idea when it came to me. It was simply a desperate way out of a bad situation."

"I know. But you know, God promises to use what we give him, however insignificant. Even a cup of cold water can be used to bring Him glory."

Kate hugged her niece and said softly, "I wish you were my daughter. I don't think either your mother or I really knew you very well, did we?"

Renn smiled. "Well, we can make up for it starting right now, can't we?"

~ * ~

The doorbell rang and Renn found a dozen familiar CPC volunteers waiting at the door. It was clear that no one felt comfortable just walking into a private home without permission.

She smiled, gesturing them in and offered drinks. Craig came toward them and said, "Have a seat, gang. I have something I want to say."

He looked at Renn, and said, "You come, too, if you would."

"Oh, I'd just be in the way. I'll get the drinks."

He took her hand and held it. "I'd really appreciate it if you sat in with us... unless you have something pressing to do."

Kate walked in with the drink tray just then, and the problem was solved.

As Renn sank down on the floor and crossed her legs, she felt uncomfortable. She didn't know these people and had no business sitting in

As he passed by where she sat, Craig whispered in her ear, "You're my moral support, all right?"

She smiled and nodded.

Craig leaned against a desk and rubbed the side of his face with his hand. It was obvious that no one knew what to expect. They all looked as if they were waiting for the other shoe to drop.

"Now don't worry. Kate isn't throwing us out. But listen, guys, I won't belabor the point. I learned something today that will change how we deal with our clients. Some of you may already know this, may even have used this approach, but we have never taught it here."

He paused, sitting still, a pencil poised, motionless in his hand. "I have never seen us in this light before, but at this moment, for the first time, I can see why pro-choicers and pregnant women see us as rabidly anti-woman. Our manuals train us to be cordial, even warm. But to save those babies, no matter what.

"That, I have come to see, is the wrong approach. Therefore, we will no longer use that training manual. But more importantly, we will begin all over again, by doing a small exercise. It's simple. It's nothing new. It's called the 'walk a mile in my shoes' approach.

"From now on, folks, we will put ourselves in the client's shoes, looking at each situation from its owner's point of view. No longer will we have any expectations of outcome."

He glanced at the faces before him. "Now, don't look at me like that. Of course, we still hope to save babies. But it's the mothers we need to reach out to in love. And I believe we have been missing our one chance to love them unconditionally and let the spirit of God do the convicting. We have been playing the part of the Holy Spirit for too long.

"Now I know not many CPC's use this approach. And I imagine it's rare to lay the outcome in the Lord's lap and the chips fall where they may. Well, it's new to me, too, but I'm convinced it's the right thing to do."

He continued, "Some of you may have a problem with this new approach. In that case, you may feel free to get up and leave, or see me afterwards if this doesn't align with your theology."

Before he could even finish his sentence, two older, gray haired women, who had come in late, picked up their purses and left, frowning. The others looked at one another, wide-eyed.

He said, "So, are there any questions?"

One young woman raised her hand, pointed toward Renn, and said, "I just wondered why you asked her to sit in on the session. Is she going to be volunteering?"

He took a breath and said evenly, "I believe she will be involved with us in some capacity, if temporarily. Does that answer your question, Lisa?"

The girl looked at Renn and extended her hand, introducing herself.

When everyone started talking at once, Craig put up his hand for silence.

He said, "Okay, now, the way we are going to approach the clients is to listen and encourage them to talk about the fears and ramifications of an unwanted pregnancy. We, of course, will let them know that they are carrying a baby and use the models and so forth. But we will no longer try to exert pressure.

"We can pray, love, give hugs and be Jesus with skin on to them. You may give them your number to call day or night. But we will not try in any way to force our values on them. We will treat them as individuals, precious to the Lord. I think when they see that, they will respond."

"There is no manual for this," he added. "It has to be led by the Spirit of God, so it's up to each of us to be sensitive. Let Him speak life through you and watch what happens. I believe this approach can literally turn the world upside down for God."

Kate came to the door and announced that lunch was ready if anyone was interested. With everyone talking at once, several gathered around and hugged Craig. Renn noticed a few girls who were weeping.

She overheard a whispered conversation between two teary-eyed young women. "I wish someone had addressed my unwed pregnancy situation this way. Even though my counselors were Christians, they couldn't put aside their own beliefs long enough to respect me as a person. I'm going to love doing it this way."

Six

Renn excused herself, after helping serve lunch, and went to her room to write. Kate appeared in the doorway a couple of hours later, looking disturbed. Her niece tried to stifle her feelings of annoyance at the interruption. Somehow people just couldn't understand that a writer was better off left alone. Renn found her concentration broken at the least distraction and had to steel herself against resentment. *Sorry, Lord.*

"Come in, Kate. Are you all right?"

She settled herself on the bed, looking exhausted. Renn waited for her to speak.

"Honey, I'm going to take your suggestion and go for psychological testing. But I don't want to go alone. I guess I'm saying I need moral support. Would you be willing to go with me?"

Renn rose from her chair and knelt beside Kate, putting her arm around her shoulder. "Of course. I'd be glad to go. Have you made an appointment?"

"I have. I paid a premium to have them fit me in on such short notice. The appointment is tomorrow morning at ten. I want to be ready with ammunition in case the children make an issue of my mental health."

Renn smiled. "I think that's very savvy of you, Kate. Fight fire with fire, as they say."

Kate returned her smile. "You know, I think you're the best thing that's happened around here in some time. I get a lift just hanging around with you."

Renn hugged her.

"So what time do we need to leave in the morning? If I know, I can plan ahead."

~ * ~

Praying in the spirit for her aunt, who would need much Holy Spirit backup for the coming days, Renn turned her attention, once again, to her writing.

Her story was really hitting its stride, and she was more than deeply in love with her characters.

At suppertime, she found Kate in the kitchen. From the kitchen window, she could see Gordy edging the walks with a long handled tool.

Kate said, "Why don't you see if Gordy would like some meatloaf and a baked potato? There's enough food here to feed an army."

Renn teased, "Well then, if Gordy comes, it should be just enough."

Kate's eyes lit up in a smile. "Do you know how much you bless me, dear?"

Gordy sat with them, his eyes radiating gratitude with his first bite of meatloaf. He had seconds of everything and looked questioningly at the leftovers.

Kate gave him an approving smile and gestured toward the food. "Go ahead, Gordy, finish them off. Martha can't seem to break the unfortunate habit of cooking for big families. We have a fridge full of extra stuff. I'm just glad it's her job to clean it out at the end of the week and not mine. I'd have a hard time throwing out all her wonderful leftovers, but there's no way the two of us could ever eat it all."

"No lie," Renn said with a giggle.

Gordy said, "I don't think I've eaten this good since my grandmother died ten years ago. After her death, things went downhill fast."

Between bites, Gordy wiped his mouth with his napkin, and said, "So what's the latest on the home front?"

Kate looked distressed, and Renn's heart filled with compassion for her. Renn said, "The cousins and lawyers sent Kate a letter demanding she see a shrink and undergo psychological testing."

He bounced out of his chair, rising to his feet in a fighting stance. "I could throttle those little twits. They scarcely know you and here they are making your life miserable."

Kate said quietly, "Now, dear, don't get yourself in a dither over it. If you were in their shoes, you might feel the same way."

He grimaced. "That's doubtful. I've never seen such avarice in my life."

Kate nodded sadly. "That's the word, isn't it? Avarice. It's a nice fit. A terrible scenario, but an apt description."

Gordy said, "If you were my mother, I'd treat you like a queen. I'd do for you what I'm doing now, only I wouldn't charge you for it."

"But that's ridiculous." Kate retorted with a frown. "You'd still have to make a living, no matter who you worked for."

He said resolutely, "Well, I would simply refuse to cash your checks if you were my mother."

She patted his hand. "Well, that's sweet of you, dear."

Renn got up to clear the table a few minutes later. Kate excused herself and headed for her room to lie down. Renn asked, "Kate, are you feeling all right?"

She smiled weakly. "Of course, dear, just tired. I think I'll read for a little while before going to sleep. I'll see you in the morning."

Gordy rinsed his plate and stuck it in the dishwasher. "She sure doesn't seem like herself, does she?"

"What do you mean? How do you think she's changed?"

"She seems depressed to me," he said thoughtfully. "What do you think?"

"Now that you mention it, she doesn't seem as upbeat as when I arrived. In fact, the reason I came in the first place was because of the tremor of fear I heard in her voice."

He frowned. "Do you think behind her bravado in front of the children, she could really be afraid?"

"She as much as told me that's why she wanted me to come. I knew she had to be desperate, since we've never been close."

"You know those three better than I do. How far do you think they'd go to get what they want?"

"I don't really know them well at all. We've never had a thing in common. But I overheard their conversation the other day, out in the yard, and…"

He looked bewildered. "How did you do that?"

She grimaced, admitting, "Well, if you must know, I was eavesdropping and it wasn't pretty. And don't you dare tell. They actually said that if she could get her hands on the money, she'd blow it just to keep them from inheriting."

He frowned. "Now where do you suppose they got a crazy idea like that?"

"I think because she was controlling, they got the idea that she'd like to control everything and leave them with nothing. But I also think Rick inferred to them that she wasn't trustworthy."

Gordy looked up from wiping the table. "Say, how long are they going to be around? Did you hear?"

"Kate thought it was only going to be a few days, but Berke seemed to think he'd find a way to stay until he knew things were under control. Evin said she couldn't stand to be here longer than a week. Couldn't tolerate being in the same room with Kate for longer than five minutes."

He scratched his head. "I sure wish I knew what they were up to. I can't bear to think they'd hurt her over money."

"Well, I'm glad she made an appointment to have a psychological test done tomorrow. That should help us if we need to fight them."

Gordy said, "So how about you and I agreeing in prayer for Kate?"

"Sure."

He led in an emotional prayer, asking the Lord to comfort and protect Kate and give them all wisdom.

Renn looked up, and said, "Oh, I forgot to tell you. We had pro-choice picketers out front for awhile this morning."

He sighed and shook his head. "It seems like the situation gets more complicated by the day, doesn't it?"

He left a few minutes later, saying he had to get the lawn equipment put away, before the dew rusted it.

A short time later, Renn got a call from her best friend from work, Deedee Presley.

She said, "Got lonely for your voice, girl. How long are you going to be gone anyway?"

"Mike said there might not be much work this summer and my aunt can really use me around here, so I'll be staying through August. Pray for us, though, okay, Deedee?"

"Of course. Why? What's going on?"

Renn filled her in, and Deedee freaked when she heard there was a CPC now open for business in the living room during the daytime.

"You've got to be kidding? It must be a circus over there."

"It does have its moments."

She told Deedee about the cousins wanting to get their hands on the money at all costs, and her friend promised she would pray.

Renn went to bed, jotting herself a note. She wanted to ask whether Kate took any medications. *Could her aunt really be in jeopardy?*

~ * ~

Renn was awakened by the sound of the doorbell at seven a.m. She opened the door to find a television crew from KRSV, Channel Fourteen, standing on the porch. Embarrassed, she tightened the belt on her robe. Feeling ill-equipped to deal with them, she simply closed the door, hoping she wasn't going to see herself in her pajamas on the six o'clock news.

She ran upstairs and found Kate putting the finishing touches on her makeup. "There's a television crew from Channel Fourteen out on the front lawn. I didn't know what to say, so I said nothing and just closed the door."

"That's what I would've done. Could you call Craig and warn him for me? His number is on the list on the fridge. I'd hate for him to walk into an ambush."

Renn found Craig's number and heard him answer, realizing she'd probably gotten him out of bed.

"I'm sorry to disturb you, Craig, but Kate wanted me to tell you that the Channel Fourteen news crew is out on the lawn, wanting interviews. She thought you ought to be forewarned."

"I'm surprised it took them this long to get there," he said with a sigh.

After a brief pause, he added, "Tell Kate I'll be over in a little while. I need to gear up for this spiritually."

Kate took the coffee Renn offered her, before pausing in front of the peephole. "Why, there must be fifteen people out there."

"Let me go up and dress, then I'll fix you something to eat," Renn offered.

"Oh, all I'd care for is toast and coffee. I'm too nervous for anything else. The test, you know."

"Okay. I'll be back to give you moral support as soon as I get dressed."

As Renn ascended the stairs, she turned to see the reporters staring back at her through the fan-shaped window above the door. It was unnerving, having them out there waiting, like dogs for a bone.

As Renn dressed, it occurred to her that Kate was looking thinner. She really needed to talk to her about her health.

Over coffee and toast, she sat down and asked, "Kate, are you feeling all right? You look a little thinner and maybe even a little pale."

"I suppose it's possible. I don't have much appetite since the ruckus with the children."

"Are you on any medication?"

"Just allergy medication and Tylenol for the arthritis in my knees and hips."

As the doorbell rang for the thousandth time, Kate checked the peephole, then sat down again at the table. Fretful, she said, "Do you suppose they'll just keep doing that all day long?"

Renn gave her aunt a sympathetic look. "I sure hope not. Just how many frightened girls are going to brave that crowd for a pregnancy test?"

Meeting her niece's gaze, she said, "Oh, my dear, you're right. I hadn't even thought about that."

Craig came in the backdoor, saying, "I parked at the end of the block and walked up the alley, to avoid the chaos."

Kate frowned. "They just keep ringing the bell. I suppose they'd be inside right now, if it wasn't a private residence."

"That's a good point, and you're probably right."

Kate said, "Craig, we were just wondering how many girls would be courageous enough to brave that mob for a pregnancy test."

He shook his head, looking doubtful. "Not many, I'm sure. Kate, do you have an attorney?"

"You mean of my own? No."

She and Renn glanced knowingly at each other and simultaneously said, "Let's call Gordy."

Gordy showed up at the back door ten minutes later. "Good grief," he said with a grimace, "you're being mobbed. Another television truck and a van from radio station KLRP just pulled up."

Kate asked, "Gordy, what can we do?"

"Your best bet would be to give the stations a prepared statement, then ask them nicely to go away. Anything else will take time and may not work at all. You might also have someone stationed out by the curb. If any clients come by... if they have the intestinal fortitude to brave the teeming hordes, have them come around to the back door."

Craig said, "I can't imagine anyone willing to darken the door under these circumstances."

Renn asked Kate, "What about the prepared statement? Do you think we should do that?"

Kate glanced at Craig. "What do you think?"

His face lit up, and he said, "I have an idea. Thank you, Holy Spirit. Hand me a phone, someone."

He dialed a number, then another and within a half hour, all of the five pregnant girls and women, who had helped move the center, appeared at the door. They picked their way through the crowd of cameras and reporters, smiling, but unresponsive to questions.

In the living room, Craig said, "Okay, gang, have a seat. Now here's what we're going to do. You all are going out on the lawn, and mingle. Some of you are going to sit out by the curb, smile and welcome anyone who might be thinking of coming in. Now, I think Kate has coffee and hot chocolate for you. Take some out to the reporters, too. If they question you, just ask the Holy Spirit for answers, all right? Remember, that's how we're operating these days."

Lisa asked, "You mean you want us to talk to them?"

"Well," Craig said, "not until we pray. Everybody join hands. Lord, we need you now, to visit this place with your presence. We need you to put a coal to our lips and words in our mouths. We pray that you would shut the lions' mouths, all of them, as we render them harmless in Jesus' name. We also ask that we would find favor with God and man in this endeavor. We believe that our presence on television will, indeed, bring these young women in, because they see the love of Jesus here. In whose name we pray, amen and amen."

As the crowd dispersed and headed toward the door, Renn could immediately see that this was the right approach. The reporters visibly relaxed. They were getting interviews from the pregnant women themselves, who were handing out beverages. The air was filled with happy banter and laughter. It looked like God had turned a potentially bad situation around for His glory.

Renn and Kate left the house at nine and headed downtown to the psychologist's office.

Kate said, "Honey, I'm so glad you're with me through all this. I don't know how I'd manage without you."

As they pulled into a parking space, Renn asked, "Before we get out of the car, could I pray with you, Kate?"

The older woman pulled her into a hug. "Of course. Nothing would please me more."

Renn said, "Lord, the cousins are challenging Kate's abilities, and it feels like a threat. It's frightening and unnerving to submit to this testing, but You say that You control the hearts of kings and rulers. Lord, we know that includes judges and doctors as well. We believe that You will give Kate Your peace and presence as she walks confidently into this place, with You at her side. And we give You praise on this side of our Red Sea, in Jesus' name."

Kate's eyes were full of tears. "Thanks, honey. I could feel God just pumping me up, squaring my shoulders and telling me to rest. So don't worry, okay?"

Making herself comfortable in the soft, leather waiting room seat, Renn pulled a Sue Grafton mystery out of her handbag and began to read. Kate had been told the test would take several hours. But within a half-hour, she appeared at the door, with a paper in her hand, smiling.

Renn frowned. "Wha…"

"Shhh… I'll tell you outside."

Seven

Inside the car, Kate was jubilant. Renn, still clueless, asked, "What happened?"

Now animated, the older woman looked ten years younger when she said, "You'll never believe it. The doctor watched the morning's live news coverage of what's happening at our house, and he was angry that they were hounding us like that. He thinks what we're doing is courageous. Said he didn't know anyone else with the guts to do such a thing."

"Wow. Do you suppose he's a Christian?"

"I couldn't tell, but we sure found favor with him. He asked only cursory questions, skipped the formal mental acuity tests and said he would testify that I'm as sane as he is, if it comes to that. This letter is to the children, and this one is for anyone else who wants to know my mental status."

Kate, without her restless, hounded appearance, resembled a contented child.

At the house, the television crews had dispersed, and there were two cars pulling up to the curb. Renn smiled at several girls, who seemed hesitant and shy.

"Welcome, girls. Come in," said Renn, touching the shoulder of one particularly shy teen.

"We saw you on the news this morning, and… well, we just had to come"

"We're glad you're here."

Kate put her arm around another girl, and said, "You aren't alone, sweetie."

The girl's frightened, haunted look softened, and she smiled briefly. "Thanks."

Several of the pregnant volunteers came and joined them, each leading the newcomers into the house and offering them drinks.

Craig came into the kitchen. "So how did the test go, Kate?"

She shook her head. "What a mighty God we serve," she said, breaking down in tears.

He put his arm around her. "Yes, but what does that mean? Why are you crying?"

Kate looked at Renn, who began to explain.

Craig shook his head and sank into a chair, "I can't believe how this is all turning out."

He rubbed his chin. "Do you know that since that morning news clip, we've had six young women in here, and it isn't even noon yet? They said they could feel the warmth and acceptance right over the air. Isn't that amazing?"

He led them to the edge of the living room, where they could see that every conversation area had its own counseling session in progress. Several of the girls were in tears. Craig and the two women backed quietly away, so as not to disturb anyone.

After most of the clients had left, one of the counselors, whose nametag read 'Mandy', came running to find Craig. Obviously excited, she threw her arms around him. "Listen, Craig, I've never worked in another CPC where this approach was used, but it's working. It's really working. They are responding to the heart of God. I've never seen anything like it."

Julie, another volunteer, joined them. Her eyes were wide as she said, "I'm totally blown away. I can actually feel the spirit move in this place since the policy change. These girls have hungry hearts. You were right, Craig, to change the way we go about this thing."

He pointed at Renn. "This is the lady you should be thanking. She's the one who showed me that we were maiming our own wounded."

Renn shook her head. "Don't look at me. That was every bit of the Lord. I guess that verse says it exactly. 'Eye hath not seen, nor ear heard, neither have entered into the heart of man, the things which God hath prepared for those who love him.'"

~ * ~

The cousins showed up just in time for lunch and immediately noticed the atmosphere of excitement. It seemed to make them even angrier.

"Mother," shouted Berke, "we demand that you dismantle this center right now. I am honestly ashamed to call you my mother."

"Well, listen, sweetie," she said, holding out her hand to him, "I'm sorry you feel that way, but this is a work of God, and I think it's taken on a life of its own. I don't think either of us could stop it now."

Brynn hissed, "That's where you're dead wrong, Mom. We will stop it if it's the last thing we do."

Kate shook her head. "Don't you all have lives and jobs to get back to? Exactly how much time and money are you willing to spend—to see this through?"

They fell silent, almost visibly receding. Evin shrugged. "Well, as long as we're here, you're going to have a fight on your hands."

"Okey dokey, dears. I hope you're prepared. You're fighting with God at this stage of the game. It no longer has anything to do with me."

Berke's face twisted in anger as he said, "Don't be ridiculous, Mother. It has everything to do with you!"

After they left, Renn wondered why no one had come to enforce the injunction. Even the cousins seemed to have forgotten it.

Gordy showed up a few minutes after lunch, saying, "I saw the news. It came across so powerfully, I've never seen anything quite like it."

Renn agreed. "I know. I'm totally in awe."

"So you've seen it?"

"No, but we heard. We had the psych evaluation to attend."

"Oh, that's right. So how did it go?"

"I can only say it was a God thing. The psychologist gave her a cursory exam and said she was fine. He said it's the other lunatics that are the problem. Of course, he didn't use those particular words."

He grinned. "I don't imagine he did."

Renn said, "Are you hungry? We've got homemade chicken noodle soup and Martha's fresh-baked bread for lunch. Want to stay?"

"Lead me to it—I'm starved. I could tell from the alley that she had baked bread. It's like a magnet."

She set a bowl of the steaming soup in front of him, along with several slices of warm, buttered bread.

"Oh, I've died and gone to heaven," he said with a delighted laugh.

After the door closed behind the last client, Renn said, "Hey, you guys, lunch is served. Homemade chicken noodle soup and fresh-baked bread if you're hungry."

She didn't have to tell them twice. She poured drinks and buttered bread, filled bowls and carried a tray into the office for Kate and Craig.

She knocked on the dining room door. Grinning, he said, "Come in. Oh, that smells terrific."

Kate said gently, "Could you sit down, dear? I'd like to run something past you."

"How about as soon as I finish helping with lunch?"

Craig said, "Please. They don't have to be served. Get yourself something to eat and join us."

She set up a tray, and carried it to the office, wondering what could be so important.

Craig stood as she entered and she blushed with embarrassment.

He folded his hands on the desk in front of him and quietly asked, "Renn, have you ever given any thought to working with a CPC? I mean in a formal capacity?"

"I guess it never occurred to me".

"Well, dear," Kate said, "Craig thinks you have a gift for it."

He smiled. "I don't *think*… I *know*. It's as clear as the nose on your face. You have compassion and a tender heart toward these girls."

Renn wrinkled her brow. "What are you getting at?"

Kate said, "Well, dear, I've been doing a lot of thinking. I can only use one bedroom upstairs and the rest just sit idle. I want to invite some of these young pregnant women to move in and use the extra bedrooms. What do you think?"

Before Renn could answer, Kate continued, "There are six bedrooms, with five baths and it's crazy to let them sit idle, when so many could use them. And there are plenty more in the basement if we need them."

Renn shook her head. "What? What are you talking about, Kate?"

"I want to make it into a shelter for those who have nowhere else to go. A place where they can feel cared for. And I want you to think about running it. I'm too old to do much of that, but we think it would be the perfect place for your gifts to be used."

"But what about my apartment, and my job?"

Kate said gently, "Perhaps you should tell me. Do they really mean that much to you?"

"The job—maybe not so much, but I'd really miss having a place of my own where I could get away when I need to."

Kate said, "Well, then, I would continue to pay the rent and utilities so you could keep it."

"Why would you do that?"

"Listen, dear, I have plenty of money and I guess I'm just asking you to pray about it. Would you do that?"

"I guess so," she said, shrugging. The Lord hadn't said a word about any of this, and it would take some time to get used to the idea.

Craig said, "You know the girl who waved at you this afternoon when she left? Her name is Linda and she is staying with a friend, because her parents kicked her out. They want her to have an abortion, and she has refused. There are many others just like her, whose families don't support them in their decision to complete the pregnancy. They need a place to live, where they can feel accepted and safe. I believe the doors are opening right here, to make it happen."

Kate said, "The Lord had given me the idea even before Craig brought it up. We were both hearing the same message."

Why haven't I heard the message?

Renn frowned in puzzlement. "But you're still going to be here, aren't you, Kate?"

She smiled. "Until the Lord has other plans for me."

Craig noted the look of confusion on Renn's face and said, "I know this is sudden. We just want you to give it some thought. Ask the Lord for wisdom. You're good at that." She wondered at the changes she saw in Craig. It seemed as if the workaholic had disappeared, almost as if by magic.

Renn excused herself and carried the dishes, including her own untouched plate, to the kitchen. Everyone had finished eating except Gordy.

He said, "I wondered where you'd gone. Hope you don't mind, but I'm cleaning up the leftovers."

She said nothing. He tilted his head, and said, "Hey, what's going on?"

"They want me to move in permanently and run a home for unwed mothers upstairs."

His eyes widened. "You mean here?"

"Yes."

"Wow." As if it were a foregone conclusion, he said, "It's the perfect job for you, you know."

She rolled her eyes. "How can you say that?"

"Because you have a heart for this stuff. You do. I can see it when you watch them coming through the door. I've seen it since the day this place opened."

"That's ridiculous."

He said, "No, it's not. Think about it. You've never been in their situation and yet you have an affinity for them that's not to be believed."

She shook her head, but said nothing. It felt like she was being sucked into something she hadn't chosen. Again.

He frowned. "So what's the long face about?"

"Nothing," she said with a sigh.

"Come on, get real with me. I want to know what's going on in that head of yours."

"I feel like I'm being coerced by Kate all over again."

He looked surprised. "Do you really feel that way?"

"I don't know."

He said, "Well, you said yourself that she's listening to the Lord now, and He changed her attitude. So could it be that you just don't want to hear the Lord's opinion on the subject?"

"Go home, Gordy," she said with a grimace, crossing her arms in front of her.

He stood up. "I will, but not before I have my say. I think you just don't like—that this wasn't your idea. It feels like they sprang it on you, and you feel trapped. Well, you're not trapped. Think of this as an opportunity to leapfrog right over the missing Master's *degree* into the Master's *work*. The real thing."

With pursed lips, she repeated, "Go home."

He turned away, frowning. "You wouldn't be so upset if this hadn't struck some sort of chord deep inside you. You know that, don't you?"

He smirked then and said, "I know, I know... I'm going."

She shrugged and turned to go upstairs as the door slammed behind him.

Eight

She pushed the ON button on her laptop and sat down to write. She had neglected it for too long.

For some reason, her train of thought derailed repeatedly with thoughts of what he'd said.

Did the Lord really want something so foreign for her? Could she just drop everything, and take on a project like this?

She sat pouting for a while, before finally saying, "Okay, Lord. I don't know about this, so I guess I'm asking for Your input on the subject. If this is from You, please turn my attitude around."

Concentrating on her writing, she was finally able to turn out ten pages of good prose. She felt pleased, when she finally left the room several hours later.

Gordy was back, sitting in the kitchen, a glass of milk and a pile of peanut butter cookies heaped on a plate in front of him.

"Don't you have a home?" she said crossly.

"I think of this as home now," he said with a laugh.

She shook her head, "You can't imagine how annoying you are sometimes."

He grinned. "I'm sure I am, especially if I'm pushing the Holy Spirit's agenda. The same one you're fighting."

She said nothing, but glanced around for Kate.

"Hey," said Gordy, "if you're looking for Kate, she's not here. She and Craig had some business to take care of."

"Oh," she said, crestfallen.

Two volunteers were visiting with clients in the living room, but the place seemed awkwardly quiet, even uncomfortable, so Renn made her way to the laundry room, where she started a load of laundry. After pulling on a sweatshirt, she heaved open the back door.

"Hey, where are you going?"

She glared at him. "What? Is she paying you to play babysitter for me now, too? I need some time to think—alone."

He looked hurt as she slammed out the back door.

The park was empty, with several swings gently swaying in the breeze. The wind was cool, and she was glad for her sweatshirt. She sat on the merry-go-round, thinking.

"Lord, what on earth are You doing to me here? Couldn't You at least have given me some inkling that this was Your will for me? You know how I hate surprises."

She stretched out on the warm, red, metal surface of the merry-go-round, realizing how well it reflected the state of her life. She looked up into the clear sky, where only a few wispy clouds wafted overhead. They looked so relaxed. Didn't they know her life was a mess? Couldn't they join in her anxiety, even for a moment?

She frowned, deciding it wasn't in a cloud's nature to be anxious, except during a severe storm, when tossed about by winds and currents, buffeted and hurled. Hmm... the parallels hit her suddenly, with their amazing accuracy.

She stared at the clouds, watching as they gently passed by, moving, but so slowly that she had to concentrate to even notice. It took a minute before she felt the breeze turning the tears on her cheeks into a cold chill. She hurriedly brushed them away, sitting up.

"Okay, Lord, You win. I guess I have no reason to say no, except my stubborn will." The tears were flowing fast now, and she let them come.

"Forgive me, Lord. Here I've been preaching to everyone else about staying in the center of Your will, and when You present me with the chance to do that very thing, I rebel… I'll go where You lead."

She wiped her face with her sleeve, noticing that all her makeup had gone the way of her tears. Great, I must look a mess, she thought.

After a minute, she slowly rose and headed back toward the house.

Kate opened the door, and said, "Come in, dear… Are you all right?"

"Sure," Renn said, pasting on a happy face.

Kate smiled. "I have something I want to tell you."

Still in a daze, Renn followed her into the office. Kate gestured her to a chair, then went to stand behind Craig.

"Sweetie, Craig and I were married by a Justice of the Peace this afternoon."

After only a second's hesitation, she stood and hugged her aunt. "Oh, Kate, Craig, I'm so happy for you both. I guess I shouldn't be surprised. I've seen it in your eyes since the first time I met Craig."

Kate said, "Was it that obvious?"

"Plain as the nose on your face, to coin a phrase," said Renn with a smirk.

Craig stood up, and pulled Renn into a warm embrace. "You know, you can call me 'uncle' now, if you want."

She made a face. "Listen. Saying *uncle* isn't something I'm particularly fond of. In fact, the Lord and I were just discussing that very thing."

"Oh darling," said Kate, stifling sobs, "you mean you'll take me up on my offer?"

"I guess if that's the direction He's pointing, who am I to argue? The hard part is being humble enough to admit that I was the last to notice."

Kate hugged her niece. "That's wonderful, dear."

Renn smiled. "So are you off on a trip now?"

Kate said, "Well, we were discussing it. The volunteers are capable of managing the day to day operations around here, but we weren't sure how you'd feel being left in charge for a week."

Renn looked around, suddenly distracted. "Excuse me. Where's Gordy? I owe him one giant apology."

"He left just as we were coming in. Didn't say a word either. Not a bit like his usual cheerful self."

"Well, that's probably my fault. Could you tell me where he lives?"

Kate said, "One thirteen Millstone Road. His is the little white cottage right at the end of the street, on the corner."

Renn was thoughtful before saying, "Well, I guess getting married takes care of your problem with the house, doesn't it, Kate?"

"I don't know. The trust agreements demand that I remain here for my lifetime. They don't seem to address the question of my remarriage one way or the other."

Renn grinned. "Well, you two just go and have a terrific honeymoon, and I'll hold down the fort. Please leave me a way to get hold of you, though, in case of an emergency. With so much going on around here, I don't want to be the answer man. Oh, and if you could, it might be nice to have something in writing, saying you give me responsibility for the property, and all that goes on here."

Kate said, "Not to worry, darling. We'll take care of it. You're sure you don't mind being left here for a week in the midst of all the commotion?"

"No." Something occurred to her. "Kate, what about your psych evaluation on Monday morning?"

"Oh my, it completely slipped my mind."

She looked at Craig. "It's court ordered, Craig, or I wouldn't give it a thought."

He looked pensive, "Well, I guess we'll just go to my place until after the exam. Then we can leave on our trip."

Renn perked up. "Craig, I'm dying to ask what your place is like."

"Well," he said with a smile, "as silly as it sounds, it's as close to a vine-covered cottage as you could get. I always thought it rather snug myself."

Renn looked at her aunt, who grinned from ear to ear. Renn said, "I'll bet it's exactly the kind of place you were hoping for, am I right?"

"It is. To a tee, darling."

Renn asked, "So, Mr. and Mrs. Steele, when are you going to tell the children?"

Kate shook her head. "Oh, I'm sure they'll find out soon enough. I'm sure not in the mood to deal with any volcanic eruptions right now. Maybe if I wait long enough, the children will simply disappear," she said with a laugh.

Renn said, "Don't worry about a thing. You do whatever you have to, just leave me your number on the fridge. Now, if you'll excuse me, I've got to go see a man about a problem."

She left them standing in the kitchen and strode down the street and around the corner. Gordy was tilling up his side yard when she caught sight of him. He looked rugged, and angry, as if he could plow up the ground with only the force of his fury.

When he noticed her standing at the curb, he stopped and turned off the tiller.

"Putting in a garden?" she asked, smiling gently.

He was gruff. "I do it every year. So?"

"Just wondered," she murmured, dropping her eyes.

"Well," he said, with an icy glare in his eyes, "if you'll excuse me, I'd better get back to work. I've been neglecting a lot of things lately that I need to be tending." With that, he turned away and restarted the tiller.

She didn't know how to feel. He might as well have tipped a bucket of ice water over her head.

She turned and left, perplexed, and stumbled back in the direction she had come. When she got to Kate's, the house was deserted. She found a note, saying they were moving her aunt's things into Craig's house and would be staying the night there. It said to call in case of emergency. Attached to the note was a letter, assigning her responsibility for the place. She refolded the letter and laid it down.

As she opened the refrigerator door, she heard the distinct sound of footfalls overhead. From the bottom of the stairs, she called anxiously, "Hello, who's there?"

Brynn came to the head of the stairs, saying forcibly, "I was just looking for Mother. Where is she?"

"I don't know exactly. I've been out."

Brynn's face turned scarlet. "You all just leave the place unlocked now, when no one's here? So just any Tom, Dick or Harry can walk in and steal us blind?"

"Listen, Brynn, I really don't feel like getting into this now. Would you just—please leave?"

"This is my house, Renn, and I'll leave when I'm good and ready."

Renn shook her head, picked up the kitchen extension and called the police to report a trespasser on the premises. Brynn was staring, wide-eyed, as she hung up the phone.

"How dare you, you little…" Brynn spat. "You had no right to do that. *You* are the interloper here, not me. I should have them arrest *you*."

"Whatever you say, Brynn. But Kate put me in charge in her absence. I have it in writing."

Brynn's eyes were blazing. "Let's see it."

Renn fought to keep her eyes from straying to the paper that lay on the table. "I'll be happy to give it to the police if they ask to see it."

"But you won't give it to me?"

"I don't think that would be wise, dear," she said, knowing she was getting in over her head.

"What would you know about *wise*?"

Renn turned away, filling the teapot and flipped on the burner underneath. "Would you like a cup of tea, Brynn?"

"No, I wouldn't like a cup of tea! I'm out of here. But you haven't seen the last of me."

"Oh, I'll just bet I haven't." Renn surprised even herself with her moxie.

A look of hatred distorted the woman's bull-dog face. "I'll take care of you, you…"

"Yes?" Renn asked.

"Never mind!" shrieked Brynn, stomping out the front door and slamming it behind her.

After bolting the door, Renn poured the steaming water into a cup and added a teabag, to steep. She wondered what Brynn had been up to upstairs. She felt shaken over the confrontation, especially after her cool reception from Gordy.

She took a minute to notify the police of Brynn's exit.

Leaving her cup on the counter, she checked the upstairs and could see nothing out of the ordinary. She must have missed noticing the smudges on the medicine cabinet mirror when she cleaned.

Renn's mind was uneasy about Brynn's visit.

She turned to leave the bathroom, then turned back. Hadn't Kate taken her things to Craig's? Then why was her medicine still in the cabinet?

She was a little lightheaded from all the excitement. The ups and downs of living here were certainly taking their toll. She could feel a headache creeping up the base of her skull. *A couple of Tylenol caps and a nap and I'll be fine.* She took two with water.

Overwhelmed by a feeling of anxiety, she descended the stairs and made sure the house was locked. She switched on a couple of lamps and a kitchen counter light, unwilling to wake to the darkness of a dusky house.

In her bed once more, she pulled the quilt over her and closed her eyes.

~ * ~

When she woke, she was gagging as she hurled herself toward the commode just in time to vomit as if there were no tomorrow. What was wrong with her? She couldn't recall feeling this bad in her life.

Renn dug an emesis basin from under the sink and retrieved a towel from the linen closet, then crawled back into bed, perspiring and chilling

When she woke to the glare of the morning sun, she still felt violently ill. Feeling weak, she didn't know whether she could make it down the stairs to seek help from a volunteer. Her heart sank when she remembered the day; Saturday. No one came on Saturdays. She would be alone all day. Even Martha had the day off.

She vomited again, wishing the process would bring relief. It usually did, but not this time. She found a washcloth and washed her feverish face. Renn swallowed a glass of water, trying to assuage a terrible thirst, but it came up less than a minute later.

She sank onto the bed, trying to think what to do. She felt the room spin around her and made it to the commode just in time.

Grasping the phone a minute later, she dialed her father's number, but no one answered. Unfortunately, he didn't believe in answering machines, so she couldn't leave a message. That was the trouble with Saturdays; no one ever stayed at home.

Light-headed, Renn hung onto the banister for dear life, descending the stairway. She sat, leaning against the wall, half-way down, overcome by an increasing feeling of weakness. She reached the refrigerator and scanned the listed numbers, dialing Craig's number. She felt too lousy to wade through Craig's monologue and hung up, annoyed. Gordy's number caught her eye, as she dragged a chair near the refrigerator and collapsed, drenched in sweat.

She dialed and after only two rings, his machine answered.

The quiver in her voice was unmistakable, as she said, "Listen Gordy, I'm sorry to bother you, but I need help…"

The room swayed precariously before she felt the floor come up to meet her.

Nine

Renn opened her eyes in a daze, disoriented.

An unfamiliar bed cradled her. Gordy sat in a chair, next to her, reading.

She put up her hand, to catch his attention and saw an intravenous needle taped in place. He noticed her movement, and said, "So, you finally made it back. What on earth did you do to yourself?"

She whispered, "I'm so thirsty, please... water?"

He shook his head. "I don't think you can keep it down, but they said to let you try."

He handed her a full plastic glass and she drank it all, hoping to satisfy her unquenchable thirst. But as soon as she finished, she grabbed the emesis basin from him and it all came up.

Frustrated, she began to cry, the room spinning. "I don't know what's happening. I've never felt so bad before."

Gordy said, "They think you may have been poisoned. Did you eat or drink anything unusual, or take any medication lately?"

She nodded. "Two Tylenol capsules from Kate's medicine chest."

With a frown he said seriously, "When was this?"

"Yesterday afternoon, when I got back from your place."

"I'd better go to the house and get them," he said, getting to his feet.

Tears flooded her eyes. "Gordy, I'm so scared."

He sat back down, and said, "I'll be right back. Really. Why don't you go back to sleep? Maybe you'll feel better later."

When he left, she felt abandoned and frightened. She had forgotten to mention Brynn's appearance at the house.

When no one came in response to her call light, she tried to get up to the bathroom. The room spun wildly, as she supported herself with the IV pole. She fell into a chair near the door, to rest. In the bathroom a minute later, she heard a knock on the door and a female voice said, "Honey, are you okay?"

The voice was Martha's. Renn wept with relief. "Martha, could you come in? The door isn't locked."

Martha stood staring for a second, then said, "Sweet Jesus, girl, what on earth is the matter?"

Tears were slipping down Renn's cheeks, as she sighed. "I'm so glad you're here. I've never been so ill in my life. I can hardly make it from here to the bed. I thought I would have to crawl back. No one answered my light… I'm just so dizzy."

She stood and would've fallen had Martha not grabbed her. Gordy's voice could be heard, "Hey, where are you?"

Renn was only half-conscious when she heard Martha yell for him. She could feel herself being tucked back into bed and was only vaguely aware of whispering voices nearby.

She woke up retching, wondering how she could still be so sick when her stomach was empty. Sweat drenched her, as Martha held the basin for her. She could read the look of worry in Gordy's eyes.

The older woman caressed Renn's forehead, gently cooling her face with a wet cloth. "Poor sweet baby," she murmured.

The cool water felt heavenly on her flaming skin.

Looking at Gordy, the older woman said, "So what are they doing for her?"

Renn's eyes closed involuntarily.

Gordy said, "The nurse injected something into her IV, to relieve the nausea and vomiting, but they said they won't really know how to treat her, except to give fluids, until they know exactly what the problem is. I delivered the Tylenol bottle to the desk just before I came in, so maybe they'll know something soon."

Renn just wished she could die and get it over with. She didn't realize she'd spoken it out loud until Martha said, "Now that's no way to talk, sweetie. You're going to get past this. Come on, Gordy, put your hands on her head. We're going to pray for her."

Renn hardly heard the prayer. She was so out of it, she hardly knew which way was up. But before long, the time came for another dreaded trip to the restroom. *That IV must be running full speed ahead*, she thought, as she sat up and pulled herself near the edge of the bed.

"What is it, honey?" Martha asked.

Her voice was weak as she said, "Gotta use the bathroom again. Oh, why does it have to be such a long way away? If only the room would stand still." Martha grabbed another gown from the drawer, and said, "You're so wet, from perspiring— that you're shivering. We'll change your gown while we're in the bathroom. Okay, sweetie?"

Gordy supported her, nearly carrying her, while Martha followed along behind, steering the IV stand, while holding Renn's gown closed.

He handed her over to Martha in the restroom. Renn was nearly oblivious to everything.

Martha said to Gordy, "Listen, don't you go anywhere, sonny. I'm going to need help getting her back to bed. You stay put right outside this door."

He laughed and shook his head. "Why is it I always feel like such a naughty boy where you're concerned?"

"Let's just say I don't want to leave anything to chance."

Between them, they got Renn back to bed, and she slept again.

The next time she woke, Gordy was gone, but Kate had arrived, and Martha was sleeping in the chair.

"Darling," said Kate caressing Ren's forehead, "I'm sorry I wasn't there for you when you called. What on earth happened?"

Renn shrugged, closing her eyes. She was vaguely aware of the nurse injecting something into her IV. The nurse said, "She was poisoned with Muscarine toadstools."

Kate sounded surprised when she said, "What on earth? How could she have gotten into anything like that?"

"Someone doctored her Tylenol."

Kate looked at Renn and took her hand. "Honey, what's going on?"

Renn opened her eyes, and said softly, "I took a couple of Tylenol for my headache, from your medicine chest. Brynn had just left. She'd been upstairs. I wondered what she'd been up to, but I had no idea she'd do something like this."

Kate looked away. "Brynn was at the house?"

Renn nodded. "Right after I got home from Gordy's."

"Did she say what she wanted?"

"She was looking for you. She acted infuriated that you weren't there and that I hadn't gone home. I've never seen her so angry. She also said she'd take care of *me*, whatever that means."

"Good heavens," Kate groaned, "will those children stop at nothing?"

Her niece closed her eyes, once again dropping off to sleep. She awoke later, to find Gordy and Kate sleeping at her bedside. He sat up, rubbing the sleep from his eyes, when Renn stirred. He said, "Can I get you anything? Are you thirsty?"

"I need to use the bathroom, please."

Kate roused, and stood to help.

When they finally tucked her back into bed, Renn said, "I'd love some Seven-Up, if you could manage it. My lips feel like the Sahara."

Kate spoke just as he was leaving the room. She said, "Honey, Gordy brought up the medications from my medicine chest while you were sleeping and they found Muscarine in my allergy medication too."

Renn saw the grief in her aunt's eyes and put out her hand to touch her shoulder. "I'm sorry, Kate."

"I know, dear. If I'd been home, I'd probably be the one in that bed right now. I wish it *were* me instead of you."

"Oh, no, I guarantee that you don't."

Gordy had slipped a straw into a cold can of Seven-Up. It tasted wonderful. And for the first time, she was able to keep it down.

There was a knock at the door just before the doctor came in. He frowned. "You had a mighty close call, young lady."

"That's what I hear."

"Well, now that you're able to drink again," he said, as he gestured toward the soda in her hand, "we should have you out of here in no time."

The next day, Renn found herself sleeping most of the time, as if her body demanded total inactivity to recover. Walking to the bathroom was no longer impossible, but it seemed that all her muscles had turned to mush, practically overnight. The following morning, the doctor dismissed her and she went home to a warm welcome.

Renn could smell the fragrance of homemade vegetable soup filling the house, and for the first time in a long while, she felt starved.

Gordy showed up right before lunchtime; she could hear his laughter echoing up the stairway. He brought up lunch for the two of them and said, "I thought you might like some company. How are you feeling?"

With a sigh, she said, "I'm just *so* glad to be home."

"I thought you'd like to know that the police identified Brynn's fingerprints on the Tylenol and allergy medication bottles, and they picked her up this morning." He paused, and said quietly, "Did I tell you how glad I am that you called me Saturday?"

"No. In fact, I wouldn't have, except that I couldn't get a hold of anyone else. You were my last resort."

A crease furrowed his brow. "I figured as much. I'm sorry I was so cold when you stopped by Friday. I was upset by the rejection I felt when you told me to go home.

"I wasn't angry with you, as much as with God. I felt that everyone was telling me what He wanted me to do—but God Himself, and I felt coerced, and forced."

Gordy hung his head. "That's partly my fault. I forced you to look at it."

She said softly, "Yes, you did, which is why I reacted so badly."

He shook his head, laying down his soupspoon. "Okay, so we were both out of line. Can we call it a draw and put down our weapons?"

Renn opened her hands. "What weapons? As far as I'm concerned, you are the only reason I'm still around to talk about it."

"You don't know how relieved I am to hear it," he said as his eyes lit up with a grin.

Soon, Craig's voice called up the stairway, "You decent, girl? I've come to pay my respects."

She laughed, as he appeared in the doorway. "Listen to you. I'm not even dead yet and you sound like you're attending my wake. Come on in. Did you get some of this yummy soup?"

"Not yet. First things first. I wanted to say I'm sorry we were out when you tried to call Saturday. We saw your number on the caller ID, but by then you were already in the hospital."

Renn smiled. "Oh, don't worry. The Lord was covering the bases."

"Hey," Kate's voice called, "where is everybody?"

Craig grinned. "Shall we tell her?"

"In here, Kate," said Renn. It's the gathering of the Peace talks, everyone wanting to make amends for past history."

The older woman appeared and hugged her niece. "You sure look better, sweetie."

Kate," Renn had a sudden thought, "I wanted to ask you how your psych evaluation went. It was scheduled for this morning, wasn't it?"

The older woman's eyes danced with laughter. "When the attorneys for the children heard about the poisoning, they dropped all action against me."

Renn smiled. "So now you can go on your honeymoon."

"We didn't want to assume anything, until you were up and around."

"Oh, I'm sure I can manage, with Martha and the volunteers coming everyday."

Craig added, "And Gordy says he'll be on-call for you. He even bought a beeper, just for the occasion."

"No kidding." A wide grin crept across Renn's face.

Gordy said, "I told you I thought you females were entirely too vulnerable living here on your own. Now you can reach me anytime and anywhere—if you can get to a phone."

Before Renn could reply, Kate asked, "Are you sure you'll be okay for a week? We don't want you to feel like we've abandoned you."

"You two *need* to get away together. It's been put on hold way too long as it is."

Craig winked at his bride. "You heard what the lady said, sweetie. Start packing, while I make plane reservations."

Renn said, "Kate, has there been any more flack from the neighbors, or anyone else, that I should know about?"

"No. Actually, I'm kind of surprised about it. I thought they'd have lawyers camped on my doorstep day and night."

The front door opened and they could hear several youthful voices, echoing up the stairway. They popped their heads around the corner and Renn recognized Lisa and the others, to whom she had not yet been introduced. When Renn nodded, urging them to come in, they surrounded her bed and knelt on the floor.

Lisa said, "I don't think you've ever met Reba or Marilyn. And this is Jackie and the redhead is Suzanne. They only get to volunteer occasionally. We'd all like to say how glad we are that you're okay."

They nodded their agreement.

Renn blushed. "Thanks. That's very sweet. I'm so glad to know you all. "

Craig laughed in delight. "This is a rare one, who still knows how to blush."

An hour later, Craig and Kate left for the airport and said they would return in a less than a week.

Martha came up to take the dishes downstairs and scolded, "Gordy, what do you mean, letting me, with my old bones, haul these dishes up and down those stairs, when your young bones are just rearing to go?"

He laughed, then apologized, "Okay, okay, Martha. I'm sorry to be such an insensitive so and so. Give them here. I'll take them down for you."

As they left the room, Renn overheard Martha say to him, "You know, you need to let that girl get her rest, or she'll never recover."

Lisa knocked on the doorframe and peeked around the corner. "Am I interrupting? Were you napping or anything? I can come back later if you need to rest."

"No, that's fine. Come in."

The teen took hold of the chintz-covered chair and pulled it around to face Renn.

Lisa said, "I'm so relieved to see you're okay. It sounded really bad."

Renn said, "It *was* really bad. You wanted to see me?"

"I was just wondering how you feel about this new project, the home for unwed mothers."

"Well, I guess I feel like it's where the Lord wants me right now, so I'd have to say I'm okay with it. Why do you ask?"

"Because one of my friends needs a place to go. Mom has had it with me, always inviting my throwaway friends to stay with us. Those are her words. She thinks we already have too many mouths to feed, and I just wondered when the house will be open for business."

"What's your friend's name?"

"Karen DeBolt. Do you remember Linda? They're best friends. When they were here, Karen didn't realize she was pregnant."

"You mean they're both pregnant?"

"Yes, by some jocks at school, who had nothing better to do than get them drunk, then pregnant. Karen's baby is due a month later than Linda's."

Renn sighed, and shook her head in disbelief. "What on earth kind of world are we living in?"

"I don't know. I'm just blessed that my parents were understanding and let me keep my baby. Here, I thought you might like to see a picture of her. Her name is Jasmine."

"Oh," said Renn, taking the picture in her hands. The infant looked like an angel, with huge brown eyes and curly dark hair. "She's adorable. Where is she when you are here?"

"Oh, my mom is nuts about her, and in a way, she's more like mom's baby and my little sister, so it works out fine. Dad thinks the sun rises and sets on Jasmine, so the only danger is that she'll turn out to be a spoiled brat," she said, shaking her head.

Renn smiled at Lisa's joke. "Hug the little sweetie for me, okay?" She paused before adding, "You were telling me about Karen? Where is she staying now?"

"She has a room at the YWCA for a couple of nights, but after that, she has nowhere to go."

Renn said, "Well, I guess now is as good a time as any to open the Martingale House, the house that love built."

Lisa's eyes widened in surprise. "Did that just come out of your mouth, or what? That's a perfect name."

Renn frowned. "I wasn't serious. If anything, it's exactly the opposite. You know what's been happening here, don't you?"

The younger woman shrugged. "It would be pretty hard not to notice something so obvious. But I still think the name is wonderful."

"Whatever you want to call it. Listen, if you don't mind getting the rooms ready, freshening them up, and airing them out, I'm more than willing to have the girls come at any time."

"Oh, thanks. It almost makes me wish I had nowhere to go."

"Please don't say that, sweetie. Your parents sound wonderful."

"You're right. I need to be grateful for what I have."

Renn painstakingly made her way down the stairs, to see Martha still there at suppertime.

The older woman frowned. "Girl, what on earth are you doing coming down those stairs?" she asked, clearly upset.

"I didn't know you were still here."

Martha pulled a chair out, and gestured, saying, "Well, sit down before you fall down. Let's have something to drink. Supper will be ready in a few minutes."

"What about your family, Martha? Don't you need to get home to them?"

"Not really. It's just me and my old tomcat, Virgil, and he comes and goes as he pleases. So it's really just me. I figured you needed me to stay later since you're not really back on your feet yet."

"Thanks, Martha. For some reason I thought you had a husband to do for."

"No, dear, I guess we've never gotten around to talking about Jack. He was the love of my life for forty years, but he died at about the same time Craig lost his wife. My Jack has been gone a year now and that house seems pretty empty, especially of an evening."

Renn asked, "Well, Martha, is there any reason you shouldn't move in here, too? Do you like having your own place?"

"You know, I thought I did, but as time passes, it seems to matter less and less to me. I guess when a person is in the Lord's will, it doesn't really matter where she lays her head, does it?"

Renn grinned, and nodded. "You're right, sweetie."

"I like my home. It's full of memories. But it's getting to be a burden to keep up, you know, what with maintenance, repairs, and taxes, to say nothing of the yard work."

"So, how would you feel about moving in with us?

Martha frowned. "Us?"

"Lisa has several pregnant friends who have nowhere to go, so I told her that we are now open for business ASAP."

"You did? Why, honey, that's wonderful. The only thing is, I've been alone so many years, I don't know if I'd be able to deal with noisy teenagers."

"Well, I wouldn't expect you to stay upstairs with us. If I'm not mistaken, there are several bedrooms and baths downstairs and even a kitchen. The family room makes it a complete apartment, doesn't it?"

She nodded. "There's even a door that can be used to close it off. But do you think Kate would mind? I mean, if I moved in?"

"Of course not. Listen, if you don't mind doing the cooking and being the chief homemaker around here, I would love to have you with us. I think we would have a ball, and when you got tired of the confusion, you could retire to your rooms, downstairs, where no one would bother you. What do you think?"

Martha's face lit up in a smile. "Honey, you don't know how good it feels to be wanted. I've been asking the Lord how He thought I'd manage alone in my later years." She paused briefly for a breath. "I'm sixty-two, and my health is good now. I can see a time coming, though, when I won't be able or even want to care for a place like mine, especially with all the stairs."

"So you'll come?"

"You won't have to ask me twice."

Ten

Martha had just set the food on the table when they heard a knock on the kitchen window.

At the same instant, they said, "It's Gordy."

Renn said, "If I know him, he's starving."

"No problem. We've got enough, even for Gordy."

Renn opened the door to Gordy, who grinned. "Any handouts for a hungry fella?"

She nodded. "Of course. What's one more mouth for our soup kitchen?"

Martha had fixed chicken and dumplings, creamed peas, and applesauce cake, like everybody's grandmother used to make.

After tasting everything, Renn exclaimed, "Oh, Martha, I haven't had anything so wonderful since I was a little girl."

The older woman chuckled in delight. "Oh, honey, I think you'd be grateful for a doggie chew biscuit soaked in broth."

Gordy laughed, slapping his hand over his full mouth, before swallowing. "You guys are about to make me fall off my chair. Now could we please have some peace and quiet while I eat?"

Renn grinned, and Martha slapped him playfully on the shoulder. "Honey, you'd better get used to racket, because this place is shortly going to be overrun with noisy young females."

He wiped his mouth on his napkin. "Mmm... She's absolutely right." With a concocted southern drawl, he added, "These vittles is great." Then he looked up. "So when is all this supposed to take place?"

Renn said, "Oh, any time now, actually. There are several who have nowhere else to go."

Martha shooed them away, after supper and Gordy said, "How about going to the park and playing on the swings?"

"I don't know."

He noted the look on her face. "Still not quite up to snuff? Okay, then, I'll settle for sitting on the porch with you. How about it? I'll swing you on the porch swing."

"I think I can manage that."

He led her out to the porch. "It's great to have you home."

"Thanks."

"When you get to feeling a little better, maybe we can actually go out and do something. You know, have a real date, that is, if you feel like you know me well enough by now."

"I'd like that."

He urged, "So fill me in on the changes around here. They're happening so fast, my head is spinning."

"Well, you know Craig and Kate are honeymooning. I have the green light to open the house to the girls whenever I'm ready, and it sounds as if I need to be ready tomorrow."

"And how do you feel about that?"

She smiled. "Great, I just wish I had a little more energy to help with the preparations." After a brief pause, she added, "But the thing that really excites me is that Martha has agreed to move in, downstairs, and make it her apartment. She'll do what she already does and have us for company, as well as a place to live."

"What about the stairs? This place is loaded with them."

"Well, it sounds like her home has plenty of steps too. She doesn't seem to have a problem with them yet. But Kate has already planned to add those stairway seats if the time comes they are needed. I just have to ask. So what do you think?"

"Y'all are movin' entirely too fast to suit me," he said, with a laugh. "No, I'm kidding. I can't think of anything I'd enjoy more than having her around. She's one spunky lady."

When it got too dark to see a short time later and the mosquitoes started their feeding frenzy on Renn's bare arms, he said, "Let's put a movie on. I know Kate has some really good ones in the upstairs den."

He held her arm as they ascended the stairway and she said, "It seems like this stairway has gotten a lot longer in the last week… Oh, I meant to tell you to give me the bill for your beeper and I'll reimburse you."

He frowned. "Nah. The beeper will be my contribution to the Martingale House, The House That Love Built."

Renn's mouth dropped open as she turned to look at him. "Where did you hear that?"

He chuckled and took her arm as they made their way up the last two steps. "Lisa told me how you came up with it on the spur of the moment. I think it's great. In fact, the name is so good, it should do wonders for our PR efforts."

He searched through the videos and pulled out *An Affair to Remember*, with Cary Grant, and Deborah Kerr. He held it up. "Don't all women go crazy for this movie?"

"I suppose," Renn said, "to a point."

Just then, they could hear someone beating ferociously on the front door.

He said, "You stay put. I'll see who it is."

Renn could hear the heated exchange all the way up the stairs. Berke had nearly broken down the door, wanting in.

He yelled, "I want you out! All of you. This is not your house. It's mine—and you are out of here right now!"

Renn heard loud banging and furniture being moved around downstairs. "All this stuff," he screamed, "is going to be out on the sidewalk when I get through!"

Renn made her way to the top of the stairs. She never dreamed he would get so out of control. She sat on the top step and said, "Berke, your mother gave me permission to supervise the house and all that goes on here."

"Well, we already know she's out of her mind, so I'm taking over. Right now."

Gordy blocked Berke's way into the living room and Berke threw a sucker punch that landed solidly on his chin. Renn knew Gordy had to be seeing stars.

"Please, Berke, come up and let's talk," said Renn.

He scowled. *"Time for talking is over, cousin."* He said it with such venom that she could feel the heat of his hatred. She noticed an odd glassy look in his eyes. *Had he been drinking, nursing a grudge?*

She slowly made her way down the stairs, as the two men continued throwing punches. Berke landed a punch on Gordy's chin that knocked him against a wall, where he slid to the floor. In two steps, Berke was in the living room, where, with superhuman strength, he began upending living room furniture and tossing magazines and pamphlets everywhere.

"Berke, stop, or I'll have to call the police," Renn said, as she reached the landing.

Gordy was trying to recover his balance when Renn lunged toward the phone, but her cousin was on her immediately. His hands encircled her throat, his eyes daring her to stop him. He pressed on her larynx as she fought, scratching his face, trying to escape from his grasp. She could feel herself starving for air.

Just then, Gordy jumped him and took him down as Berke gave a piercing screech. He shook Gordy off and suddenly jumped to his feet, glaring.

"If the two of you think you're going to cheat me out of my father's estate, you're wrong. I'll see you dead before that happens. I'm giving you fair warning." He was calm now, with a crazed look in his eyes.

The glass in the door rattled as he slammed it on his way out.

Gordy picked up the phone and dialed 911, reporting the threats. The dispatcher said a patrol car would be out shortly.

Renn was rubbing her bruised neck, when Gordy said, "Are you okay? Let me take a look. You will probably have a dilly of a bruise tomorrow." After a brief pause, he added, "I don't think it's safe for you to stay here alone tonight. Call Martha to come and spend the night. I'm staying, too. In the morning we're having the locks changed, and I'm buying you a big dog."

Renn shook her head in disbelief. "Gordy, we can't have a big dog around here with strangers coming and going."

He shrugged, and said resolutely, "Then we'll rent one."

"Haven't you heard a word I said?"

He frowned. "I heard."

She repeated, "A dangerous dog isn't going to help our already frightening situation."

"Well, it'll make me feel better."

She shrugged, sighing. He had obviously made up his mind.

She stared at his swelling face. "So how's your jaw?"

"Don't ask," he said, gingerly touching his cheek.

She pulled an icebag from the freezer and handed it to him. "Here, this will keep it from swelling."

"Thanks. You know, I don't think that guy is playing with a full deck. Honestly. He was totally nuts."

"You're right. His eyes were creepy."

Shortly, Martha appeared at the door, and frowned at the mess in the living room. Two bored male police officers showed up just then, took their statements and said all they could do was increase police presence in the neighborhood. An officer would drive by every couple of hours instead of once a day.

After making a few phone calls, Gordy left, saying he'd be right back. A huge Doberman was straining against the leash Gordy held when he returned a short time later.

Renn shook her head. She felt uneasy with the dog's obvious aggression. "Do you think I'll feel safer with that thing around? He looks like he could eat me as easily as look at me."

"Well, that's just until I tell him who you are. Listen, Romeo," he said, crouching beside the dog and pointing to Renn, "this is Renn. Renn is a friend, so you let her be. And this dear lady," he pointed to Martha, "is Martha, who is also a friend. You be nice to her. She's doing me a big favor being here. Your job, Romeo," he said, with a laugh, "if you decide to accept it—is to guard the place from nut cases like Berke."

Renn couldn't contain a giggle. "I can't believe a dog like that could be called Romeo. Talk about a misnomer."

Gordy and Martha moved their things into the upstairs bedrooms while Renn rested at the kitchen table. A few minutes later, they supported her trek up the grand staircase.

"Thanks, you guys. Sleep well," she said at the door of her room. She showered and spent a few minutes journaling about the fast-moving events of the day. After a short quiet time, she fell into an exhausted, dreamless sleep.

She awoke in the dark, aroused by a soft scuffling noise and flipped on the light. Romeo had made his way into her room, though the door was closed when she went to bed. At least she thought it was.

The muscled-canine glared at her with glazed eyes, and she was unsure whether he had understood Gordy's definition of *friend*. She involuntarily let out a piercing scream when the dog lunged straight for her. Immediately, he began digging into her bed for all he was worth, trying to pull the covers back. Finally he grabbed the quilt in his teeth, pulling, as she tugged on the other end.

Gordy appeared in a flash and said, "Romeo, heel. Good boy. What on earth? How did he get in here? I thought you closed your door."

"I did."

Renn could feel her heart hammering a crescendo in her ears.

Gordy said, "Are you okay? You look pale."

Her teeth were chattering as she said breathlessly, "Well, what did you expect? He scared ten years off my life."

He laughed at the look on her face. "Oh, I bet I know what happened. Romeo is used to sleeping with Dale and I'll bet he got cold and went hunting for his bed. Come on, boy. We'll make you a bed downstairs." He turned to her, "And I'm going to lock your door on my way out."

Renn grimaced, shaking her head. "Good plan."

She turned off her light, but sleep refused to come. The clock read two-fourteen when she grabbed the robe off the end of the bed and threw it around her shoulders. She made a bathroom stop, then sat down at her computer and began to write.

Her writing career had suffered, living here, but maybe nights would better accommodate keyboard work. *At least there would be no interruptions.*

She readied a proposal for an article and finished another piece for a women's magazine, stamping them for mailing. It felt good to be back in the swing of things. Somehow it released the tension pent-up inside her, almost as if she'd run a marathon or done a two-hour workout. A while later, she was annoyed to notice a progressive feeling of weakness and fever as she shut down her laptop.

The clock gonged six times as she finally crawled into bed, feeling terrible. She still felt awful when she was awakened within the hour, by the doorbell, accompanied by Romeo's ferocious barking. Renn felt flushed and lightheaded as she threw on her robe and ran to the door of her room. She yelled, "Gordy, I forgot about the girls moving in today. Romeo will scare them to death."

He already had. When Gordy opened the door, he saw that they had scattered off the porch, tossing their belongings to the winds.

Gordy looked chagrined and said, "Sorry, ladies, this is our loaner watchdog, Romeo. He's friendly, honest. I'm sorry he frightened you. Please, come on in. After I put him somewhere out of the way, I'll retrieve your things from the lawn."

Romeo barked and howled, clearly unhappy to be stranded in the mudroom.

Gordy looked properly embarrassed, as he sat at the breakfast table, listening to the dog's plaintive yowling. A few minutes later, he swallowed the last bite of toast and drained his coffee cup. "Listen," he said to Renn, "I don't think he's working out all that well. What do you think?"

She shook her head and burst out laughing. "I think he's homesick. And to be honest, he's made me a nervous wreck. You know, if he bites someone, we'll be liable for their injuries."

"Say," Gordy said with a knowing nod, "I hadn't given that a thought, but you're right. Even if he bit Berke, we'd be liable, wouldn't we?"

"You're the law man in the house, so you'd know better than I about that."

Gordy had Romeo by the leash as they left, and it was a toss-up as to which direction they would take, with Romeo straining his muscular hulk against Gordy's massive frame.

When Gordy returned a while later, he wiped the sweat from his brow and said, "Dale was in the same shape as Romeo. I guess they've never spent a night apart since he was six weeks old and that was four years ago. They're basket cases, both of them."

Renn giggled as she dried her hands on a dishtowel. "Since who was six weeks old? Dale or the dog?"

He laughed, and mussed her hair. "You know, you're a funny gal. You keep me on my toes."

"Well, somebody has to."

Gordy nearly inhaled a second breakfast of ham and eggs, with toast and fried potatoes. He poured his fourth cup of coffee and headed for the door.

"I've got to get the mowing done." With a shake of his head, he said, "I'll be losing Renn in it shortly if I don't make quick work of it."

Martha grinned at Renn, after the door closed behind him. "I think he's got feelings for you, sweetie."

The sound the mower filled the air, ushering in the fragrance of fresh cut grass. Not long after, he took a coffee break, poured a refill and offered, "Anything more I can do to help the girls move in?"

Renn said, "I think they just brought clothes, things that would fit in a duffel bag. Thanks for the offer, though."

The girls were happily making girl-noise upstairs and Gordy smiled at the sound. "It's nice to have kid sounds in the house, isn't it?"

"Well, it is now, but we'll see how we feel about it after a week or two."

"Say," he said seriously, "maybe you'd better get yourself a chalkboard and list the house rules".

"No, that's too much like school," she said. "They're all sharp girls who just need to be told once. I'm sure they'll be great."

He grinned in awe. "Whoa, I'll bet you'll get the housemother-of-the-year award, thinking like that."

"Listen, I'll be doing good just to keep up with them. I don't want to hinder the Holy Spirit by trying to take His place. Know what I mean?"

Gordy took her hand, as she turned away. "Hey," he said, "I have a locksmith coming to change all the deadbolts at ten this morning. Thought you'd want to know."

"Thanks, Gordy. You're a really handy guy to have around."

"I do what I can," he said with a mischievous twinkle in his eye.

Renn added, "Just give me his bill when you get it, and I'll write him a check." She was grateful that Kate had put her name on the checking account.

~ * ~

Renn felt progressively worse, as the day wore on.

The deadbolts had all been exchanged for shiny new ones by four o'clock, giving Renn a heightened sense of security.

Martha was working on laundry, hauling a load of towels up from the basement. Her face reflected her exhaustion.

Renn couldn't help but be concerned as she asked, "Martha, are you okay?"

"I think so. It's just those doggoned steep stairs. They get to my knees."

"Listen, I'll do the hauling from now on, all right?"

"Honey, you're as weak as a kitten. No way I could ask you to do that."

Renn frowned, thinking. "Well, we just acquired several energetic young folks, who have nothing better to do than to help with laundry. What do you think of that idea?"

"I'd say," she said with a nod, "it's a winner."

Renn slowly climbed the stairs, as Gordy watched. At the door of Linda's room, she saw Karen sitting on the bed. They both stood as she knocked. "Oh it's okay, don't get up. I just have a small favor to ask. I guess I should introduce myself before asking for favors, though, shouldn't I?"

They giggled timidly.

"I'm Renn, but then, you already knew that didn't you?" After a pause, she added, "I hope you'll feel welcome here. Okay, now for the favor. Martha… you've met her, right? Well, she is having a hard time negotiating the stairs and needs some help hauling the laundry up from the basement. Would you guys be willing to take care of that? She or I will fold it, if you can just get it up here, okay? Right now, I'm still a little under it, so I may ask your help now and then until I'm feeling on top of things if that's all right?"

"Sure, no problem. I'll be happy to do my part," said Linda. Karen said nothing, just smiled and nodded shyly.

"Thanks. And I meant to extend my welcome to you long before this."

Karen gave a timid nod. "I just want to say thanks for letting us stay. We'll be on our best behavior. And if there's anything you need, just yell."

"Thanks, guys, and I sure appreciate your help. In about an hour, you can change the laundry and haul it up for Martha, if you would. Now if you'll excuse me, I think I'll go lie down."

Karen held out her hand. "Are you okay, Renn? You don't look so good."

All of a sudden, the room turned upside down and she was gone.

Eleven

She woke up on her bed with Gordy patting her hand.

She chuckled, shaking her head. "They only do that in the movies, Gordo."

He was serious. "Listen, you scared me. What is going on with you?"

"I don't know. One minute I was fine and the next, that was it."

He looked perturbed when he said, "Well, I don't think that's normal. I think you should see a doctor."

"No way, Gord. I just fainted."

"Well, any more of that and you're going, whether you like it or not."

"Excuse me," Renn asked, "but who crowned you king around here?"

"No one, but someone has to use good sense when you're not."

She felt the color rise in her cheeks. "You know, you're welcome to go back to your place whenever you're ready. We girls will be just fine now that the locks have been changed."

He glared at her. "What, you think I'm butting in and you resent it?"

"In a word, yes. And I'd appreciate it if you'd stop."

"So—what?" he asked, "so you can scare those poor girls out of their wits, blacking out at their feet?"

She frowned, feeling defensive. "Well, it's not exactly an everyday occurrence."

He shook his head. "You haven't got the good sense God gave a chicken. Something is wrong, and you just don't want to see it. So don't, but just remember what I said. I think it's lousy of you not to care about the girls more than that. I'll be leaving after supper, for your information."

"Fine," she retorted, "see ya."

"Maybe, and maybe not," he murmured.

She worked at her writing for a short time, but felt so rotten, she finally closed her laptop. She requested a supper tray be sent up, so she wouldn't have to deal with the stairs again. The truth was that she didn't want to see Gordy again today, and maybe never. After two bites, she set the tray aside.

Martha sought her out and said, "Gordy's terribly worried about you, honey. He only acts angry because he's afraid."

"I don't care how he feels. He's acting entirely too possessive. I hate that stuff. I can take care of myself."

"Are you sure, honey?"

With a frown, she said, "Martha, what are you saying?"

"I'm saying I think he's right. You shouldn't be having this kind of trouble. And you should be bouncing back a lot faster, if you want my opinion. Your color isn't that great, and your appetite isn't either, from the looks of those dishes. Now why won't you get it taken care of?"

"I'm fine, Martha. If it continues, I'll go to the doctor. But I really think I'm fine. Maybe you could take the tray now."

The older woman pointed to the tray. "This is exactly what I mean. You hardly touched a bite. You used to eat better than this."

"Please… I don't need a mother hen telling me what to do." Immediately regretting her harsh words, she said, "Oh Martha, I'm sorry. I shouldn't have said that."

The older woman sat down on the bed and gathered her into a hug. "Honey, you're about as close to a daughter as I've got. You forgive a meddling old woman for worrying, but I *am* worried. Ask the Lord for wisdom, will you?"

"Thanks, Martha. I'll try to have a teachable heart. Sometimes I get so stubborn, I can hardly stand myself."

The older woman turned just before leaving the room. "Anything you'd like me to tell Gordy?"

"No, thanks. And shut the door on your way out, okay? I'd appreciate it."

Her throat was scratchy and she noticed tender, swollen glands in her neck. She stuck a thermometer under her tongue. It registered one hundred two point two. She lay down for a nap soon afterwards and didn't wake until morning.

Something really *was* wrong. A nap shouldn't last over fourteen hours. The truth was, she felt like she hadn't slept at all.

She got up, brushed her teeth and started down to make breakfast. She was going to eat whether she felt like it or not.

Martha was already up, folding laundry, fragrant and warm from the dryer. She gave Renn an odd look before commenting, "Kind of a long nap, wasn't it, sweetie? The girls were worried about you. And so am I. I had just decided to call Gordy if you weren't awake in the next fifteen minutes."

"I'm glad you didn't. I'm calling the doctor this morning."

"Got any appetite?"

She sighed and shook her head. "Not much."

Three volunteers came in just then, happy and giggling. They weren't much older than the girls upstairs, who joined them a few minutes later.

"Hi, Martha. Hi, Renn. Mmm… what are you cooking?"

"Beef stroganoff."

"Oh, I wish I lived here," Lisa commented with wide eyes.

Martha grinned and offered, "I'll feed you whether you live here or not, sweetie."

"All right!" Lisa cheered.

The mower started a few minutes later and they had to close the windows, and turn on the air conditioning to shut out the sound. Gordy didn't appear at the door at all, and Renn knew he was still smarting over her angry words. They were getting to be a habit with her, and she wasn't proud of the fact.

The doctor's office was able to squeeze her in for a late morning appointment, which a cancellation made available. Gordy looked in her direction as she slid into her car. She waved and smiled apologetically. He waved briefly, unsmiling, and watched as she pulled out of the drive.

The doctor greeted her with a frown and tilted his head, adjusting his bifocals to take a closer look at her face and neck, "My nurse thinks you're being abused. Are you?"

She explained the circumstances surrounding her injuries and the fact that she was now in charge of a group of pregnant girls. He said, "Well, if I didn't already know you, I'd wonder what was going on. Come out in the hall. I want to weigh you." She hesitated only a moment before complying. As he pushed the small weight further toward the left, he asked, "So have you bounced back from the poisoning?"

"Not completely, I guess."

He frowned at the numbers on the scale. "Renn, I don't believe you're anorexic, but something is going on. What is it?"

She burst into tears, as he followed her into the exam room and closed the door behind her. He helped her onto the exam table and sat down, tilting his head thoughtfully.

The lab girl came in, and drew several vials of blood from Renn's arm a short time later.

When Renn had composed herself, she explained the emotional strain she'd been under. He said, "Do you want me to prescribe an antidepressant?"

"No. I'll be fine."

His tone was unbending as he said, "I want you back here to see me in one week." He excused himself to retrieve the results of her lab work. She felt angry at his demanding tone and was glad he wasn't there to see her struggle with it.

When he returned a few minutes later, he was frowning. He said, "You have mono, girl. Now, you may be wondering if there's any danger to the girls or their babies, but mono is not easily contracted, so there shouldn't be a problem.

"Now, getting back to you, you're bordering on anemia and dehydration. Haven't you been eating and drinking?" He barely paused before rushing on. "Now, if you don't want to be hospitalized for IV's, forced feeding and vitamins, you'll get busy, and start taking care of yourself. I mean it," he added sternly. He dug into a drawer, and handed her a handful of sample packages. "Take these vitamin and iron supplements everyday, without fail." He fished the pen out of his coat pocket and began writing on her chart.

Only minutes later, she tossed her handbag onto the front seat of her car and fished the keys from her pocket. As if things weren't bad enough already, her Camry engine failed to turn over for several minutes. *What else can go wrong?*

She felt an overwhelming sense of relief when it finally stirred to life. She pulled out of the parking lot and edged into heavy traffic, feeling terribly fatigued. *I'll nap at the first opportunity.*

She was approaching the driveway, where Gordy was still mowing, when she felt her vision growing fuzzy. In front of the house, she slammed on the brakes, too late to avoid hitting something. A cold feeling of terror momentarily enveloped her before blackness descended.

Gordy was sitting cross-legged on the lawn, holding her, when she came to. He was irate. "What in tarnation is the matter with you?" As he stroked her cheek, his harsh tone softened, "You could have killed yourself. Why can't you ask for help like any normal person?" She glanced over to see that she had bounced her car over the curb.

She felt achy and feverish. Exhaustion overwhelmed her until she could hardly keep her eyes open. Tears slid down her cheeks and she just shook her head.

He stood, cradling her in his arms and said softly, "It's going to be okay, babe. Just rest. I'll take care of everything. She let her eyes close and though she heard the sound of soft voices around her, she couldn't hold on to a single word.

Later, she was aware of the comforting sound of the mower in the yard, but that was all she knew until morning.

~ * ~

Martha brought up her breakfast at nine the next morning.

She said, "The girls tried to wake you last night, but you wouldn't wake up. Did you know that? What did the doctor say?"

"I have mono. He gave me some vitamins and iron pills and yelled at me for not eating and drinking adequately."

"Well, let's get you fed, then." The older woman uncovered the plate to reveal poached eggs on toast and orange juice.

Renn smiled and looked up to meet the other woman's gaze. "Martha, did you know that's what I used to make for my mother when she was sick?"

Martha settled into the chair and crossed her ankles. "Well, what did your mother make for you when *you* were sick?"

Matter-of-factly, Renn said, "Oh, she was always sick, so there wasn't time for me to be sick."

The older woman frowned, and fidgeted in her seat. "You mean your mother never mothered you?"

Renn took a sip of her juice and shrugged. "Not to speak of, I guess. She had a heart condition, and always needed me to look after her."

Renn took a bite of toast and chewed thoughtfully.

"Well, no wonder you can't bear to let anyone mother you. It's foreign and frightening."

Renn frowned, unable to think of a word to say.

Martha continued, "That's why you give Gordy such a hard time, you know. You just can't stand for someone to take care of you. Am I right?'

Renn grimaced before she said, "I guess I never thought about it quite like that."

Martha stood to her feet and softly caressed Renn's hair. "Well, think about it, sweetie, because I think it's the key to everything, if you don't mind my saying so."

She added, "The girls have been folding all the linens. They've been wonderful. I think I'm going to love having them around." After a pause, she said, "You realize, don't you, that to be a good housemother, you need to settle your own issues first. You know, take the log out of your own eye, before trying to take the fleck of dust out of someone else's."

Renn flinched at the blunt words.

Martha's eyes filled with tears. "I'm not trying to hurt you, honey. But honestly, there are just some things a body can't see without help from the outside."

When the older woman left the room, tears nearly choked Renn.

She couldn't eat another bite and covered the tray with her napkin. She forced the juice down her sore throat, adding tears

135

of pain to the tears of heartache that threatened to drown her. She curled up, closing her eyes.

When Martha returned a while later, she stood looking at the tray. She removed the napkin that covered the plate, setting it aside.

"Why you've hardly touched a bite." Seeing the look on Renn's face, she said, "Okay, okay, I'm leaving. I'll be around if you want to talk."

Renn got up long enough to take the vitamin samples the doctor had given her before crawling back into bed. He had suggested rest and minimal physical activity. She had no trouble with that concept at all. She turned over and went back to sleep.

When she woke, it was already getting dark and for the first time, she was afraid. She had never felt this out of control before and found it unnerving and frightening. Her entire self-image centered on her competence and sense of self-reliance.

She left the room and, holding tight to the rail, descended the stairs, in search of Martha. The main floor was deserted; she had evidently gone to her rooms in the basement. Renn gazed at the stairs. Even if she went down, she wouldn't have the strength to climb them again.

She turned to go up the stairs to her own room and suddenly realized that they loomed larger than the pyramids of Egypt. She collapsed on the steps in tears.

When she finally calmed down, she sank onto a kitchen chair to think. *Okay, this should not be that difficult to figure out.*

~ * ~

After a minute, she made her way to the library, turned on a lamp and made herself a cup of herb tea, then snuggled under the thick afghan on the couch. With the television sound on low to comfort her, she fell asleep.

Sometime during the early morning, Martha came in and turned off the television, waking her. "Honey, what are you doing in here?"

All at once Renn's tears started and refused to stop. Martha sat down and put her arm around the younger woman's shoulders, caressing her hair. "Honey, what on earth?"

"I'm sorry to fall apart on you this way. I came down to find you last night, but you had already gone to your rooms. I knew I couldn't go downstairs after you and I couldn't make it back upstairs to mine. So I just came in here and curled up."

"Oh, honey," Martha said gently, drying Renn's tears with the hanky from her pocket. "I'm sorry this happened."

Renn whispered, "I've never felt so helpless in my life."

They could hear the front door slam and knew, by Gordy's whistling, that he was headed for the coffeepot.

"Say, what's going on here?" he said, appearing at the library door, looking confused.

"Renn came down to find me last night, but I had already gone to my apartment. She knew she couldn't manage the stairs, or even make it back up to her room, so she came in here and slept."

He frowned, looking annoyed. "Well, for heaven's sake, let's put in an intercom system. Having pregnant girls here, we probably need one anyway."

Martha asked, "Is that something you could do?"

"It's just wiring, so it should be no problem. Hey, Renn, I don't think it's a good idea for you to be stuck upstairs with this going on. You really need a bed on the main floor. What do you say?"

Martha nodded and Renn smiled briefly. "Thanks, Gordy. Sorry to be so much trouble."

"Listen," he murmured, suddenly perking up. "We macho types have to do stuff like this on a more or less regular basis just to keep from feeling totally worthless. Don't worry. I'll have you fixed up in no time. There's an extra bed or two down in the cedar closet, isn't there, Martha? And a good mattress or two?"

The older woman nodded. "There should be several, if I recall. I'll get the linens and we'll get it ready for you, sweetie."

Feeling comforted, Renn curled up and dropped off to sleep.

She woke again to the sound of Gordy's voice and the touch of his hand ruffling her hair. "Hey, sleepyhead, I've got your room all set up. Come and see what you think." He helped her up and escorted her down the hall to the library, which was set up with all her essentials, including her laptop and books. "Thanks, Gordy. I really appreciate it."

He hauled a big wedge-shaped pillow from the closet and set it next to the bed. "Thought this might be helpful, so you could use the laptop while you're resting."

She sank onto the bed, covered her eyes and burst into tears.

He sat down beside here, put his arm around her and said, "What's the matter, girl?"

"I don't know how you can stand to keep coming back for more abuse from me. I'm so sorry. Martha made me see that I have a problem letting someone care for me. I guess I don't know how to act when someone reaches out in that way. I know I've hurt your feelings and I feel terrible about it."

"Listen, I'm learning to develop a thick skin being around you. Don't worry about it. Nothing you can say or do will make me care for you less. Right now, you just feel sick, kiddo. Things won't look so glum once you feel better. Crawl in and rest now, okay?" He pulled back the covers and helped her get situated, before covering her and gently caressing her hair.

He added, "I promise, in a couple of weeks, you'll be feeling much better."

She said sarcastically, "What a comfort that is. A couple of weeks? Just how do you know so much?"

"I looked it up on the Internet. It takes two to three weeks to get over this, so just be prepared to be down, then it will be over." He tilted his head, and grinned, looking like a giddy child. "And by the way, you just finished apologizing for your last outburst. So let's try not to let it happen again, all right?"

Renn laughed in spite of herself.

He joined in the laughter, once again ruffling her messy hair, and said, "Go back to sleep. It'll do you good."

He didn't have to tell her twice. She was out like a light again in no time.

The next two weeks, surprisingly, went very quickly, with her sleeping twenty hours out of every twenty-four. By the end of the first week, she decided she would need physical therapy to ever resume a normal life. She made it a habit to walk around the entire first floor several times a day, after the crowds dissipated, just to regain her strength.

At the end of the second week, Gordy, who had been popping in frequently to visit, during her few waking hours, said, "So do you feel like your old self yet?"

She was thoughtful, before saying, "I don't know. I don't think I'd recognize her if I met her on the street."

He couldn't stifle a laugh, and it made her smile to see him so happy.

"Well," he said, as he made himself comfortable on the end of the bed, "tomorrow is the end of your second week and if you feel up to it, I think we should celebrate."

"By doing what?" she asked skeptically, "herding buffalo?"

"I'm not sure that even I would be up for that. How about dinner and a movie?"

"Okay. It will certainly be good to see something besides these four walls, hallowed though they be."

He made a face. "You're something else. Do you know that? Well, then, you're on. Be ready by five. We're going out for Chinese. Does that suit you?"

"Ooh," she said, involuntarily smacking her lips.

Watching her blush sent him into gales of laughter. She apologized, "Sorry. It's my all time favorite, so you can see why I can hardly contain myself."

Twelve

The next morning, Renn got out of bed and tested her sea legs. She couldn't believe it; except for a little remaining weakness, she felt pretty good.

Martha came to the door, and knocked. "So what would you like for breakfast, sweetie?"

Renn said with excitement, "Well, just how much are you willing to cook?"

"What?" Martha asked, bewildered.

"I'm starved, Martha. For the first time in a month, I'm actually hungry. Feed me. I'll eat it all, whatever it is, if it has gravy on top."

Martha chuckled, and enveloped her in a warm hug. "It's so good to see you smiling again, sweetie. Just give me ten minutes and I'll bring you a tray."

"Martha, I want to eat in the kitchen, with anyone else who's up. I feel like I've just found my admission ticket back into the human race."

Both Linda and Karen were having breakfast when Renn joined them. She ate like there was no tomorrow, feeling like every bite of Martha's biscuits and gravy were manna from heaven.

Renn said, "So how are you guys doing upstairs on your own? I hope you're beginning to feel at home."

Karen's smile was warm when she said, "Oh, this place is like a dream. Everyone is so wonderful. I feel like I belong to a real family for the first time in my life."

Linda added, "Well, I always thought I had a loving home, until I messed up. Sometimes it takes a crisis to show you what a relationship is made of. As far as I'm concerned, this place is one in a million. We want you to know we aren't taking it for granted either."

Renn said, "You've been a godsend, helping out the way you have, and I want you to know how much I appreciate it. I also need to apologize for blacking out in front of you. It had to be frightening."

"Well," said Linda, "it's not like you could really help it, now, is it?"

"We've been praying for you, Renn," said Karen.

"Oh, honey," Renn burst into tears, "you don't know how much I appreciate hearing you say that."

Karen sprang from her chair and laid her head in the older woman's lap, enveloping her in a fervent embrace. Renn smoothed the girl's soft hair and said, "You are such a blessing to me. Both of you." The girls left, encouraging her to rest.

She had just crawled back into bed when Lisa knocked, saying, "I hope I'm not disturbing you."

"Not at all. Come on in."

"Renn, I just wanted to say how much I appreciate you taking in the girls. My mother and father thank you too."

"They're such sweet girls. They've really been a help in the past few days, in case you haven't already noticed."

"Oh, I heard. So how are you feeling?"

"Great. Now if I can just get my strength back, my mind would love to run around the block."

"Wow." The young girl's eyes widened in awe. "That's a pretty big leap from where you are now, isn't it?"

"Sure," Renn said with a smile, "but I can dream, can't I?"

When Gordy came inside for his morning coffee, she was sitting cross-legged on the floor, reading. He brought two cups to her room and sat down beside her. Handing her a cup, he said, "Be careful. It's really hot." After a pause, he looked at her and asked, "So, how are you feeling? You look a little better."

She said, "I was actually hungry for the first time in over a month."

He raised an eyebrow, and smiled. "All right! Good for you."

Renn was thoughtful for a moment before asking, "Hey, Gordy, do you think you could move me back upstairs today? I'm tired of being by myself."

He frowned. "You probably don't want to hear this, but I think it's too soon. Why don't we give it a couple of days and just see how well you get around. You've been down a long time."

She grimaced. He was telling her what to do again, and she could feel her ire rising.

Stifling a laugh, he gave her a warning glance, raising his index finger. "Now don't start. I'm just trying to get you to be sensible about this. You always have such high expectations of yourself. Give it a rest, why don't you?"

She felt furious, but said nothing. She let out of big breath in frustration, which he immediately noticed.

"Listen, kiddo, you don't have to tackle the world in a day. It's okay to pace yourself."

He suddenly tilted his head and gently took her chin in his hand, turning her to face him. "Somebody had very high expectations of you as a child if I'm not mistaken. Who was it?"

She frowned in irritation. "So what are you *now*, my therapist?"

"I'm going to overlook that statement because I care about you. Now I'm going to ask you again. Who was it?"

Frowning, she stuck out her lower lip, as he continued, "It was your dad, wasn't it? I can picture the scenario right now, from what little you've already told me. Your mother has a mild heart condition and a few close calls. It scares your father and he puts you in charge at a very young age. He tells you not to let anything happen to your mother. Is that accurate?"

She folded her arms and silently refused to answer. He added, "You were the mother and your mother was the child. You never got to be a kid, Renn. Don't you see? That's why you have such a hard time letting others care for you. Your dad did you no favors, putting you in a position like that."

She pursed her lips, and an ache began to build in her chest. "Don't say that about my dad. He did the best he could."

"I'm sure he did, but it was still a heavy load for a little kid to deal with. So let me guess how old you were at the time. I'd say six. Is that right?"

She grimaced, emphasizing every word. "Wrong. I was four. Just turned four."

Anger burned in his eyes, and he blew out a puff of air. "Good grief, that's even worse than I imagined. Okay, so let's review the facts. Here's this four-year old girl-child, put in the role of caretaker by her father and you said yourself your mother milked it for all it was worth."

Angry tears filled Renn's eyes, but she shook them away.

He took her hand, kissed it and said softly, "You never got a chance to be a little girl. You always had to be a grownup with grownup responsibilities. What a lousy thing to do to a four-year old."

She fished a tissue from her pocket and held it in a white-knuckle grip. "My life wasn't so bad," she said defensively.

He wiped the tears from her face with his hands. "Then why are you crying?"

She sobbed, "I don't know. I don't know."

"Well," he said, "I do. You're grieving the loss of your childhood."

"Who made you so smart?" she cried.

"Well… God—if you want to know the truth. I asked Him for insight into this situation. Now are you going to say He is wrong?"

She sighed, running her hand through her hair. It occurred to her that she must look a mess. She didn't answer his question.

He said evenly, "Now, stop wandering off in your head. Get back here and deal with this."

"What if I don't want to?"

He looked her in the eye and said sternly, "Then all that talk about God being your top priority had better cease this instant, because you're shoving Him to last place in your life, if you refuse to deal with this."

She shuddered, sobbing. "Gordy, I feel like you're killing me. Like you're shoving a knife through my heart, tearing me to pieces."

He hugged her to his chest. "I know. But think of this as surgery and the diseased tissue has to go, before the healthy stuff can thrive. Now talk to me."

She sighed, leaning her head back against the bed. "I'm so tired. I feel like I'd like to go to sleep and never wake up."

Again he took her chin in his hand. "Well, that's not going to happen. So talk to me. Tell me what your childhood was like. I think the Lord wants to do a work of healing in your spirit today, if you'll stop refusing to look at things the way they are."

She tipped her head back, staring at the ceiling, as tears poured down her cheeks. She said, "I'm going to cry buckets over this. Are you ready for that?"

"I've got my rain gear ready and my boat filled with fuel. Now get on with it."

She sighed again, and said, "Okay... I think my mom had her first episode just after my fourth birthday. I recall so clearly that she felt her heart fluttering and passed out. I was alone with her and it scared me. I found a wet washcloth and a paper fan and washed her face and hands and fanned her as if that would do any good."

She frowned, swallowed tears and continued, "She wouldn't wake up and I had to run to a neighbor's for help."

She hiccoughed. "The neighbor, Mrs. Phelps, was really old and couldn't hear very well. She didn't understand what I needed until I started crying."

When she didn't continue, he said, "How did you make her understand what you wanted?"

Renn's tears continued unabated. "I grabbed her hand and pulled her down the porch stairs. She hung onto the railing as if she thought I was trying to kill her. She didn't want to come."

"And how did you feel about that?"

"Terrified that my mother would die while I stood there arguing with her."

He reached over, put his handkerchief to her nose. "Blow... Okay. Then what happened?"

"Well, I guess when I became hysterical, she finally figured out something was wrong. She found Mom and called for help. I felt so sad and alone when they finally took her away in the ambulance."

Gordy's mouth fell open. "Why? Were you alone?"

She nodded. "My dad went straight from work to the hospital to be with Mom and didn't get home until after dark, and by then I was terrified. I'd never been alone in the dark before. I was way too little to reach the light switches. It was like I was paralyzed. I just sat on the floor in the dark and cried."

"Why were you alone?"

"I don't know. For some reason, Mrs. Phelps just… went home."

She sobbed wretched heart-wrenching sobs; he held her as she cried.

He said gently, "It's okay. You'll feel better if you let it go."

It was several minutes before she was calm. She was so still that Gordy lowered his head to look into her eyes. "You still with me, kiddo?"

She looked at him, shaking her head. "I don't think I can do this."

"You're doing great. I know it feels like you're going to die, but that's not so. You're going to make it. And I'm here for you, now go on."

She paused, with a sigh before she added, "Dad was furious with me when he got home. He yelled, upset that I was feeling sorry for myself when mother had practically died, and he shook me and said couldn't I see how selfish I was?"

"You were barely four years old, for God's sake. That's barely out of infancy."

She went on, "He spanked me and put me to bed with no supper. I felt so condemned. I knew it would be my fault if she died."

She covered her face and shook with silent sobs. After a minute, she calmed herself and continued, "In the morning, he came in and said that now I had to grow up and basically get with the program. He didn't use those words, but the meaning was infinitely clear. I was not allowed to feel sad, or needy in any way."

When tears suddenly filled Gordy's eyes, she covered his hand with hers. She continued, "Mom came home from the hospital and I did everything. Dad even made me a little yellow stool so I could do dishes at the sink, and fix sandwiches. You know… get stuff out of the refrigerator."

She went on, "He would make the meals, do the real cooking, but I had to fetch and carry for my mother. And later, I don't know at what age, I learned that she just had an irregular heartbeat. *Now* I realize that people live for years with that. For a long time, I was confused, wondering whether her condition was really life threatening or not."

He raised his eyebrows. "And was it?"

"I don't think so. She died last year at age fifty-seven. But it sure had me on pins and needles for most of my life, thinking she could die at any minute. Dad said she was my responsibility."

He was livid. "How could anyone do that to a little kid? You were just a baby yourself! Somebody was supposed to be looking out for you."

They were quiet for a minute, before she said quietly, "I've never seen myself this way before, Gordy. I just felt I was extremely independent."

"Well, it's no wonder, is it?"

Her voice was sad. "I guess not."

"So later, how did you feel about your mother?"

"Oh, I loved her. But I knew she was also a great actress and used me to fill her emotional bucket."

He looked into her eyes and caressed her cheek. "But who filled yours, little girl?"

She threw back her head, wailing, "Nobody. Nobody!"

He held her securely while she wept, and she knew she sounded pathetic. She could feel his tears in her hair and felt comforted that he cared. Something was breaking deep inside her. Before, any show of caring had made her angry, but his tears now felt warm and embracing and she wished he would never let her go.

She sobbed until there were no more tears and he finally said, "I think you need to sleep for awhile. You're exhausted." He lifted her up and settled her in her bed. She felt him pull the quilt over her shoulders as she closed her eyes and dropped off.

~ * ~

Martha came in just as she was waking up and said, "So how about some lunch?"

"Okay," she agreed quietly.

Martha's eyes were questioning. "Are you all right, honey?"

"I'm fine. Thanks for asking."

Martha brought a tray and set it on the table. After a few bites, Renn pushed the tray away and curled up under the quilt.

Gordy came in, and pulled up a chair. He set his lunch on the desk beside the bed, and said, "Come on, now. We're going to eat together."

When she didn't respond, he said, "Sit up, we're going to have a nice companionable lunch. Now, don't make me wait. I'm starved."

She did as she was told. He made conversation about the flowers he was mulching and some silly things the girls were doing upstairs. He finally looked at her, and said, "You haven't heard a single word I said, have you?"

"I heard," she said quietly.

He took the fork out of her hand and set it down. He pulled her chin up so she was facing him. "Now, listen to me. I can see where you might be feeling grief, knowing you missed out on your childhood. But I think you've forgotten something. You serve a God who makes up for all the deficits in our lives. You can't go around feeling sad the rest of your life about what happened thirty years ago. I won't let you."

He went on, "You have spunk and drive and we need those commodities right now. So choose. You can snap out of it and get on with life, or withdraw and get yourself committed to a mental facility for treatment of chronic depression. Now what's it going to be?"

She shook her head. "You don't give a girl a break, do you?"

He grinned, and said, "Nope, not a chance. I've gotten a glimpse of who you can be when the Lord has control of you and it's a mighty appealing sight, if I do say so myself. But it can go either way, depending on how long you want to continue this little pity party of yours."

"Okay, okay, I get the message. Now would you shush and let me eat my lunch?"

His eyes lit up in a delighted smile. "Dig in."

She yawned, stretching like a cat, then took a bite of the roast beef sandwich in front of her. After a single taste, she felt hungry and finished every bite, leaving only a spoonful of potato salad on her plate.

Gordy picked up the dishes, carrying them toward the kitchen and said, "Get dressed. I'm getting you out of here for awhile."

Renn made her bed for the first time in a month, thinking what a wonderful privilege it was. She took a leisurely shower, washing her hair. She did up her face and noticed for the very first time that her clothes hung on her frame. *How long have I gone without eating?* At that moment, she remembered the doctor's comments about her weight loss. Why had she never seen it herself?

Gordy came to the door and knocked, "Ready?"

"I guess. Where are we going?"

"To the park. We're going to play."

As they walked, the air was warm and the sun seemed to fill her up after a great emptiness. At the park, she sat on a swing and he started pushing her. Before long, he had her high over his head. Up to his old tricks, he ran underneath the swing at its peak. She laughed and squealed, "Gordy, didn't I ever tell you I'm afraid of heights?"

With a mischievous grin, he said, "No, you never mentioned it."

He finally slowed her swing and sat down beside her. He said, "It's good to hear you laugh again. It's been such a long time."

She said, "Thanks for sticking by me, Gord. This is the first time in a long time that I felt I was going to make it."

"Oh," he said with a cheerful smile, "that's music to my ears, girl."

She said, "I'm embarrassed to have fallen apart like I did."

He gazed at her seriously, for a long minute before saying, "You know, don't you, that saying that—means you aren't through processing this stuff yet."

She shook her head, biting her lip. "What do you mean?"

"When you fell apart, you let yourself be vulnerable for the first time. When you say it embarrassed you to let me see your pain, it means you still can't handle feeling vulnerable."

She frowned and sighed.

He said seriously, "Now cut that out. Those facial expressions are a sure sign of a rebellious and independent spirit, neither of which are pleasing to the Lord."

She shuddered and he stood, pulling her into his arms. She shook her head, tears overflowing and said, "So tell me what to do about it."

He held her against his chest, and whispered, "Just be like a little kid, resting against someone she trusts. God is trustworthy and so am I, and we both care about you."

He held her, until she quieted. He said, "Learning to trust is the first step toward healing. I want you to remember something whenever you feel yourself frowning and sighing, or folding your arms to protect yourself. Those feelings and behaviors are your clue to choose to turn it around. It's a choice. No one will make you do it, so you never have to feel coerced. But if you want to walk in truth, this is the first step toward getting there."

She said softly, "It's terrifying to be so vulnerable. To let anyone see what's inside. I feel like I'm going to die in the process."

He tilted his head and nodded. "You're exactly right. It feels like dying and in a way, it is. It's dying to our agenda and stepping toward God's. Does that make sense?"

She nodded.

He continued, "I promise you, that once you get this into your spirit, God will show Himself so big to you, that you'll wonder why you waited so long to change."

He grinned and said, "How about I push you in the swing one more time? Ready?"

She looked uncertain, then said, wide-eyed, "This is a test, right? Even though I'm afraid of heights, I'll find out I won't die if I just hang on?"

With a chuckle, he said, "Well, I hadn't really looked at it that way, but it sounds right to me. Okay, sit down, hold on tight, and trust. And you never know, you might even enjoy soaring."

She frowned and was ready to sigh, when he laughed, "Oh-oh, there it is, doubt and fear. Come on, walk out of it. You can do it."

"You're bound and determined to see this through, aren't you?"

"Yup. It's why they pay me the big bucks."

She giggled as he pushed her higher on the swing. She wasn't sure she could ever love it, but she wanted to give it a try.

Just then, Lisa came running to the park, looking for them.

"Lisa, what's going on?" Renn demanded.

"Karen has gone into labor and I think we need you."

Gordy took Renn's arm and they hurried home to find Karen curled in fetal position on an upstairs bathroom floor.

Renn yelled, "Did anyone call nine-one-one?"

Lisa said, "They're on their way."

"Karen, "Renn asked, "have you had any bleeding?"

"No, just cramping. Terrible cramping. I hurt so bad, I wish I could die."

"Hold on, honey. The ambulance will be here shortly. Somebody get a pillow and a blanket for me."

She stuck a pillow under Karen's head and covered her with a blanket.

"How far along are you, honey?"

"Four months. I can't be in labor yet. My baby's too small. It can't survive."

"I'm going to pray, okay, sweetie? Lord, you know exactly what's going on here and we need you to comfort Karen, sustain the baby and make a way through this. We trust you, Lord, for you know us intimately."

Karen started screaming, and Renn said, "What's going on, Karen?"

"I feel like I have to push. Help me."

"Okay, Karen, pant. Like this."

She demonstrated the pant and Karen followed suit.

"You're doing great, babe. Keep panting." She gently caressed the girl's forehead.

Karen cried, "Renn, is my baby going to die?"

She squeezed Karen's hand."I don't know, sweetie. But you need to trust God right now and just take this a moment at a time, all right?"

"I'll try, but it hurts so bad, all I want to do is push."

The ambulance pulled up outside and Renn said, "Gordy, can you carry her downstairs?"

He picked her up and hurried toward the ambulance, where the crew had bags of IV solution and supplies torn open, ready to start treatment.

Karen held tight to Renn's hand, and said, "If I don't make it, I want you to know that I love you, Renn."

"I love you, too, sweetie. And I know you're going to be fine. Just hang on, okay?"

"Will you ride with me in the ambulance, Renn? Please?"

Glancing up at the paramedic, she said, "I'm not sure they'll let me."

He said, "It's okay with us, lady, if you want to ride."

They pushed the stretcher in, locked it down and Gordy handed Renn up into the squad, saying, "We'll be right behind you."

The door had barely shut, when the attendant said, "She's bleeding. Step on it, Dave."

Thirteen

With lights flashing and siren screaming, the squad pulled into the ambulance bay ten minutes later. By then, Karen was barely conscious.

Gordy pulled up, as the crew rushed Karen through the door. Tears were streaming down Renn's cheeks as he ran to her, and said, "So what's going on?"

"She's hemorrhaging. I'm so worried about her. They had her IV open all the way and they still couldn't keep up with the blood loss."

Lisa and Linda, just exiting the car, were both crying. Renn pulled them into a warm embrace and said, "Now, we know our God is bigger than this and we need to pray and trust, okay, girls?"

Lisa said, "You pray, Renn. I feel better just hearing you pray."

"Lord, You are the lifter of our heads and You love us. You love Karen and her baby and we ask that You would protect them and turn this situation around. We know You can pull off the impossible and we stand in agreement that You would do that right now. And we give You praise before we even see the answer. In Jesus' name."

They seated themselves in the waiting room and shortly the doctor came out, asking for the family of Karen DeBolt. Renn said, "She's living with us."

He said, "She lost the baby. She's hemorrhaging and we need to get her to surgery. Where are her parents?"

"They won't come. They threw her out," said Lisa.

"Then we'll have to do this as an emergency life-saving measure, without permission. A hysterectomy. We'll keep you informed." Then he turned and hurried away through the double swinging doors.

Renn felt as if she'd been hit in the stomach with a battering ram, but dared not let the girls see her fall apart.

Linda said, "But Renn, we prayed. Why didn't God answer our prayers?"

Renn knelt down in front of the devastated teen and pulled her into her arms. "We did pray, honey and God is answering. He doesn't always answer in the way we want, but He is here and He hasn't forsaken Karen or us."

Linda laid her head on Renn's shoulder and wept.

In a few minutes, Gordy handed Linda a hanky and gently helped her into her seat. He pulled Renn up and steered her toward a chair.

He whispered, "You aren't in any shape to be on a cold, dirty floor. Now, come and sit down and let me get you some juice."

He brought juice for everyone and Renn was grateful for his protective presence.

It seemed like hours before the doctor finally swept into the room. He said, "Karen is going to be fine. She'll be in recovery for forty-five minutes or so, then you can see her."

Gordy stood up and shook the doc's hand. Renn followed his example. "Thanks for all your help."

Linda looked up at Renn, then came to stand in front of her. "So that means Karen will never have any other babies, doesn't it?" Tears were sliding down her cheeks.

"Oh, honey, I'm sorry," she murmured as she gathered the weeping girl into her arms.

Gordy said, "Okay, guys, we need to get some fresh air, get out of here for a few minutes. Let's take a drive. We'll be back by the time she wakes up."

Renn looked at Gordy like he was crazy.

He put up an index finger and shook his head briefly.

Against her better judgement, Renn said, "I think Gordy is right. Let's go get ice cream cones and take them to the park. We'll be back before Karen even wakes up."

They found a Dairy Barn a couple of blocks away and a park a short distance beyond that. They sat on the merry-go-round, eating ice cream, and Gordy ended up pushing them high on the swings and running underneath.

They were laughing and giggling before they knew it.

As they piled into the car a short time later, Renn squeezed Gordy's hand, whispering, "Thanks. It was a good idea."

He laughed, and said, "I have lots of good ideas, if you'll only trust me."

She smiled, and whispered back, "I want to try."

He closed her car door and slid in behind the wheel. "Okay, gang, are we ready to go see Karen?"

"We are," came the chorus from the backseat.

Karen was just waking up when Renn went in alone to see her. "How you feeling, baby?" she asked, squeezing Karen's hand.

"I hurt, Renn."

Renn pushed the call button and used the intercom to tell the nurse that Karen needed pain medication.

There were tears in Karen's eyes when she said, "My baby's dead, isn't it?"

"Oh, sweetie, I'm so sorry."

"I knew it, even before they brought me in, that my baby wasn't going to make it. Is this God's way of punishing me, Renn?"

"Of course not, sweetie. You were forgiven the minute you turned your heart toward God. He doesn't punish the repentant. He gathers them into his loving arms."

"I don't feel worthy of His forgiveness, Renn. How could he forgive me after what I did?"

"Sometimes we feel like that, sweetie. But that is not the way God intends for us to feel. He believes we are worth salvaging. He promises to make something beautiful out of our broken pieces. He just wants us to believe what He says about our value. Then He wants us to live in righteousness and obedience."

Tears slipped down Karen's cheeks as she said, "My baby is in heaven, isn't it, Renn?"

"Of course, darling. The Lord has the most tender heart toward his precious little ones."

"So what did they do to me, that I hurt so much?"

Renn took a deep breath and prayed silently for words.

"Honey, you were hemorrhaging and they couldn't stop it. So they did the only thing they could and took your uterus. I'm sorry, baby."

"So what does that mean?" Karen paused, grasping the harsh facts. "That means that I'll never be able to have children?"

She burst into loud sobs, sounding as though her heart would break.

Renn just held her, as her own tears fell. She was so tired she could hardly stand.

By the time Gordy and the girls came in a few minutes later, Karen had calmed herself. She grinned at the girls, who looked terrified. "Come on, guys, I won't bite. Anyway, I need some hugs."

They huddled together, and began talking, as Gordy took Renn's hand. He said, "You guys take your time. We'll be waiting down the hall."

Renn looked at him, and he said, "I think you've had enough for one day. Come and rest awhile."

She sank into a soft chair and rested her head on the wall, with closed eyes. She was quiet for a long time, when he finally asked, "What are you thinking?"

"I feel so bad for her. She has her whole life ahead of her and now, because of one tiny blunder, she'll never have children of her own."

"And you told her?"

"Yes"

He frowned, with a compassionate look in his eyes. "How'd she take it?"

"About as you'd expect. She was devastated."

"And so, of course, were you."

She fixed a piercing gaze on his eyes. "Are you saying I shouldn't be?"

He put his arm around her. "To a point, it's normal. But don't get so emotionally submerged that you let them drown you right along with them."

She said evenly, "Is that what you think I'm doing?"

He shook his head. "I don't know. You tell me."

She let out an audible sigh. "Listen, I'm just going by instinct right now. If I figure anything out, you'll be the first to know."

He gave her a wide grin. "Okay, chief. Just a thought."

The girls came out a few minutes later, saying Karen had fallen asleep. Renn tiptoed back into Karen's room and planted a tender kiss on the girl's forehead. "I'll be back again, sweetie." She gazed at the gentle girl with the big brown eyes, and soft blonde hair.

Karen stirred. "Thanks, Mom," she murmured before dozing off again.

Renn was surprised at her feelings of elation at being called Mom, even by mistake.

Gordy noticed the look on her face and said, "So what are you grinning about?"

"I kissed her, saying I'd be back later, and she stirred just long enough to say, 'Thanks, Mom.'"

"Wow," he said, taking her hand and leading her toward the car, with Lisa and Linda tagging some distance behind them.

By the time they got home, Renn felt as if she'd been struck by a freight train. Nearly too exhausted to see straight, she let herself be steered to the library, where she felt her shoes being removed and a quilt tucked over her.

At suppertime, she woke, smelling the enticing fragrance and sizzling sounds of chicken frying. Martha stood in the doorway and said, "I heard about Karen's loss. How is she holding up?"

"She's doing okay. At least she's able to cry over it. It's going to take time to get through the grieving process, but I think she's going to be all right."

Martha tilted her head, wide-eyed. "What about you? How are you doing?"

"I'm fine. Is that chicken I smell?"

Martha grinned, looking pleased. "You finally getting your appetite back or something?"

"Or something is right."

"Well, it will be ready in a few minutes. The girls are setting the table now. We sent Gordy to get rocky road ice cream."

The sound of girlish laughter, coming from the kitchen, made Renn smile. She commented, "From the sound of things, Linda and Lisa are doing okay."

Martha said, "I told Lisa she was welcome to stay until Karen gets back. So what happens now that Karen is no longer pregnant? Are you going to let her stay?"

"I guess it depends on her home situation. We've got plenty of room and she's such a dear. But if her parents welcome her back, I think home would be the best place for her. I guess it will be my responsibility to investigate the options, won't it?"

Martha sighed and turned to look out the window. "Looks like your job description gets an overhaul every time you turn around, doesn't it?"

In the kitchen a few minutes later, Martha cut up a crisp Granny Smith apple and said, "Here, eat this, girl. It'll keep you from starvation until the food's on the table."

Renn said, "Thanks, Mom."

The older woman couldn't stifle a grin. "You're welcome, daughter."

Gordy came in and put the ice cream in the freezer. He lifted the skillet lid and said, "That smells great. When do we eat? I'm starved."

Renn laughed at the yearning look on his handsome face, like a little boy with his nose pressed to the candy shop window. "You know, Gordy, I don't think I've ever seen you any other way."

During the meal, she observed the girls, who alternated between lighthearted banter and quiet thoughtfulness. After supper, Martha begged off with a headache and went to her quarters. The girls helped do dishes and Renn was surprised to feel herself the recipient of a dripping sponge on the neck. "Sorry Renn," said a giggling Lisa, "that was meant for Linda."

Things got a little too feisty and just as Renn had decided to escape to her room, Gordy grabbed the wet sponge and squeezed a sloppy stream of warm water down her neck.

"Gordy! Get a grip. You're not a kid anymore."

"Who says so?" he cackled with glee.

She changed into dry clothes and left for the hospital. Gordy was just putting away the gardening equipment and called to her, "Hey, where you headed?"

"Going to see Karen. I'll be back in no time."

"Want me to come?" she heard him call, but she already had her car door shut and the engine running. She smiled and waved, anxious to see Karen.

Less than a minute later, she had an overwhelming sense that she should have brought him along. She ignored the feeling, by then too deep into traffic to turn around.

The hospital parking lot was full and she had a long walk to the front door. The air smelled fresh, as if it had rained, and she savored its sweetness.

Karen was now feeling good enough to complain. "I wish they'd let me out of here. I'm ready for some of Martha's cooking. The stuff they serve here is disgusting."

Renn lifted the metal lid on the tray to stare wide-eyed at a liver colored meatloaf dish. "Did you choose this?"

"No," Karen said with a laugh, and ended up wiping her tear-filled eyes on the backs of her hands. "I think they brought it to me because no one else would eat it. Looks like it's been around the block a few times, doesn't it?"

Renn laughed and after a pause, said, "So how are you doing?"

"Oh, I think I'm going to cry and have sad moments over this for a long time. It sort of washes over me, then disappears, if that makes sense. I think that's probably normal, don't you?"

"Sounds like it to me.

Renn hesitated before gently asking, "Karen, I just wondered if you phoned your parents yet."

She looked thoughtful. "I thought about it, but I was afraid to, since they were so hateful the last time I saw them. They said they never wanted to see me again. I guess I wasn't sure how I'd be received."

"Do you want to try to contact them while I'm here?"

She looked doubtful. "I guess I could."

Renn handed her the phone. Karen anxiously twisted the cord as she waited for it to be picked up. Renn prayed silently, as Karen said, "Hi, Daddy, it's me."

She watched the girl's face crumple. "But Daddy," she cried, "I lost the baby. I'm in the hospital."

She pulled the phone away from her ear and covered the mouthpiece with her hand. She cried, "He doesn't care what happened. He says I made my bed and now I can just sleep in it."

Renn took the receiver and placed it gently back in the cradle, waiting for the Lord to give her the words. She put her arms around the girl, "What about your mother, Karen? Would she feel the same way?"

"Oh, well, she might not feel the same way, but Daddy is such a tyrant, she wouldn't dare go against his wishes."

Renn sat on the bed and said, "Karen, would you like to continue to stay at the house?"

The young girl burst into tears. "I thought it was just for unweds. I thought I'd have to find somewhere else to go. I'm only sixteen, too young to live on my own and too scared." She hesitated. "You mean you'd keep me, even though I'm not pregnant?"

"Of course. I love you, sweetie. Here," she murmured as she handed her a tissue.

Karen laid her head against the headboard and whispered, with tears sliding down her cheeks, "I didn't dream I'd ever have anyone who could ever love me the way you do."

"Come here, baby," she said, pulling the teen into her arms, where she rocked her.

After the girl had quieted, Renn asked, "Did the doctor say when you could go home?"

"Tomorrow, if all goes well. One thing, though, he doesn't want me lifting, or climbing stairs for six whole weeks. Who ever heard of that?"

"I've heard about that. But that's okay, because I'm going to move upstairs to my old room and you can take the room on the main floor. And if you don't want to be alone, I think Linda will bunk in with you."

"Are you sure, Renn? Can you manage the stairs okay now?"

"I'm doing great. We've switched places, haven't we?"

Karen moved and winced.

"Are you hurting, honey?"

"Only when I move or laugh. They're sending me home with a wrap deal. What's it called?"

"A binder?"

"That's it, a binder—to wrap around my tummy."

"That's good. Those things are a godsend. You'll see. So when will you be ready to leave?"

"I think by nine or ten."

"Well, I'll let you get some sleep, then, and I'll be here by nine, okay?"

Karen whispered, "I love you, Renn. I really do."

"I love you too, sweet pea. Now get some sleep."

Driving home, Renn's heart overflowed with gratitude to God for the dear people she had grown to love. She pulled into the driveway, surprised to find the house ablaze with light.

What on earth?

She hurried into the house and found Berke just inside the entryway, looking crazed. She wished she'd looked through the window before thoughtlessly throwing open the door.

"You. Cousin," he snarled. "Get in here."

She glanced around. Linda and Lisa were huddling together at the kitchen table, with terrified, reddened eyes. They rushed toward Renn when they saw her and she gathered them into her arms.

"I'm sorry," Lisa whispered anxiously, "I didn't know who he was. When I opened the door, he burst in, waving a gun."

Renn whispered quietly, "Where's Gordy?"

"He went home about an hour ago."

"Shut up and sit down," Berke was deadly serious when he spoke to the girls.

As the girls resumed their seats, Renn asked, "Berke, what do you want?"

The girls stared at her as if she were crazy.

He shouted, "How many times do I have to say it? I want you out of here. You and I are going to start moving furniture out, and I'm moving in tonight."

She could tell he was less than lucid. His eyes glistened with an unnatural light that she had seen in other psychotic visages, including his, the last time he had come.

"Okay. Tell me what to do," she offered.

He turned toward the living room and she whispered to the girls, "When we get the first piece of furniture outside, you slam and lock the door. Run downstairs to Martha and *stay there*. And call nine-one-one. Do you hear me?"

They nodded. He looked back with a furious look in his eyes. "You shut up!"

He gestured, and said, "Renn, you take that end of the loveseat. We're going to dump it out on the front lawn."

She made sure to give the girls a subtle nod, as she passed by with her end of the sofa. They were just outside the door, when it slammed and Berke heaved his end of the loveseat toward her, slamming Renn off the porch. She scraped her face on the concrete and bit her lip, tasting blood. The pain brought tears to her eyes.

Berke was immediately beating on the door. Where was the gun? Renn wondered. She hoped the girls had done as she instructed and were safely downstairs.

Berke finally realized he wasn't going to get the door open, but noticed the sidelight, which he immediately smashed with his fist. Sticking his hand inside, he turned the deadbolt and opened the door.

"Come on, Renn, you've got work to do." When she let her head droop in weariness, he ran toward her and grabbed her arm.

"Don't you understand English, lady?"

She meekly followed him.

They stood in the entryway, when he announced, "Now, we each take a chair. We're going to do this piece by piece. And when the living room is empty, we'll go out to the garage and bring in the family furnishings that belong here."

He seemed amazingly strong for some reason. *Is it true that lunatics are stronger because of their lunacy, or is that just a wives' tale she had heard somewhere? She couldn't recall.*

He stood in front of her, glaring. "You know, I wish you had died from the poison. It would've been the perfect plan. With you gone, and mother married, I could've reclaimed the house." *How did he find out about her remarriage?* Renn realized, immediately, that it had probably been in the local newspapers.

Where were the police? Renn thought. Hadn't they called for help, as she'd instructed? Where was the gun? She hadn't seen it since before they moved the loveseat.

She tightly closed her mouth, trying to staunch the blood coming from her lip. He said, "Oh, yeah, I forgot to tell you. If you think help will be coming, forget it, because I cut the phone lines."

She sighed. She hoped everyone had gotten out the back door. *Please keep them safe, Lord.*

Glancing at him, she suddenly saw him grow pale.

Berke said, "Get me something to drink," and sank down into a kitchen chair. For the first time, she noticed the blood seeping from his wrist, no doubt, a result of shattering the sidelight. He was staring at it, detached. She watched, awestruck, as he looked from her to his wrist. He was bleeding out and didn't even realize it.

She didn't know what to do. Would he accept her help if she offered?

She said, "Berke, you're bleeding." He looked at her, uncomprehending.

With adrenaline pumping, she grabbed a dishtowel and the phone, before remembering he had cut the lines. She found a hot pad that was thick and absorbent. Wrapping the wound, she tied the large cotton tea towel around it as tightly as she could.

"Berke," she said, "I've got to get you to the emergency room. Your arm is bleeding."

He gazed vacantly, as she led him to the car. The trip to the hospital seemed interminable.

"Stay with me now, Berke. Don't go out on me."

She saw his eyes roll back into his head, as he slumped down in the seat and banged his head on the window.

Fourteen

She pulled into the emergency entrance right behind a squad and jumped out of the car. Running through the E room door, she screamed for help.

Several emergency room workers followed her to the car and pulled Berke out onto a stretcher, rushing him inside.

She dictated his name and pitifully inadequate vital information to the clerk at the desk. "That's all you know?" the woman asked with a frown.

"Sorry, yes. He's not from around here."

"Okay," she said with a shrug, "have a seat."

Renn found a phone, and dialed Kate's number.

"Kate, I'm at St. Luke's with Berke. I think maybe you'd better come."

Fifteen minutes later, Craig and Kate appeared at her side and immediately noticed her bruised face and swollen, split lip. "Honey, are you okay?" asked Kate.

"I'm fine. It's Berke. He slashed his wrist, when he slammed his fist through the sidelight trying to get through the front door. He's in with the doctor now."

"I don't understand, dear. What was he doing there?"

"He demanded that we get out of the house. He wanted me to help him throw all the CPC stuff onto the lawn and move all the family furniture back in. He said he was moving in."

"He can't do that. The house is to be sold, so none of the children can live there after I'm gone. Their father knew the scrapping that would go on, so he planned for that in the trusts."

"Well, evidently no one told Berke. He was very clear about his intentions," she said, touching her hand to her bruised cheek.

"What happened to your face? Did he hit you?"

"No. He knocked me off the front porch after the girls locked him out of the house."

I'm sorry about all this, honey. Where was Gordy while all this was happening?"

"At home, I guess. I don't know. I sent Linda and Lisa downstairs to Martha, and told them to call for help. But Berke had cut the phone wires, so they're probably still down there, worrying. Craig, could you go let them know everything is okay?"

He nodded, "Of course," and turned to go. Kate pulled Renn into a chair.

She said, "Honey, I'm sorry he threatened you. I think he's going to have to be committed. He's tried to hurt several people, as it turns out."

Renn felt shocked. "What do you mean? When did you find out about this?"

Kate said, "Evin called the house today and said she thought he was psychotic. She's been afraid to be alone with him the past few days. I talked to the attorneys and got a court order to institutionalize him, with his insurance covering expenses. If he doesn't improve within a certain length of time, his estate will be liquidated to pick up the tab for long term care."

Renn shook her head. "I'm sorry, Kate."

The older woman sighed and said, "I should've seen it coming long ago. He was supposed to return to his job several weeks ago, but seemed to be obsessed with the house long before that. I guess I just didn't want to face reality."

Renn nodded. "There seems to be a lot of that going around."

"So did he wreck everything?"

"No, just threw a few things out on the lawn. I guess I need to ask, how does Evin feel about us being in the house?"

"After all that's happened, she would have no problem if I decided to sell, but I think I like things just as they are."

Renn said, "I can't believe the neighbors haven't kicked up more of a fuss."

"I guess they decided they could have worse neighbors, and they're right.'

Gordy strode up to them and took both of their hands. He shook his head, "If only I'd stayed a little longer…"

Renn asked, "How did you find out?"

"Craig called me on his cell phone and told me to come. Renn are you okay?"

Before she could answer, he said, "You look rough."

"I'm fine."

"Kate, how about letting me take her home? She's been through a lot in the past twenty-four hours. In fact… in the last month."

"Of course, dear. You two go ahead. I'll be fine until Craig gets back."

Renn let Gordy lead her to his car. He said, "We'll have someone come for your car tomorrow."

He turned her to look at him, as he opened her car door, "Why didn't you call me?"

She shook her head. "He cut the phone lines. I just can't forget the terrified looks on the girls' faces when I came in. They were so vulnerable, and I wasn't there for them."

"They handled it. The Lord protected them and as soon as possible you did what you could. Everything turned out. You have to let it go."

He closed her door and slipped behind the wheel. On the way home, she was quiet. He said, "What are you thinking?"

She couldn't stifle a sigh. "Nothing much. Just that I wish things could get back to normal. Whatever normal *is*."

He patted her hand.

At home, he pulled the ice bag out of the freezer and gently laid it on Renn's cheek. "We're certainly giving this thing a work out. I'll bet you're going to have a million dollar shiner tomorrow. Does it hurt much?"

"Only when I laugh."

He laughed, ruffling her hair. He said, "You sit tight." He checked the doors and rounded up the tool pouch, boarding up the sidelight again, and was back at Renn's side as she made coffee. He handed her the icepack. "You were supposed to keep this on."

She said, "Want a cup?"

"Sure, only add lots of creamer. That stuff is bothering my stomach these days."

"What? Getting old, are you?"

He playfully put a hand around the back of her neck, before seeing the look of terror on her face. "Oh, sorry. You still have bruises from Berke's last visit. Insensitive, aren't I?"

She was quiet, until he finally said, "Listen, I'll be by early, to help Craig move the furniture back in."

She frowned. "Can't you and I do it tonight?"

"Are you serious? It's after ten and you're not in any shape to be moving furniture or anything else."

"I can do it. Please, Gordy. I don't want the neighbors waking up to see that mess on the lawn. We have enough PR problems without that."

He headed toward his car. "Where are you going?" she asked.

"Out to get my cell phone." She followed him out to the porch.

"When did you get a cell phone?" she asked, puzzled.

"Today. You guys are entirely too vulnerable here without a male in residence, so from now on, I'm on call."

She laughed and shook her head. "We're costing you a fortune, aren't we Gord?"

"Hey, will you do me a favor and stop calling me Gord? A gourd is something hollow that grows in a garden. My name is Gordy. Not Gord. Okay?"

She smiled, stifling a giggle. "Okay. Who are you calling? I thought we were going to move furniture."

"I'm calling Dale. I'm moving furniture *with Dale*. You, my fine feathered friend, are going to bed."

She was so exhausted that she couldn't stifle the hysterical giggles that bubbled up inside her. "Hey, just tell Dale to leave man's best friend at home, okay?"

He grinned and asked, "You sure?"

Dale appeared in the doorway ten minutes later, while Renn was doing dishes. She finished the last pot and knelt down to wipe up the blood Berke had spilled on the floor.

"You must be Dale. Please excuse the mess. We had a little incident earlier tonight." After a pause, she realized she sounded like a Chatty Cathy doll she had once seen. "You didn't bring the dog, did you?"

The blonde man rolled his eyes, "No. He's probably climbing the walls by now. Or tearing the place to shreds. Maybe eating the sofa. But see...? ...no dog."

She waved at him with her dishrag. "Nice to meet you. I'm Renn."

Gordy said, "Now, you need to let us men folk get this work done sometime before dawn, okay?"

She looked at him with raised eyebrows. "So who's stopping you?"

Renn cleaned up glass *again* and knew she'd be finding stray shards for some time to come.

They had everything put to rights within fifteen minutes. After thanking Dale, Gordy finally saw his friend to his car. Back inside, he warmed his now cold cup of coffee and sat down, watching her wipe counters.

Renn sank into a chair after filling her cup. She suddenly stood and said, "I'll be right back. I forgot to go check on Martha."

She made her way down the stairs and knocked at the apartment door. "Martha, it's Renn. I just need to make sure you're okay."

Martha answered the door, looking pale. She fell into Renn's open arms, tears cascading down her cheeks. "Are you okay, honey? I thought he was going kill you, hearing the furniture thrown every which way." She paused, noticing Renn's injuries and said, "Good land, child. Did he do that to you?"

"He knocked me down when he tossed the sofa at me. But I'm okay. I might be sore for a couple of days. Kate said they're going to have to commit him."

"Honey, I'm dying to know. How did you get out of the situation?"

Renn looked at her wide-eyed. "You were down here praying, weren't you?"

"We were, sweetie."

"Well, as soon as the girls locked the door, Berke slammed his fist through the sidelight, letting himself in. And though I didn't see it right away, he cut his wrist and was bleeding."

"Oh, my."

"When I finally noticed, he was already fading out on me. I tried to staunch the blood flow with a potholder and tied the whole thing in a tea towel, but he was bleeding out. With the phone out of order, I had no choice but to rush him to the ER."

Martha shook her head solemnly. "I thought it got awfully quiet up there."

Renn hugged the older woman. "I'm just glad you guys are all right. I'm sorry he had everyone so frightened."

"I'm just relieved to see you safe. Does your face hurt?"

"A little. Does it look bad?"

She laughed and shook her head. "Looks like you went a couple of rounds with Mike Tyson."

Renn smiled, then grimaced at the pain it caused. Then she added, "Oh, Karen is moving back in. She can't handle stairs, so she's taking the den and I'm moving back into my old room."

"So you've decided to let her stay. "

"Yes. I love her and if I have to, I'll go to court and get custody of her. Martha, she called me Mom when she was dropping off to sleep. I just can't let her go."

Martha wiped Renn's tears with her hanky and said, "I think you two were meant to be together. I think she comes from a very abusive home."

"How did you know that?"

She shrugged. "It's written all over her face."

"She called her dad from the hospital tonight and he said he didn't care whether she lost the baby or not. He still didn't want her back. Can you imagine anyone being so cruel? And Karen is so sweet."

"Poor thing. Well, it's the right thing that she should be here."

"Martha, I'm counting on you to help me raise her. She's just turned sixteen, and I've never been anyone's mother before."

"Listen, I think it's normal for a mother to wish each child came with an owner's manual. But if she already loves you, you'll have no problem, sweetie."

"Are you comfortable down here, Martha? Do you need anything?"

"I'm fine. I'm really beginning to feel at home."

"Well, tomorrow Gordy is installing an intercom system so we won't feel so isolated if we need help, all right?"

"I think that's a fine idea."

"And I'm going to ask Kate to install a chair glide or whatever they call those things, on each stairway, so they won't kill us off young."

"That'll be a blessing. I vote yes."

"Okay, good night, Martha. I'm going to pick up Karen at nine in the morning."

"Good night, sweet girl. Sleep well."

Gordy was still sitting at the kitchen table when Renn returned. She said, "Oh, I thought you'd be gone by now."

He frowned, looking annoyed. "Does that mean you want me to go?"

"No, I just wouldn't have kept you waiting if I'd known you were still here."

He gave a noncommittal shrug.

Renn said, "I hope you won't mind, but I need to check on the girls for a minute."

"Don't you think you've tackled enough stairs for one day?"

Noting the look on her face, he sighed, and nodded in assent.

She opened the door to Linda's room and could hear her regular breathing."

Lisa's lamp went on as soon as she heard the door open.

She whispered, "Oh, Renn, are you okay?"

"I was just going to ask you the same thing."

Lisa threw her arms around the woman's neck. Renn gently smoothed the girl's long dark hair.

Lisa whispered, "We were so worried and didn't know what had happened, until Craig came by. He said you sent him."

"I knew you would be worried. But everything is okay now."

"Karen is coming home tomorrow, and I want you and Linda to help her get situated in the library.

She looked puzzled. "You mean she's coming back here to live?"

"Yes. Her parents won't take her back and I love her, so she's going to stay with me."

Lisa beamed through tear-filled eyes. She tipped her head back and let out a huge sigh. "You don't know how I've prayed for someone to love Karen. She's so sweet and her parents have been just awful to her. This is definitely a God-thing."

"Well, you'd better get some sleep. You going to be okay?"

"Sure. Now that I know *you're* okay."

Renn joined Gordy in the kitchen and sank into a chair. He got up, dumped her cold coffee down the sink and poured a fresh cup.

"So, are they okay upstairs?"

"Linda was asleep, but Lisa was awake and worried. I think she'll be fine now."

"Like I said, you have a way with these guys. So, when is Karen going home?"

"Tomorrow. I'm picking her up at nine and bringing her back with me."

"Do you mean she's coming here? What's going on?"

"She phoned her father while I was with her, to tell him she had lost the baby. He told her she made her bed and to lie in it, so she has nowhere else to go. I can't just throw her out into the street."

"But the home is supposed to house unwed mothers."

"I know. But what about the rest, who, through no fault of their own, have nowhere to go?"

"She has no relatives?"

She shook her head. "I guess not. She was living at the YWCA when she came to us."

"She should go into foster care, then."

"Please don't say that, Gordy. She's a dear, and I told her I want her with me. I'll even go to court to get custody if I have to."

His eyes widened in disbelief. "Are you serious?"

"I am."

"I don't get you. Less than a month ago, you couldn't wait to get back to your apartment, and now you want to adopt a teenager?"

She giggled, mostly out of fatigue. "You said it yourself, Gordy. Follow the Lord's leading."

He was quiet for a while, before saying, "You need to get that ice back on your eye. Thanks for the coffee. I'll let myself out."

"Gordy, before you go, could I ask you for one more favor? Karen can't do stairs for six weeks and she needs to move into the library. Could you help me move my things back upstairs and her things down here? And I need to find another twin bed. If Linda doesn't mind, it might be good if they room together, so Karen won't be alone, at least at first."

"Okay, sure. I bought an intercom system to install tomorrow anyway, so there's no reason I can't help move, too."

"Thanks, Gord, I really appreciate it."

At his raised eyebrow, she smiled, and said, "I mean, Gordee. Oh, and bring me the receipt for the intercom tomorrow and I'll write you a check."

After he locked the door with his key, Renn dragged her weary frame to bed. She crawled under her quilt, just hoping for a little boredom in the future.

~ * ~

Before it was even light, Renn woke, feeling stiff and sore. With her eye discolored and swollen, she walked toward the sound of dishes rattling in the kitchen. Martha was starting breakfast and shortly Linda and Lisa popped in, "What can we do to help?" They noticed Renn's face at the same time and said simultaneously, "Wow, does it hurt?"

"I think I'll live."

"Hey, Martha," Renn remarked, "you must've done something to get on their good side. They offered to help."

The older woman's eyes lit up in a smile. "They like my cooking. What can I say?"

Renn swallowed her coffee, refusing anything but toast, in a hurry to get to the hospital.

As she left, Gordy was on his way in, his arms loaded with bags. She waved, and yelled that she'd be right back.

At the nurse's station, she said to the nurse, "I came to pick up Karen DeBolt?"

The nurse looked up, and said, "Wait…" as Renn proceeded to her room. It was empty and cleaned.

Suddenly fearful, she turned to the nurse, "Where's Karen?"

"I tried to tell you—she's been anxiously waiting just down the hall."

Renn nearly ran to the waiting room. She broke into a grin when she saw the young girl's eager face, and she said, "Ready, sweetie?"

Karen gave her a worried frown. "What happened to you? You look terrible."

"Oh, I had a little accident."

"Accident? What kind of accident?"

"I ran into some pavement outside the front door."

"Does it hurt?"

"Not bad. Okay, so are you ready to go home?"

"Sure am. I've been sitting here waiting for two hours. The doctor even had to send someone to look for me."

Renn laughed at the girl's eager face. "Excited to get home, are you?"

"Boy, you can say that again. Maybe Martha will feed me. I'm starved."

Renn carried the bags to the car and came back to where the nurse had settled the girl into a wheelchair. As she stood to get out of the chair, Renn noticed she was having trouble standing up straight.

"Honey, did they give you that binder?"

"They did, and I'm wearing it. It's just that I'm having trouble standing up straight."

She gathered the girl into her arms. "Well, you've got nothing but time to mend once I get you home."

Karen's face lit up in a wide smile. "I knew you'd say something like that."

~ * ~

Gordy ran to the car and grabbed the bag. "Your room is ready for you, Karen."

Renn said, "She shouldn't be doing this steep hill. Gordy…"

He handed Renn the bag, and Karen giggled as he gently swept her into his arms and carried her inside. He deposited her on a chair in her room and said, "Home sweet home. If you need anything, just ring this bell. We found it in a drawer. This room has obviously been used as a convalescent room in its past life."

After a pause, he grinned at Renn. "Too bad we didn't find the bell sooner, huh?"

She shook her head, feigning a pout. "Yeah, too bad. Oh, well, it's the story of my life."

She put Karen's things away and sat down beside her. Linda came in and said, "I don't want to stay upstairs without you, so I hope you won't mind having a roommate."

Karen said, "I was wondering how I would do down here all by myself."

Lisa came in after her CPC client left and hugged Karen. "I'm so glad you're back. This place is like a tomb when someone's missing."

Renn helped Karen into bed, noticing how frail she looked. She covered her with the quilt and said, "You rest now, okay?"

"Renn," she asked shyly, "would you mind if I called you Mom? I know you're not my real Mom, but I want to call you Mom more than anyone I've ever known."

"I'd be honored, sweetie." Karen was already drifting off when Renn quietly closed the door.

Fifteen

When Renn wandered into the kitchen, Lisa was leaning against the counter. The girl pushed her long dark hair behind her shoulder, and said, "My parents think I've been gone too long. So now that everything has calmed down around here, I'll be moving back home." She hugged Renn. "I'll miss you guys something fierce. You know?"

"Well, you tell your parents we appreciate them letting you stay when we needed you so much, all right?"

Another young blonde knocked at the front door and Lisa welcomed her with a warm smile and brought her to the kitchen for a soda. Lisa said, "Renn, this is Dena."

It occurred to Renn that the kids-reaching-kids technique was working out well, even though it was unplanned. They seemed at ease with their peers, when they might not be as comfortable with adults.

"Hi, Dena. Welcome. Make yourself at home."

Dena had the look of a pregnant, embittered rebel. Trying not to make any snap judgments, Renn began praying that the Lord would use Lisa to minister to her.

Lisa approached Renn in the kitchen, a few minutes later, to say that Dena had nowhere to stay. Renn was quiet for a few seconds, before whispering, "Come into the office, will you?"

She gestured to a chair, and said, "Do you think we can handle Dena? She looks like a pretty tough cookie."

Lisa shrugged. "I know she'll be a challenge. I can't imagine her being cooperative. But what else can we do? Throw her out on the streets?"

Renn said, "Honestly, I don't know if we can afford to add any more stressors to the equation right now."

The girl said, "Maybe you could just talk to her and tell her what is expected of those who live here. See if she agrees to cooperate."

"Okay. Show her in."

As the girl left the room, Renn put her head in her hands, and said, "Please Lord, help me. I don't know if I have the energy to deal with a rebel right now."

A minute later, Dena sat down, crossed one mini-skirted knee over the other and snapped her chewing gum. *Help, Lord.*

She saw the girl eying her face.

Renn said, "I took a fall."

The girl replied doubtfully, "Yeah? I hear there's a lot of that going on."

With a slight shake of her head, Renn said, "Dena, I hear that you have nowhere to live. Would you mind if I ask why you aren't living with your parents?"

The girl raised her left eyebrow and said, "My parents and I don't see eye to eye on much these days. I'm old enough to make decisions for myself." When Renn said nothing, the girl continued, "They don't like it when I have my boyfriend stay over. They want me to do all the work. You know. They're abusive."

Renn prayed for the right words. She took a deep, calming breath, before saying, "Well, I don't imagine you'd like living here either. We have exactly the same rules as your parents."

"Like what?" the girl asked, her lips pursed in a frown.

"Well, first of all, we don't allow males here either. And the girls do chores to help out. They do laundry, make their beds and take care of their rooms, clean up the kitchen and do dishes after meals. All the things it takes to keep a house going."

"I thought you had a maid for all that."

"Nope. She just does the cooking. The rest of the work falls to us. And we divide it up equally."

The girl snapped her gum, surveyed her inch-long shiny silver acrylic claws, and said, "Bummer. Well, listen. I have all the grief I want at home. I sure don't need it from *you*."

Renn stood and gently touched the girl's shoulder. She flinched. Her eyes blazed. "You're not going to jump into that Jesus speech on me now, are you? I've heard it before, and if you don't mind, I'd just as soon skip it."

"Whatever you say."

At the door, the girl turned and studied Renn for minute before saying, "I'll keep you in mind if I ever get that desperate."

Renn said evenly, "Do that, Dena."

After the girl left, Renn buried her head in her hands, suddenly exhausted.

Lisa appeared at the door a minute later.

"What happened, Renn?"

"She decided that if we didn't have a maid to do the work, this wasn't the place for her."

"Whew. That was a close one. Maybe you'd better come up with a list of rules or something."

Renn looked up and said, "Gordy mentioned that a while back, but I said I thought the girls would do fine if I just expected them to do the right thing."

Lisa said, "In Linda and Karen's case, I think you might be right. But otherwise... well, all I can say is, *if only it were so*," the younger girl lamented.

"You know," Renn added, "I'd appreciate *your* ideas about what should be included in a list of house rules."

Lisa gave the older woman a sad smile. "I can do that. Sorry to burst your bubble, but I have a feeling heaven is the only place where rules aren't necessary."

"I guess you're right. Thanks for all your help."

Renn took the opportunity, a few minutes later, to inspect the furniture that had been tossed on the lawn. Actually, except for a tiny grass stain here and there, it was none the worse for wear.

A telephone man appeared at the door, saying a Mr. Craig Steele had ordered repair service. Bless Craig, he thought of everything. Within a half-hour, phone service was restored.

Gordy hauled in a good-sized box, filled with intercom equipment and started unloading it on the kitchen table. Martha piped up, "Oh, no you don't, sonny. I'm gonna be fixing lunch and you're gonna be *in my way*. There's a card table in the pantry. You set it up over there, out of the lane of traffic."

Gordy laughed good-naturedly. "Aye-aye, sir."

A few minutes later, Renn found him deep in concentration over a huge page of instructions. She said, "I thought you knew how to do this already."

He looked up and gave her his most winning smile. "I do, but you know, it never hurts to read the directions first."

Martha was fixing barbecued beef sandwiches and potato salad and the fragrance had Renn's stomach growling.

Even before noon, the volunteers were peeking around the corner. Martha said evenly, "Now don't y'all be gettin' in a hurry. It'll be ready when it's ready. If you want something to tide you over, have an apple.'

Valerie glanced at Lisa and frowned. "Doesn't she ever stock any good junk food around here? No candy or cookies?"

Lisa said, "She absolutely draws the line at potato chips. Occasionally she'll let me buy ice cream, but she won't stock the freezer with it."

Val said, "Bummer," as they each walked away with a newly washed Red Delicious apple.

Renn heard the sound of a bell and knew it was Karen. When she stepped to Karen's door, the teen said, "I hope it's okay if I eat in the kitchen. Is there room for one more? I'm sick of being in here by myself."

Renn said, "Sure, sweetie. I know exactly how you feel. Do you need any help?"

"Nope. I can make it. I just need you to pin a sign to my back that says: *slow-moving vehicle.*"

Renn laughed, hugging the girl. "I'll go set one more place."

The kitchen table was good sized, but from the looks of it, it was going to be crowded from now on. Making room for nine people at lunchtime was crowding everyone.

After lunch, the girls played a rousing game of Uno, until Karen said she was too tired to sit up anymore.

The sound of power saws and drills filled the air for most of the afternoon as Gordy played Mr. Good-wrench, only occasionally ceasing when a client came in for counseling.

Renn made her way down to the garage and turned on the light, inspecting the massive, much-despised dining room table. It was sturdy, with two center supports. It was much too large for the kitchen in its present state. But upon closer inspection, Renn discovered two removable leaves in the center, each about two feet wide.

Re-entering the house, she found Gordy just finishing up his intercom installation. He grinned, pushed his bushy hair out of his eyes and said, "Hey, you're just in time to help me test this thing. You go into the upstairs hall and I'll call up to you. The buttons are self-explanatory. Make sure the power button is on, before you push the one that's labeled *talk*. There's one each for six labeled sites, including the basement, upstairs hallway, kitchen, entryway, garage and front porch."

"So you just push the button of the place you're calling to the ON position, then press *talk*. Can you spare a few minutes to help me make sure it works?"

"Sure, if you can spare me a few minutes, after we're through, for a project I'm working on."

After the intercoms passed the test, Renn said, "Listen girls, you need a lesson on using the intercom. Come and let Gordy show you the ropes."

Soon Linda and Lisa found the intercom system to be a source of endless entertainment, and ended up sending messages back and forth like children playing with two cans and a long string.

Turning with a smile, Renn said, "I think it's a hit. Great job, Gord. Thanks."

With a grimace, he said, "I thought we decided you weren't to call me that anymore."

"Hmm…" she said, rolling her eyes. "If you recall, I never promised you anything."

"Hey, girl," he teased, in a gruff voice, "Them's fightin' words. You better be watchin' your back."

"Get a grip, *Gordy*. Now I need your help in the garage."

He frowned and raised an eyebrow. "Exactly what is it we need in the garage?"

She made a face at him. "That huge dining room table that will seat twelve."

"I hate that thing," he complained, etching deep lines between his eyes.

He followed her into the garage and flipped on a dim overhead light.

"So do I, but have you noticed how crowded the kitchen table is getting?"

"Yes, I have."

He took a closer look at the table and said, "Hey, this thing has leaves that are removable. I never noticed them before."

"I just noticed them myself. It won't fit in the kitchen the way it is, but what if we took out two leaves? That would take off four extra feet. Maybe then we could use it in the kitchen."

Gordy fished a tape measure out of his trusty tool pouch and measured it. He asked, "Aren't there any more lights we can turn on in here? It's like we're living in a cave or something. I'll bet we could get bats to take up residence if we tried."

Renn found the light switch and turned it on.

"Thanks," said Gordy. "That's more like it. Here, you take this end and we'll dump these leaves."

A few minutes later, they trooped into the kitchen, where Gordy measured the space in front of the window. It was twelve feet long.

Renn could see his face light up, as he said, "That table would be perfect, if we leave out those two leaves. It's not as kitchen-y as this table, but it would sure make room for more people, wouldn't it?"

"My thoughts exactly, Sherlock," said Renn, with a satisfied smirk.

They returned to the garage and re-measured, then lowered the drop leaves, which left the table four feet long, with a twenty-four inch drop leaf on each end. With the leaves out, it was possible for the two of them to move it.

Linda held doors open as they hauled the smaller kitchen set to the garage and replaced it with the dining room table, where they raised the drop leaves. That brought its size to eight feet long by forty inches wide. It was a perfect fit.

Lisa came in, grimaced, and said, "Yuck. It sure is ugly, isn't it?"

Martha frowned, noticing it for the first time. "Boy howdy, you can say that again."

The wood was stained a dreary looking dark brown, nearly black. Renn said, "Listen people, for right now, it's size we're concerned with, not aesthetics."

"Well," said Martha, "Y'all better put on your thinking caps and soon. Figure out something, 'cause I don't know how long I can tolerate being in the same room with that thing. May just sour my cookin'."

"We'll work on it, Martha," Renn assured her with a hug.

Gordy was out in the yard a few minutes later, trimming around bushes and trees. He turned off the trimmer when Renn tugged on his arm.

She said, "Gordy, it hadn't occurred to me, but you've been here so much lately, you surely can't be caring for other peoples' lawns as well. Am I right?"

"Well, I had to change days, so I'm working two jobs on Saturday. I actually had to give up my biggest account."

"Oh, Gordy, you can't give up your income. I'll tell Kate that we need you as a full-time gardener/handyman. I know the trustees won't have any trouble with that."

He looked at her open-mouthed. She said, "You can close your mouth now, unless you're planning on catching flies."

"Thanks, girl. With so much on your plate, I can't believe you found time to give it a thought."

She looked apologetic. "If I'd been on top of things, I wouldn't have let it go this long. I'm really sorry, Gordy."

"Don't worry about it. I'm not starving."

"I know. You've got tuna and soup." She paused. "But that's not the point and you know it." She had started back toward the front door, when his voice reached her.

"You know," he called, "we never really had that date to celebrate your 'coming out.'" He joined her near the front steps.

"Yes, we did, sort of. You took me to the park, remember?"

"Well," he said, as he raised his eyebrows in a hopeful glance. "I can see you're going to be an easy woman to please, if an hour at the park counts for anything."

"You know, with all that happened that night, I don't think I even remembered to thank you. It was really fun, at least most of it was."

"Glad you enjoyed it. But how about going on a real date? One where I actually buy you a meal? You know... in a restaurant?"

She gave him a wide smile. "Do people still do that?"

"Not around here, apparently. Not that Martha isn't a great cook and you too, for that matter, but it's pretty tough for two people to be alone together around here."

"So you want to be alone with me, huh?" she shot back, unable to resist teasing him.

He flushed a bright red and stammered. "I do. Yes. Now, let me get some work done, why don't you?"

She looked less than contrite when she said, "Sorry, Gord. Didn't mean to embarrass you. If you'll let me know when, I'd love to go to dinner with you."

When she phoned Kate to ask about making Gordy a full-time handyman, her aunt asked to speak with Gordy. He took the call in the office and came out smiling a few minutes later.

Renn returned his satisfied smile. "I take it the news is good?"

"I can quit all my other jobs for the money she's going to pay me. Bless God. He answers the prayers of those who love Him."

He grabbed Renn's waist from behind, and swung her around, to the delighted amusement of the rest of the household.

"Lisa and Linda whistled and clapped, grinning, as Renn felt a rush of heat creep up her neck. She rolled her eyes. "Gordy, put me down."

Karen stuck her head in the kitchen door, and said, "What's all the commotion? What am I missing? Sounds like y'all are having a party without me."

Regaining her composure, Renn said, "We're celebrating. Gordy has a new job. We've just hired him to work here full time as the handyman, so he can quit all his other jobs. As you can see, he's a very happy man." Renn tipped back her head and laughed.

Gordy scowled and said, "Hey, lady, what's so funny?"

"You are. And we're going to love having you here, aren't we, ladies?"

Everybody laughed, cheering and clapping, enjoying his discomfort. It was again Gordy's turn to blush a deep pink. He skittered out the back door, mumbling something about putting away tools.

A minute later, Renn found Lisa staring at the ugly table and chairs, in deep thought.

She finally said, "You know, Renn, I paint."

The older woman turned to look at her. "Paint what?" she asked.

"You know—things. It's called tole painting. I guess they call it decorative painting these days."

"Really?" Renn's eyes lit up. "Do you think you could do something with this stuff? It's the product of another era. The Dark Ages, would be my best guess," she said facetiously.

"It's not really very old, but it sure is ugly. It looks like it came out of Frankenstein's castle, doesn't it?"

"Oh, no," Renn said as she made a face. "I'd say it was much earlier than that. But it does have good bones, doesn't it?"

Lisa giggled and shrugged. "Have it your way. Anyway, what would you say if I painted it?"

Renn looked around. "Could you make it coordinate with the wall paper? You know, florals and checks?"

"Ooh, that would be darling. I can picture it now. The only trouble is, I'll have to paint it in the garage and we'd have to use the other table until this one is finished. And it would need lots coats of acrylic sealer if it's going to be for everyday use." She paused, thoughtful, then added, "The fumes need to be kept out of the house. Maybe we could find some fans, to keep the smell in the garage to a minimum."

"Sounds good to me. What else have you painted?"

"Hmm… let's see. I've painted cupboards, chairs, and small tables. A few dressers. A bathroom vanity. Nothing quite this large, but the concept carries over, no matter what. So what do you think?"]

"Listen Lisa, you have my full and enthusiastic support. When can you start? Would now be too soon?"

The girl laughed at the twinkle in her friend's eyes. "I almost think I'd need to move back in again, just to have enough hours to do it. Would that be all right?"

"Hey," Renn said, waving her hand in the air. "I vote yes for whatever works."

Lisa said, "Listen, hand me the phone and pray, okay? I'm not sure my parents are going to like the idea of my spending more time here than I do now. Especially when I just moved back home."

A few minutes later, Lisa gave a high five to Linda, hanging up the phone. "My mother said it's okay as long as it's a worthwhile project and not just 'jacking around'. She did, however, make me promise to call home at least once a day."

"Sounds fair to me," said Linda.

As they ate supper at the ugly table, Renn could hardly wait for the metamorphosis. After the meal was cleaned up, the group helped haul the monstrosity back to the garage and exchanged it for its smaller counterpart. They agreed unanimously that a little temporary crowding was a small price to pay in exchange for the transformation.

Lisa headed home, saying, "Okay, guys, tomorrow, after my shift, I'm painting and I need complete privacy. No one is allowed in my workshop until I've finished the creative process, that is, unless I need advice, or something." After a brief pause, she added, "Hey, Renn, can I get reimbursed for the supplies?"

"Of course. That's the least we can do. Here's the charge card. If you give me a minute, I'll write a note authorizing you to use it. Just bring me the receipts, all right?"

Lisa's eyes were bright with excitement as she left.

Sixteen

The next morning, Craig was in bright and early, with his bride on his arm. They made an adorable couple, making eyes at each other when they thought no one was looking. The entire household was in a high humor, just watching.

Lisa said to Martha, "It's kind of funny to see people their age so much in love. Know what I mean?"

Martha chuckled, "Looks purely crazy from where I stand. But it also looks like fun." She winked and the girls, who sat around the table playing cards, broke up, giggling again.

Kate exited the office and said, "Where's Karen? I want to hug on her awhile."

Renn followed Craig to the office, handing him a cup of coffee. "So how was the trip?"

He grinned and wiggled his eyebrows. "Oh, you know... sweet."

"She seems really happy."

"She's not the only one. Say, I need to ask a favor. But first close the door..." An embarrassed flush crept up his neck as he said, "Could you do me a favor and ask Martha for some of her recipes? Kate's had a cook for such a long time, I think she's forgotten how to make her way around a kitchen. It's like she's never touched a stovetop before." He grinned, putting his finger to his lips as he added, "I trust this will remain our little secret."

She winked. "My lips are sealed." She went to find Martha, who was busy washing pots and pans.

Renn whispered, "Listen, Craig needs a tactful way of getting your recipes into Kate's hands. He says it's like she's never ventured near a stovetop in her life, and has forgotten how to cook."

Martha raised her eyebrows, and giggled. She whispered, "Honey, she doesn't know how to cook. Doesn't he know that?"

Renn looked dumbfounded. "What do you mean she doesn't know how to cook? She had a family to cook for, for years."

The older woman became animated, gesturing and shaking her head. "I'm telling you, she doesn't know how to boil water. She never cooked for them. *I* did all the cooking. From the time she married Rick, he paid me to make meals. The children bought school lunches and of course, breakfast was no problem after corn flakes came onto the market."

Seeing Renn's look of doubt, she crossed her chest with an index finger, ready to erupt into laughter. "If I'm lyin', I'm dyin'. Cross my heart, and hope to die."

The younger woman frowned. "Well, I guess we have a small problem, then, haven't we? He gave me the impression that she was trying, with discouraging results. Let's put our thinking caps on and see what we can come up with, okay?"

Martha shook her head in disbelief. "I can't believe she didn't tell him she couldn't cook. I wish I could've been a mouse in the corner to watch that. I gotta tell you, I do."

Kate had already left the house when Renn approached Craig's desk. She whispered, "Don't worry, Craig, we're working on the problem. Pray, too, will you?"

"Oh," he laughed lightly and added, "one of my first silent prayers was, 'Help me swallow this, Lord.'" He tugged at his belt, and added, "Lost a few pounds these past few days, but there is a limit. I thought it was odd that she had no idea what to do in the kitchen."

She put her hand up, and whispered behind it, "She didn't forget how to cook. She just never learned."

He gave her a dumbfounded stare. "You're kidding, aren't you?"

"For your sake, I wish I were."

"Me, too."

She laughed, patted his hand and turned to leave the room.

Laundry was piling up now that the census was increasing. There were more dishes and pots and pans, and of course, more messes. Renn collected and sorted towels, threw in a load of laundry, and cleaned bathrooms, which were looking a little grungy.

Poor Martha was having trouble keeping up.

~ * ~

Renn found the older woman cleaning out the refrigerator. She laughed. "What, no leftovers?"

"Not anymore," said the older woman, with a shake of her head. She tossed several plastic wrapped items in an already overflowing black trash bag. The younger woman held the bag for her as she continued her task.

Renn said, "Well, have you given any more thought to Craig's little dilemma?"

Martha rubbed her cheek with an index finger, leaving a distinct black smudge. Renn smiled, and pointed. "Uh... you might want to check the mirror."

"Later. I need to finish this." After a pause, she changed gears. "Listen. The only thing I can think of to do is to give Craig my recipes and let him prepare them, with her help. At least that way, the meals would be edible. Now, this assumes Craig knows his way around the kitchen, at least a little bit. What do you think, sweetie?"

"Oh Martha, you're a gem. I'll let him know the plan. Until we can get recipes together, though, he might want to order take-out."

"An excellent suggestion," Martha agreed.

Renn found Craig poring over catalogs at his desk. He looked up as she knocked. "So what have you come up with?"

She closed the door. "Well, I'm afraid we have no magical answers, but Martha had an idea. She suggested that you say you want to try Martha's recipes and have Kate help you. In the process, you can teach her how to cook. Until then, we thought it might be good to eat take-out."

He grinned. "I like it. I think it just might work. I'd hate for Kate to be humiliated over this… I really do love the woman."

"I would never have guessed."

~ * ~

Martha was elbow-deep in soapy water, scrubbing food storage containers and refrigerator racks when Renn returned to the kitchen, poured herself a cup of coffee and doctored it. "I was wondering—what did you decide to do with your house?"

With a wet hand, Martha pushed a lock of hair from her face before resuming her task. "Well, my son, Charlie, has moved in temporarily and is doing the fix-up work that needs to be done before I can put it on the market. He thinks he'll be finished in a week or so. He took vacation time from his job at the meat packing plant to do it. Makes me feel terribly guilty."

She frowned before continuing. "It needs interior painting and repairs. There's a dead tree that's got to go and bushes that are overgrown. He needs to paint the garage and just between you and me, I think he's got a lot more than one week's work on his hands, but we'll see. He's always been a go-getter, so he may just do it. After he's finished, I'm listing it with a Realtor. It's not in the most desirable part of town, so pray for the Lord's buyer, okay, sweetie?"

Renn hugged her. "You bet I will. Hey, you've mentioned Charlie a couple of times, but I don't have a sense of who he is. Are the two of you close?"

Martha shook her head. "I wish we were. But he's not crazy about spiritual things, and that's always left a huge gap between us. He's sweet and he helps when I need him, but I'm still yearning for him to know the Lord. You can add that to your prayer list, too."

Renn nodded. "He's your only child?"

"Well, I had three, but the twins were killed in a drunk driving accident when they were seventeen. Their names were Mike and Dean. They've been gone so long, I can hardly remember their faces."

"Oh Martha, I'm so sorry. What year was the accident?"

"Nineteen seventy-six. It's a funny thing about loss. It seems like yesterday and yet it seems like forever, too. Does that make any sense?"

"It does. Time sort of skews perception, doesn't it?"

"No doubt about it. Oh, honey, I saw you folding laundry. Just want you to know how much I appreciate it."

"No problem. I think I'll look in on Karen."

Martha smiled. "She seems pretty chipper this morning."

Renn knocked on the library door, and Karen called out, "Is that you, Mom?"

The new mom smiled as she met her daughter's gaze. "So how are you feeling today?"

She slowly stood up. "See, I'm working on the posture thing. It's a stretch, but I'm going to do it if it kills me."

"Wow, you already look much better. How's the pain?'

"Not so bad that Ibuprofen doesn't kick it."

Glancing at her watch, Renn asked, "Can I get you some breakfast, sweetie?"

"Thanks, but Martha already offered me some. It's probably kind of late for breakfast, but I just want a bowl of cold cereal, I think."

"I'll bet she had something to say about that."

Karen laughed. "You got that right."

Linda came in, and smiled. "She sure looks a lot better today, doesn't she?"

Renn nodded. "I'll say. Come on, let's go get some cereal."

After a quick breakfast, Renn left them sitting at the kitchen table and went to Craig's office.

At her knock, Craig said, "Come in, Renn. Have a seat. What can I do for you?"

She sat down, tilted her head, and said, "Well, I guess I need to know, are you going to stay with the CPC, or find something else to do?"

He folded his hands on the desktop and met her gaze. "I've given this a lot of thought and talked it over with Kate. To be honest, I feel like God is changing me into the man he wants me to be, just being with all of you. So I'm staying."

Renn was overjoyed. "Oh Craig, that is such a load off my mind. I just can't imagine this place without you, and I agree that God has been working. I can see the workaholic, hard-driving salesman slowly being replaced by someone entirely new. I'm glad you're staying."

"You know, my dear, I think you are the best thing that's happened to any of us."

She could feel a crimson flush creep up her neck. "Would you stop saying that? It has nothing to do with me."

"I won't stop saying it, because it's true. You're the glue that keeps things together around here, and you're good for everyone. Now just say thank you, and let me get back to my work," he said with a playful grin.

She shook her head and shrugged.

Lisa came bounding in the door, with bags lurching in every direction. "Help me, somebody. Grab that bag quick."

Renn grasped two parcels and said, "Good grief, how much stuff did you try to carry in one load?"

Lisa frowned and said, with a loud, exaggerated, sigh, "Obviously too much."

Gordy stuck his head around the corner.

Renn said, "Gordy, you're just in time to help a damsel in distress. She needs her things moved upstairs again."

He picked up everything as if it weighed nothing and had it upstairs in one smooth motion. Lisa sighed. "I'm impressed. Maybe I should start working out."

A young girl rang the bell just then, and Lisa invited her in. The girl's face was streaked with tears and mascara, as the older girl drew her into her arms. Renn silently withdrew, leaving them alone.

Gordy took the stairs two at a time before he stood at Renn's side. "So how about you and me tonight?"

"Tonight what?" she asked.

"You know—going out to dinner. Now that I have full-time employment, I'm flush and I want to blow my wad on you, girl."

She laughed at the mischievous look in his eyes "Oh, Gordy, what would I ever do without you to keep me laughing?"

He put his face close to hers, tilted his head, and smirked. "I don't know, but I never want you to find out."

He was out the door, then turned around, saying, "Six o'clock sharp. Be ready. Dress nice."

"Nice-ly," she corrected automatically.

He laughed and winked at her. "Okay then, dress nice*ly*."

"Wait Gordy, I don't have anything but jeans to wear."

He came back in, with his hands on his hips. "What do you mean? Where on earth are your clothes?"

"Well, I've lost so much weight since I moved here that I really don't have anything that fits."

"I thought you had lost more weight when I picked you up in the kitchen. It's like you're fading away before my eyes. How much have you lost?"

"I don't know. I don't get too excited about it. I've needed to lose for so long that it feels good to be losing."

His tone was resolute. "Well, listen. There's a point of no return, girl, and I think you've reached it. Don't lose any more." He turned to leave, before adding, "And go buy yourself something that fits." He turned, and headed for the shed. *He was telling her what to do again.*

Renn phoned Kate to mention the stair glide chairs. Her aunt said she'd order them right away.

Martha was folding laundry, when Renn joined her. The pile of sheets and towels had grown into a mountain.

Renn frowned. "Good grief. This is too much. Maybe we should just ask everyone to take care of their own laundry, including sheets and towels. Would that help?"

"It would, but remember, Karen can't do stairs."

"I know. I can take care of her laundry. I've heard that's what mothers are for."

Renn finished putting laundry away, so Martha could get to work on lunch.

By the time she could smell the savory fragrance of lasagna, she had written several pages of prose on her pc, and she felt starved.

Gordy saw her on the stairs, and said, "I could smell lunch clear from the alley. It smells great." He paused, tilting his head. "Did you get yourself anything to wear yet?"

"Oh, no. I completely forgot. Anyway, I hate clothes shopping. It's not my thing."

Gordy raised an eyebrow. "I thought all women liked shopping."

"Not me. I hate it."

"Well, you'd better get cracking if you want to go out. I'm not taking you anywhere in jeans."

She frowned, cut a piece of lasagna and filled a plate for Karen.

After a late lunch replete with plenty of silly girl chatter, Renn helped with dishes before she excused herself and grabbed her purse. She sighed and slid behind the wheel. Where to go shopping? She knew of a great little consignment place a few miles away, but it occurred to her that she had no idea what size to buy.

The consignment store, called, 'Twice Around the Ballroom,' was a small shop in a deserted strip mall and had a nice selection of outfits. She chose several, finding that she was now a size ten. She hadn't been that thin since high school. She piled an armful of things on the counter, including: two silk shirts, one mauve and one white, black slacks, a creamy bulky knit sweater, two pairs of jeans, a white blazer and two dressy two-piece floral print outfits, either one of which would do nicely for a dinner date.

She stopped at WalMart and did other necessary shopping before heading home.

She carried her bags of clothes into the house an hour later and noticed that the house seemed deserted. *Where is everyone?*

She set the bags down on the bottom step and noticed a note on the table. The note was signed *Lisa, and gang*, and said they were treating Martha to pizza and would be home later.

After a shower, she pressed one of the new two-piece outfits and slipped into it. After curling her hair, and doing her makeup, she surveyed herself in the mirror, pleased with her appearance. Her bruises were nearly invisible now, and she felt her confidence returning.

Renn had just applied a second coat of mascara to her eyes when the doorbell rang. Thinking Gordy had forgotten his key, she eagerly descended the stairs and threw open the door.

A stranger stood there, frowning. "May I help you?" she asked, cringing at his intimidating size.

With a craggy growth of beard, and stringy dark brown hair, he reminded her of a fierce mountain man. But it was his eyes that frightened her the most.

When he barged past her, she could smell alcohol on his breath.

He growled, "Where's Karen?"

Instantly on guard, and with her heart pounding in her ears, she moved to where she blocked his way.

"She's not here."

"Well," he raised his voice, his eyes piercing hers, "where is she?"

"I'm sorry. I don't know. Now if you would please leave?"

"I'm not leaving without Karen. She's my kid, and I'm haulin' her home."

His eyes were threatening. A big man, he probably stood six-three, and weighed two-seventy. She tried to memorize his face for the police report she'd be filing.

They were at a standoff. He pushed her out of his way, bellowing, "If you run this place, you should know where my kid is."

"You need to leave now," she said evenly, gesturing to the door.

He frowned and nearly spat, "I said I'm not leavin' without my kid. If I have to tear this place apart, I'm not leavin' without her."

Renn's heart sank. *Where on earth is Gordy?*

Karen's father started hurling himself from room to room, slamming doors and swiping tabletops clean with one swing of his hand, smashing and breaking whatever he could reach.

She grabbed the phone, ready to speed dial 911, when he turned on her, and snatched the phone from her grasp. With blazing eyes, he tore it out of the wall, hitting her with the back of his meaty hand. The impact sent her flying, and her head hit the kitchen table with a resounding crack. She fought to stay alert, knowing he was out of control, but felt herself falling, as darkness descended.

She woke up, feeling suddenly fearful, as Gordy knelt over her, calling her name. He gently placed a wet cloth on her forehead.

"What happened?" he asked, frowning. She tried to sit up, but the pain in the back of her head was searing as she touched it. She brought back a hand covered with warm blood.

"Don't get up. Hey, where's all the blood coming from?"

She grimaced in pain. "Karen's Dad was here, drunk and he wouldn't believe me when I said she wasn't here. He's gone isn't he?" she asked with a shudder.

"He did this? Turn your head."

He sighed. "You need suturing, girl. Let's get you to the ER. Wait… I need to find something to stop the bleeding."

"A hot pad usually works pretty well."

"And how would you know that?"

"I used one for Berke's wrist the other night."

He gave her an annoyed grimace. "I'm afraid to leave you alone for five minutes. Do you know that?"

"Don't worry about me. I'm worried about what will happen to Karen if he comes looking for her. I think he would've killed her if she'd been here.'

He mumbled, "Well, he sure did a number on you."

Gordy steered her toward the car, his hand on her upper arm. She was having trouble with balance and dizziness and nearly stumbled a couple of times just getting to the curb.

In a no-nonsense tone, he said, "Here. Now keep this hot pad pressed against your head."

She could feel Gordy's anger and felt tears fill her eyes.

A minute later, he said, "What?" as he threw the car into gear and screeched out of the driveway.

"It feels like you're angry with me. Are you?"

"Not with you, just with life. One person shouldn't get as many bad breaks as you have—not in one lifetime."

"Please Gordy, slow down. You'll kill us both, driving like this."

Without warning, he pulled the car to the side of the road and gently drew her into his arms. "Did you know that tonight was going to be special?"

She smiled, "I know. We were going to have a real date."

She let her tired arm fall to her lap and felt warm blood trickle down her neck.

"No, now you've got to hold the hot pad to your head. Here, use your other hand."

She did as he said, sighing deeply. She felt very sleepy.

"Renn, don't go to sleep. Talk to me."

Her voice faded, as she blinked and sighed. "Sorry, Gord, I'm just so tired all of a sudden. Don't know what's the matter with me."

She could feel him jam the car into gear and floor it. She felt herself slammed back into the seat just before she remembered nothing.

Seventeen

Renn woke up in a hospital bed with her head bandaged. She shook her head, immediately deciding it was a bad move. This was getting ridiculous. She was alone, but someone had brought her extra clothes, which were piled on the end of the bed. She sat up and started getting dressed. Her head was splitting, and the room spiraled out of control.

I'm not staying here. No more of this.

Gordy came in just as she stood to pull on her jeans under her long white, bulky sweater. She struggled into the jeans, as he frowned.

"What do you think you're doing?"

"I'm going home. I don't want to stay here, Gordy."

His eyes flashed. "You aren't going anywhere. Now sit down and let me get a nurse to help you get undressed. Why on earth did you do this?"

"I told you. I'm fine, and I'm not staying," she said, getting to her feet.

He pushed her down on the bed and said sternly, "Now you stay put. Do you hear me?"

As he left the room, she could hear him mutter, "Hasn't got the sense God gave a chicken…"

Tearfully, she realized she was too tired to move anyway, so she tipped over on the bed, fully dressed and let her eyes close.

A short time later, he was back, pulling her into a sitting position. She opened her eyes.

"What…"

"Martha's here. The nurses are too busy to be bothered with stubborn patients tonight. She'll help you get undressed."

"But Gordy, I don't want to stay. I want to go home."

"You're staying put, so don't give me any flak about it."

This was obviously no time to argue with him, so she held her peace.

Martha stopped at the door, "Gordy," she said, covering her mouth with her hand, "you didn't say what happened. What on earth is going on?"

He frowned. "Karen's Dad came looking for her, drunk as a skunk, and… well you saw the house. He went wild."

"He did this to Renn?"

"Nice job, huh?"

Martha sighed. "Okay, Gordy, I'll take care of everything. You can go wait in the hall."

He stomped out, looking furious. Even in her semi-stupid state, Renn could feel his anger.

"Honey," Martha said, "how are you feeling?"

Renn murmured, "About like you'd expect. I have a terrible headache."

"Let Martha help you, sweetie. Can you stand for just a second?"

She stood, then heard Martha scream, "Gordy, help me. She's losing it."

~ * ~

It was dark outside when Renn woke again. Gordy and Martha slept in chairs, one on either side of her bed.

Glancing at the door, Renn was horrified to see Mr. DeBolt's face peering through the glass. But she blinked, wondering if she had imagined it, and he was gone the next time she looked. Gordy was holding her hand and woke when she moved.

He sat up, pushed the call button and said, "So how are you feeling?"

"I'd like to go home now, if you don't mind."

He shook his head, with an annoyed sigh. "Renn, you can't go home." He emphasized his words slowly, but distinctly. "Repeat after me. '*I can't go home.*'"

She burst into tears. "Why can't I go home? I'm too scared to stay here."

Martha woke and pulled the younger woman into her arms.

Gordy said, "You have a severe concussion and you need to stay until they know you're okay. *Then* you can go home."

She said, "My head hurts so bad, it feels like it's on fire."

Martha pushed the call button and said, "The nurse will be in, in a minute"

Renn lay back and closed her eyes. A few minutes later, Gordy flew out of his chair. "Why can't they answer the lights when we call? What's the matter with everybody? A person could die waiting. In fact, I'll bet it happens all the time."

Martha said softly, "Now, dear, don't let it get to you. You'll upset Renn, and she doesn't need that just now."

Renn knew she must have slept, because it was daylight, and she was alone the next time she opened her eyes.

She felt confused and fearful. "I want to go home," she cried to no one, with tears running down her cheeks and wetting her gown.

Renn couldn't see her clothes and supposed they were in the closet. Trying to stand, she hung onto the wall, keeping her eye on the goal—the closet door. With her clothes in hand, she was headed toward the chair, when Gordy came into the room and said, "Oh, no you don't."

He grabbed the clothes and threw them in the closet, keeping one hand on her arm. Then he scooped her up and carried her toward the bed.

He scowled. "I really can't trust you alone for a minute, can I?"

"Please, Gordy, I just want to go home!"

In a slightly gentler tone, he said, "I know you do. Just lie down and rest. Close your eyes. That's a good girl." He pulled the covers over her, and caressed her forehead.

Even in her twilight, she could hear the soft murmur of voices. A nurse came in and shined a light in her eyes and made her follow directions and answer silly questions. Vaguely she recalled someone doing it before.

A little while later, a doctor came in and did the same things over again. Renn felt disoriented and dizzy. When the doctor pressed on the suture line on the back of her head, she heard herself cry out. *What on earth is the man's problem?*

She woke some time later to someone violently shaking her by the shoulders. "Do you know what you done to me, girl?" A man's deep voice growled. She opened her eyes to see Karen's Dad and realized she didn't know his name. She stared at him, wide-eyed, as he said, "The cops came to my door and accused me of assault. They put me in jail because of you, lady, and nobody gets away with that. Nobody causes trouble for Jake DeBolt. I'll make you pay." His breath reeked of alcohol.

She couldn't believe this could be happening. Maybe she was having a nightmare; maybe she was hallucinating. His voice was real enough and his eyes were scaring her. Where were Gordy and Martha?

She closed her eyes to see if he would disappear, but when she re-opened them, he was still there, his eyes glittering with hatred.

The door slammed open suddenly, and Martha and Gordy saw him at the same instant and flew into the room. Gordy pinned Jake's arms behind him, before he could react, and marched him into the hallway.

Martha pulled Renn into a hug. "Honey, are you okay?"

Tears slid down Renn's cheeks. "I feel like I'm in a nightmare, and I just can't wake up. Help me, Martha."

The older woman rested Renn's head against her shoulder, hummed a lullaby and rocked her gently, like a mother would a frightened child. Renn fell into a deep, dreamless sleep. She had never felt so tired in her life.

When she woke in the daylight, her headache was a little better, but she was once again alone and afraid. Each time she woke during the night, Martha had been holding her hand, either praying or sleeping. *Where is Martha now?*

She tried her sea legs and made it to the bathroom, fighting dizziness. On her way back from the bathroom, she saw someone look through the door glass and recognized the fierce countenance of Jake DeBolt.

She frowned in puzzlement. *I thought he'd been hauled away.* She knew her thinking was fuzzy, so she couldn't be sure of anything. She felt grateful for a racket in the hall, right outside her door that probably deterred him from coming in.

Suddenly terrified, she decided she couldn't stay and let Jake catch her again. She hung onto furniture as she made her way to the closet, grabbed her clothes and dressed, sitting on the lid of the commode.

If they wouldn't let her go to Kate's, she would go to her own apartment. Maybe she'd find some peace and quiet there. Certainly Jake DeBolt would never find her there.

Renn hung onto the sink as ran a comb through her hair and gently washed the mascara from under her blackened eyes. She bore a striking resemblance to *The Wreck Of The Hesperus*.

She slipped into her shoes and checked the hallway, before exiting her room. She wasn't in the mood to argue about this and she wasn't about to let anyone change her mind. Including Gordy.

Inside the stairway door, she stopped and prayed silently, *Lord, please. Help me make* it *the two miles to my apartment.*

It couldn't have seemed farther if it had been two hundred miles.

At the first floor of the hospital, she began to breathe a little easier. She found an exit on the far side of the building and let herself out. The day was overcast and blustery, as if the skies would weep at any minute. Renn had no purse, or identification, but there was a spare key outside her apartment door, underneath an ornamental potted bush.

She hadn't remembered the bush until just that second. It hadn't been watered it for more than six weeks and was probably dead by now. She could only hope the key was still in its place.

Less than a mile later, she sat down on a bus bench to rest, feeling feverish and exhausted. Her headache was back, in all its glory, pounding and throbbing. Dizziness threatened her balance. She tried to decide which limb she would forfeit for the use of a pillow for an hour.

She happened to glance up at a beat up, rusted Chevy, sitting, not ten feet away, at a stoplight. She instantly recognized the driver, Jake DeBolt. He stared at her, with malice in his eyes. She got up and began to hurl herself in the opposite direction, but kept looking back, terrified that he was following.

Less than an hour later, shaking with exhaustion and soaked with perspiration, she staggered up the flight of stairs to her apartment, pulling herself up with the handrail. She dug for the key. Someone, probably a kind neighbor, must have watered her bush, which was still green and thriving. It was covered with lovely azure blooms. *Maybe it's a sign.*

She pushed through the door, flipped the deadbolt and turned on a lamp. The place was stuffy, so she clicked on the air conditioning. Exhausted and relieved to be home, she kicked off her shoes, pulled a lightweight blanket over her and collapsed in a dead sleep on the sofa.

~ * ~

Renn was slammed into wakefulness by the sound of someone beating on her apartment door. She just wanted them to go away. She didn't care if she ever woke up again. *Please Lord, just go ahead and kill me now. I'm sick of life. I want to come home.*

The pounding stopped and she drifted off, only to be awakened again some time later, by the sound of a key in the lock.

Seized by panic, her heart thudded in her ears. *Help me, Lord.* Tears stung her eyes as she tried to make herself invisible by covering her head with a quilt. She shuddered in fear and could only hope it was a nightmare that she would wake from soon.

The door opened, and a familiar voice called, "Renn, it's Gordy. Don't be afraid."

She was sobbing now as he approached the sofa.

"Oh, babe, how did you get here? I've been looking everywhere for you. I'm so glad you're all right."

She sobbed so hysterically that she was unable to answer. He sat down and pulled her onto his lap, where he brushed the hair out of her eyes. Rocking and murmuring to her, he said, "It's okay now. You're all right."

He stroked her cheek until she closed her eyes.

When she opened them again, she couldn't tell how much time had passed, but he was still holding her, whispering to her, and she felt warm and protected.

"Are you awake, Renn? We need to talk. I want you to tell me what happened. Why did you run away from the hospital?"

She tried to sit up, but he just said, "Shh… you're okay where you are. Just talk to me."

"Gordy, did you beat on the door just before you came in with the key?"

"No." He looked perplexed. "Why on earth would I do that if I had a key?"

She wailed, "He knows where I live!"

He dried her eyes gently with his thumbs.

"Gordy," her shaky voice cried, "Jake was at the hospital. I saw him looking through the window in my door. I had to get out of there. Then I saw him in his car while I was sitting on a bus bench on a corner, catching my breath. So I ran. I didn't know what else to do. And just before you let yourself in, someone beat on the door for several minutes. I thought they'd break it down. It had to be Jake!"

Gordy said, "He must have made bail somehow. I was hoping he'd be locked up for awhile. He probably hocked his wife's wedding ring, or something."

She asked, "Why is he after me?"

He shook his head. "I think he's been on the verge of being in trouble with the law, and out of control, for a long time. Until now, no one has ever forced the issue, because they were afraid of him. But now that you reported him, he has a police record for the first time, and it's made him crazy. I think he knows his days are numbered. Karen said this is how he acts when he's been drinking, and it sounds like he's not much better sober. The only way she's been able to cope with him was to comply and stay out of his way. I guess you got *in* his way and he's not letting you forget it."

"What am I going to do, Gordy? He's going to find me," she mumbled as the tears started again.

"Well, first things first. Let's get you home. Do you need anything from the apartment?"

She looked bewildered. "You mean you're not going to force me to go back to the hospital?"

"I think the doctor was going to dismiss you in a day or two anyway and I think you're better off at home. *At least you'll stay put there*."

She heaved a huge sigh of relief.

He asked again, "Is there anything from here that you'd like to take with you?"

"No. I'll be fine."

He asked, "How did you happen to come here instead of going home?"

"I thought you'd force me to go back to the hospital, so I couldn't go home, and I couldn't think of anywhere else to go."

He frowned. "You could've called me."

She shook her head and flinched at the movement. "I had no idea where you were, and I could hardly think straight."

"Okay, babe, calm down. Nobody's faulting what you did, but I don't imagine it helped the healing process much."

With Gordy's assistance, she wandered around the apartment, noticing a few things she wanted, after all: her boom box, her address book, perfume, some shampoo and conditioner. She had Gordy pull her favorite shirts from the closet, along with a worn, faded nightshirt that said, *Sandman's a comin'*.

She noticed her vitamins and pain relievers and added them to the pile in his arms. She had him pull out several bottles of herbs that would help her heal, then found the coffee cup with her name on it.

A couple of favorite paperbacks, like old friends, begged to be taken along, so he added them to the pile. She had him open the closet and pull out her favorite sheet sets. Her stereo was added to the growing pile, as well as her cell phone and charger.

She found her crossword puzzle books on the coffee table and her extra pair of sunglasses in the medicine cabinet.

Gordy laughed, holding his side, as he surveyed the pile he had stacked by the front door. "Are you sure you've got everything? Okay, then, where are the garbage bags?"

She frowned. "What do we need those for?"

"We have to have something to put all this stuff in, don't we? Or do you expect me to make twenty-seven trips to the car?"

She laughed at the word picture that conjured up. "Up in the top of the hall closet."

He returned with a large, tweed duffel bag and started filling it.

"There," she said, "now you can carry it all in a single trip."

He lifted it and set it down again, making a face. "I didn't know I'd be needing my Wheaties this morning. I'll be lucky if I don't have a hernia after this."

She laughed, flinching, holding onto her head. "Ouch. Stop complaining. You're the one who's always looking for a way to show off your macho muscles."

A short time later, she sighed, tired. It felt good to laugh even though it hurt. And once again Gordy was responsible for the improvement in her mood. Someday she'd have to find a way to thank him properly. *Maybe a nice tuna salad sandwich.*

He did love the way she fixed it, didn't he? She knew her thinking processes were skewed, but couldn't help herself.

"Oh, wait, Gord. I need to water this plant one more time, okay?"

He said, "Well, I'll take these things to the car. Now don't go anywhere without me, okay? Promise me."

"I won't."

"You won't what?" he said, looking puzzled.

"I won't go anywhere without you."

With eyebrows lifted, he said firmly, "Make sure you don't."

She had just returned the watering can to its place under the kitchen sink, when she turned around to face Jake DeBolt, who stood, not five feet away. She threw back her head, and wailed, "Help me, Jesus."

Jake was moving toward her, threatening her with a small knife. She retreated a couple of steps, and screamed, "Gordy, help!"

He came flying in, and Jake turned to face him. The raging man lunged at him.

"Gordy," she screamed, "he's got a knife!"

The two men fought like wild animals and Renn looked around for something heavy to use as a weapon. She could see nothing that would stop the raging bull that was Jake DeBolt. They wrestled and shoved their way out the front door and onto the porch. She saw Gordy skitter out of the knife's path, as DeBolt tried to plunge it into his chest. Her head was splitting.

Then she remembered the planter. She sidestepped the two scuffling men and picked up the planter. It was so heavy, it threw her off balance and she lurched toward Jake. He saw her coming, but couldn't get out of the way fast enough. The planter crashed into his midsection, and sent him sprawling over the second story railing, onto the concrete below. He made no sound as he fell. She rushed to the railing and gasped, staring at the body of her pursuer, lying among the shattered wreckage of the planter. The vacant look in his staring eyes made it clear that he would never pursue her, or anyone else again.

She started to say, "Gordy, are you ok…" right before she went down.

She was on the sofa, covered with her quilt, her head in his lap once more. He smiled. "You know, this is getting to be a habit."

She smiled tiredly up at him. He said, "You're quite a gutsy lady, to go after him with that thing. It had to weight a ton."

"It did. It was adrenaline that did it, I swear. It had nothing to do with me."

He laughed, with a sardonic twinkle in his eyes. "It's okay. You can take credit for it."

She sat up. "Don't we need to call the police or something?"

Just then, the cacophonous sound of sirens broke the silence, as he said, "They're on the way. We'll get out of here as soon as they get through with us, all right?"

She sighed. "I'm ready. I'm tired enough to sleep for a week."

"That might be the best thing for you."

She tilted her head. "Did you call Karen?"

"No, I thought it would be better if we told her together."

Several hours elapsed before the police took their statements and the coroner finally rolled the body away, zipped into a black plastic body bag. With Jake's history of assault, there was no question of it being anything but self-defense.

~ * ~

Renn heard one of the younger officers on the scene say to another officer, "I was there when he was arrested. I've never seen anyone that I felt was more of a threat. I can't say I'm sorry he's gone."

It was dark by the time the planter debris had been cleaned up, and Gordy led Renn to the car, closing the door after her. She was quiet on the way to Kate's.

Shortly, he said, "You still with me, Renn?"

She nodded sleepily.

"How's the headache?"

"Bad. Really bad. I don't think lifting that thing helped my head at all."

He patted her hand. "That was my line, remember?"

"Well, you were right."

"Listen," he said softly as he put his arm around her, "just lean against me, and we'll be home in no time." She laid her head in the hollow of his broad shoulder and once again closed her eyes.

"Are you hungry?" he asked.

"No, I just want my bed."

It was nearly midnight when he finally parked in the driveway and pulled her bag from the backseat, opened her door and took her hand.

"Come on, little warrior, let's get you situated."

She sat there and laughed tiredly. "You're crazy, Gord. Do you know that?"

Feigning upset, he said, "There you go again, calling me Gord. Remember, we just had this conversation the other night. A gourd is a something you dig out of a…"

"I know, a garden."

Eighteen

Renn woke, before daylight, to the soft sound of weeping in the room.

She switched on the lamp and blinked her eyes, trying to focus. Her head was swimming and her vision refused to cooperate.

Karen wept, curled up in the overstuffed chair by the door.

"What's the matter, sweetie? Are you okay?' Renn asked.

Karen flew to her side. "It's me who should be asking you that. My father almost killed you. How can you still want me around after that?"

Renn sat up straighter and beckoned Karen onto the bed beside her.

"Honey, listen to me. You are not your father. You had nothing to do with his behavior. None of this is your responsibility."

"But I know him. He'll stop at nothing once he's enraged."

Renn rolled her head on her shoulders, feeling very old and stiff. She said, "Karen, I have to tell you something." She paused, then said succinctly, "Your father is dead."

"What?" The girl's mouth dropped open in shock.

"I'm sorry, sweetie, but he's dead."

Karen buried her face in her hands and shouted, "No he's not. He's like the devil. He can't be killed. I gave up long ago, even praying for him to die. It's like he has a thousand lives and can't be killed. Not that many haven't tried."

"Karen," Renn repeated, "he's dead. I saw him myself."

Agitated, the girl demanded, "Who killed him? How did he die?"

Renn looked down, solemnly regarding the quilt covering her. "I did, sweetie, and I feel terrible about it, but he was going to kill Gordy. He had already tried to kill me."

"I knew he'd try. How did you kill him? He's as strong as an ox."

"I knocked him off a second floor balcony with a forty-pound planter."

Karen looked shocked. "I can't believe it. He was killed by a woman." She shook her head. "He'd be so mad if he knew that."

Renn, feeling giddy, said, "Well, then, let's don't tell him. We'll just let it be our little secret, okay, Karen?"

The girl gave a slightly hysterical giggle, then frowned. "You going to be okay?

"I'm fine. How are you feeling?'

Karen sighed, looking relieved. "I think this is the first time in my life I haven't felt afraid."

"Of your dad?"

"Well, wouldn't you be, if you were me? We never knew what state he'd be in. But usually it wasn't good. My mom has the worst case of abused woman syndrome I've ever seen. We saw a video about it in Family Life class. She's textbook."

Renn shook her head in disbelief. "I still can't believe I am responsible for someone's death. It's a stunning thought. It's like I pushed someone over the brink right into hell itself. Now that's something a girl could have nightmares about, wouldn't you say?"

Karen hugged her. "Renn, if you had really known my Dad, you would be dancing for joy, like my mother probably is right now. He was a cruel, vindictive man."

"I understand, sweetie. But I'm pretty sure the Lord and I will still have to process this for some time to come."

Gordy knocked on the doorframe. Renn said, "Gee, Gord, can't you even give a girl a chance to dress?"

He covered his eyes, in a mock shock gesture.

"Well, cover up, because I'm coming in."

Renn threw the quilt over Karen, and said, "We're decent. You can come in now."

He sat on the bed. "Did you tell her yet?"

Karen nodded. "She told me and I can't believe it. I mean that a small woman killed him. A lot of really big men have tried, and no one could ever do it."

Gordy nodded. "I can believe it. He was like a roaring lion…"

Renn shrugged. Tears filled her eyes. At that moment, the magnitude of her actions hit her like a gunshot between the eyes.

Gordy watched, frowning, then said, "What are you thinking, Renn?"

Karen crawled out of bed, gave Renn a hug, then excused herself and slipped out, leaving them alone.

Tears slid down Renn's cheeks as she shook her head. "I don't care how bad a man he was, I hate being the one to push him over the brink of eternity. I don't know if I can handle it."

Gordy sighed. "Oh, I knew this would happen. Why couldn't it have been me who did it? At least I could have handled it better than you."

He sat down in the chair next to the bed, set his coffee mug on the bedside table and took her hand. He looked thoughtful for a minute. "You remember the story of David and Goliath? Do you think God would have let that little teenager kill a giant if he hadn't ordained it for his glory?"

There was pain in her voice as she said, "But that was back in The Old Testament where everyone was killing everyone else, and it didn't seem to matter."

Renn rolled her head, trying to relieve the tension in her neck. Gordy noticed the gesture, and scooted her down, to rest her head on the pillow.

He gave a raucous laugh. "Are you listening to yourself? That's ridiculous. I'm sure even back then, there were tender-hearted folks who hated killing just as much as you do and yet, God called on them to strengthen their hands and do the next thing, which was to rout the enemy for His glory."

She practically shouted, "Are you saying you think it glorifies God that I pushed a man to his death?"

After a brief pause, he answered, "Well, let's just say that it glorifies God when you are obedient to do the hard things. Things that go against your nature."

He continued, "In fact, I imagine David, being a shepherd, had a pretty tender heart himself, don't you suppose? I wouldn't be at all surprised if he felt just as you do about killing until he gave those feelings to the Lord. Of course, he had to kill wild animals just to protect his sheep. You killed Jake DeBolt, to protect Karen. In fact, if it hadn't been for you and that crazy planter, he might've killed me. I was worn out, but he still had plenty of fury fueling his brute strength."

Silent tears chased each other down her cheeks, before she said, "I don't know how to live with this. I don't."

He stroked her cheek, saying firmly, "You'll talk to the Lord about it and He'll help you figure it out."

"I don't think so, Gord. Honest."

He caressed her hair. "I know, babe. That's the way it feels right now, but the Lord is much bigger than this. He can handle anything you lay at His feet."

She sighed, thoughtful.

He grinned. "Come on. Don't you think you've lolled around in bed long enough? Get dressed. We've got things to do and places to go."

She shook her head. "I don't feel like it, Gordy."

He took her hand. "Listen, I'm not going to sit around and watch you beat yourself up over this. Now get up and get dressed. I'll give you five minutes to get dressed, or I'm sending the troops in after you."

"My head is splitting."

"You're coming if I have to carry you out of here."

She frowned in irritation. "Can't you just let me be?"

He gave a rueful laugh. "You need me to make your life miserable. You do. Now get dressed."

"All right. That's just about enough. You are excused."

He saluted, turned several quarter turns and left, closing the door behind him, laughing.

As he shut the door, she yelled, "Where are we going, Gordy? It's hardly even daylight out yet."

He yelled back, "You'll see. Just trust me."

She stepped out of the shower, feeling a little better, but wished for all the world that she could wash her hair. Just as she finished dressing, Martha knocked, and yelled through the closed door, "He says you're going to be AWOL if you don't get the lead out. His words, not mine," she said with a laugh.

Renn blew the hair out of her face, and said, "Tell him to go soak his head."

Martha called through the door. "I'm not getting in the middle of this war of words, no sir. You'd better tell him that yourself."

Gordy yelled, "I heard that."

"Martha, tell him I'll be there when I'm good and ready."

Kate knocked on the door and stuck her head in. "It's just me, dear."

Her aunt smiled, giving her a hug, "Honey, you're a sight for sore eyes. I heard about your harrowing close calls the past couple of days. Are you all right?"

"I think it's going to take a little time. I just wish I could crawl into a hole and pull it in over me."

"I'm surprised you don't feel like you've been cursed since moving here. Nothing much happened before that."

"Well, I'm really trying to stay positive."

Kate hugged her again, and said with a sigh, "I'm glad you're okay, dear. If you need to talk about anything, you come and find me, all right?"

Gordy waited outside the door, knocking impatiently. "What did you do, start from scratch?"

She opened the door to glare at him. "Don't you give me a hard time, *Gord*," she emphasized his name.

He asked, "Are you hungry?"

"No."

"Okay. Now, come into the other bathroom. We're going to see what you weigh."

Her eyes flashed angrily. "What? What are you talking about? It's none of your business what I weigh," she said, stubbornly digging in her heels.

"Yes, it is. I've been lifting you a lot lately, in case you haven't noticed, and I can feel you disappearing in front of my eyes. Now get on the scale... please."

"I am not getting on the scale. What... you think I'm anorexic or something?"

"I didn't say that. Even if you don't tell me, I think you need to see how much you've lost."

She turned on her heel and said plaintively, "Gordy, this is absolutely the last straw. I've put up with just about as much as I can stand. Now, just leave me alone. If I hear one more word..."

"Yes?"

"I'm serious."

He grinned. "I don't doubt it for a minute."

She turned and faced him, hands on her hips. "What is it with you? Why do you feel you have to order me around? I'm perfectly capable of running my life, and making my own decisions. Now if you'll excuse me, I have some things I want to do... alone."

Renn shut the door on him and flopped angrily down onto the bed. Her head throbbed. She flipped open her laptop and began writing, with tears blinding her eyes.

She grabbed her address book and let it fall open. She hadn't talked to her friends in so long, she wasn't even sure she still had any.

After picking up the phone, she dialed, getting Deedee's answering machine. *Nuts,* she thought, *I don't even know what day it is.*

She walked into the kitchen, where everyone, including Gordy, was quiet, watching her. "What's the matter with everybody?"

Lisa smiled and said softly, "We're just glad you're okay, Renn."

Renn asked, "What day is it? Martha, what day is this?"

Martha put her arm around Renn's shoulder. "It's Tuesday, honey. Can I get you something to eat?"

She said firmly, "I'm not hungry, Martha."

Renn closed her bedroom door, and crawled under her quilt, feeling like an outsider. She didn't belong anywhere. She suddenly wished all the meddling people in her life would just leave her alone forever.

After a few minutes, she knew what she had to do. She heaved her belongings, one by one, into the duffel. She would move home and just go back to her old job, or find a new one. She didn't fit in here; she felt worse than useless here.

She hauled the bag to the kitchen, where Martha stood alone, doing dishes. "I'm packed, Martha. I've got to get out of here. Really, I can't stand it here another minute. I'll be fine. I've just got to have time to figure things out for myself. Bye."

Martha stood wide-eyed, watching her walk out the door.

Gordy ran toward her, looking alarmed, but she ignored him. Her Camry refused to start.

Gordy approached her car. "What's going on?"

She shook her head violently and bit her lip, silent. She kept pumping the accelerator and she could smell gas. She had flooded it in her rush. When the engine finally roared to life, she slammed it into gear and fled. She knew, even without looking, that Gordy was standing there, in open-mouthed shock.

Twenty minutes later, she unlocked her empty, dark apartment, and opened the shades, turning on every light. *I will find my answers here. I can feel normal here.*

No one could make her feel uncomfortable in her own place. *Maybe I just need to get a cat.* That was it. She'd do it today; get one of those strays from the humane society. Cats didn't make any demands; they just loved you.

Even with all the lights on, the day seemed unusually dreary and dark for summer. The sun was out. Why did its light feel so dim? And where was its warmth? What had happened to blinding sun and bright, white-hot summer days? *Why can't I feel anything?*

She pulled out her favorite Christmas CD and turned it on. It was somehow comforting, like a lullaby. But even that didn't comfort her the way it used to.

Renn pulled the sheets off her bed and made it up clean, tossed a sprinkle of perfumed talc onto them, then pulled them off, deciding that everything smelled stale. *The world smelled stale.*

She swallowed eight hundred milligrams of Ibuprofen, trying to get her headache to subside. When it started to ease she got busy.

Pulling out every towel, sheet and stitch of clothes, she heaped them by the door. She began working her way through six loads of laundry, one at a time. Then she pulled out the spray cleaner and scrubbed everything that didn't move. She washed windows, pulled down curtains, polished surfaces, cleaned the oven and vacuumed everywhere her wand could reach. She pulled down every cobweb, daring them to build again.

Finally, she flipped open her laptop and e-mailed her four closest friends, whom she hadn't seen or talked to in so long, they'd probably forgotten her very existence.

By then her head was killing her.

She put on another Christmas album and began to cry. *When did my life fall apart? I used to feel so normal. I think I was a pleasant person to be around. I even had friends, not just people who needed me for some reason. I was smart, even vaguely attractive, and more or less physically fit. There was even a time I felt competent and capable to handle life. Where did that girl go, and who is this bizarre stranger who has replaced her?*

She laughed at herself, through tears that refused to stop and wished she could buy Prozac over the counter. What on God's green earth was the next best thing she could get without a prescription?

Shortly, she dug in the bottom of the duffel for her Bible and let it fall open.

It opened to Psalms 145:14-15: "The Lord sustains all who fall and raises up all who are bowed down. The eyes of all look to Thee and Thou dost give them their food in due time. Thou dost open Thy hand and dost satisfy the desire of every living thing."

"Lord," she began quietly. She didn't know how to pray. When tears fell on her Bible, she hurriedly brushed them away. "Lord," she said again, "are You there? I'm so messed up now, I don't know up from down. I'm scared, Lord, and I need You to satisfy me with what I need. The trouble is, I have no idea what that is. Is this making any sense, Lord? You might just have to read my mind, because I have no idea what I'm talking about right now.

"I just feel so out of it. I don't know where I belong. I don't feel loving, or lovable, or anything else good, right now. I hate who I am and who I'm becoming. Oh, yeah," she giggled a little hysterically, "and don't forget to add *killer* to the list, too. Now there's *a goodie* that not many folks can put on their resume' of Christian works. I want to die, Lord. I honestly want to die."

She sighed, turned off the music, which had replayed over and over until she could barely stand it. Then she went to retrieve the next load of laundry.

She sat there, staring vacantly, with the heaping laundry basket in front of her, feeling overwhelmed with pent-up frustration. Then she checked her e-mail. Three of the four e-mail messages were returned as undeliverable, making her wonder if the twilight zone was a real place, in close proximity to Kansas City.

Digging through the cupboards, she found a box of stale crackers, some peanut butter and a warm bottle of unopened Diet Coke. She swallowed a few bites, before pulling her nightshirt over her throbbing head at seven-fifteen. With no reason to stay awake, she swallowed another eight hundred milligrams of Ibuprofen and slept.

She woke late, to a hot, sticky day. The sun still seemed dim. She got up, turned off the air and opened the windows. Somehow she felt starved for air and light. Her windows were streaked. But streaked was good; at least it was a sign of life.

She was drenched in sweat at only eight-thirty, so she closed the windows and turned on the air. After showering, she dressed, folded more laundry and went shopping for groceries. Before she realized it, she was parked at the Humane Society and she watched as someone turned the *OPEN* sign around. Window shopping was definitely the order of the day. Cute animal signs and caricatures were plastered everywhere, but they didn't cheer her as she'd hoped.

She stood near the door, trying to decide whether to go in. "May I help you?" asked a young red headed woman.

Renn said, "Well, I am considering getting a cat."

"If you'll follow me, I'll show you to the cat room."

"The cats have a room all to themselves?"

"They sure do." She followed the woman to a long narrow room, lined floor to ceiling with cages, about half of which were inhabited by cats of all sizes and colors.

The woman asked, "Were you looking for anything specific?" When Renn looked confused, she asked, "Male or female... you know, that sort of thing?"

"Well, it needs to be affectionate, declawed, and neutered, I guess."

"Well, then, these are the ones you'll want to see. These are neutered males and these six cages house the ones with the most easy-going dispositions."

Renn perused each cage, but they somehow all looked alike, except one. A large, laid-back male regarded her intently, through brilliant green eyes. He had thick, peach and white colored fur, with a smushed-in nose. The woman smiled, "That's Friday. He's a tom. He's a sweetie. Do you want to hold him?"

"Yes," Renn answered, "I think I'd like that. Thanks."

The woman talked baby talk to the cat, as she laid him in Renn's arms, where he snuggled.

Renn grinned happily. "Friendly, isn't he?"

The redhead answered with a delighted laugh. "Friendly Friday. I'll have to remember that."

He was immediately purring and chewing on his right forepaw.

Renn asked, "Is something wrong with his foot?"

"Oh, no, I forgot to mention it, but he sucks his thumb when he's happy."

"You're joking, right?"

"No, I'm serious. He's doing it now. He does it every time you hold him."

Renn smiled and said, "He's wonderful. I'll take him."

A minute later, Friday paced slowly back and forth over the paperwork she filled out on the counter. He swished his tail in her face, making her laugh.

The woman said they guaranteed him for thirty days, and if for some reason he didn't work out, she could trade him in on a another model of her choice.

Renn laughed at the idea and said, "I'll keep that in mind."

She and Friday stopped at the Pets R Us store, and he waited patiently in her arms, while she bought cat food, and toys, kitty treats, a litter box, forty pounds of litter and dishes. She found a catnip ball, which had always intrigued her and added that to the cart as well.

Friday began purring loudly when she finally slid behind the wheel of her car.

"Do you think you'll like belonging to me, boy?" She scratched between his ears, and he arched his back in pleasure.

She said, "Thanks Lord. I think I'm feeling a little better already."

Unlocking her apartment door, she set Friday down and watched as he investigated every nook and cranny. She dropped the paper sack on the floor and began to fill the litter box with litter. When she looked for him, she found him deep in the sack, curling up for a nap.

She sat down to read and decided Friday had the right idea. She snuggled into the quilt on the sofa and slept. The phone rang, waking her with its foreign sound. She hadn't had a personal call in so long that she had no idea who would even be calling. When she picked it up, she heard an oddly modulated voice, giving a computerized pitch for siding, asking when they could schedule her appointment.

She laughed, sounding slightly hysterical, even to her own ears; somehow the robotic telemarketer fit nicely into her "Twilight Zone" existence.

Flipping on the television to an old movie channel, she watched some slapstick comedy, while she made popcorn. She dropped a few kernels and watched as Friday grabbed them from midair with his mouth. Before the movie was over, he was on her lap, sucking his thumb. She could feel herself relaxing, her *normal-meter* rising a degree or two in the process.

She dug the catnip ball out of the kitchen drawer and dropped it on the floor for Friday. He responded as if he were a pile of iron shavings drawn to a magnet. He batted it around playfully for a few seconds, before falling down, rolling around, and batting his feet in midair, acting like a drunken sot. She began to laugh at his antics and watched transfixed, as she felt her spirit grow lighter.

She flipped the calendar to the correct month and realized that summer was more than half gone. She would call Mike, at the office, and ask if her job was still available. She noticed that it was Thursday. She tried to remember the last time she actually felt acclimated to time and place and couldn't recall.

She thought fondly of her job, its predictable and peaceful routine. There were no surprises and that appealed to her more than anything right now.

Feeling hungry, she pulled out some chicken breasts and browned them. She put one in the freezer and stuck a potato in the microwave to bake. She opened a can of green beans and when one slid to the floor, she was tickled to find that Friday was also a green bean fan.

Setting her plate on the computer desk, she poured out a journal full of self-pity that made her feel ashamed. She just couldn't get past the horrible reality that she had killed a man, sending him to hell forever. The thought was overwhelming enough to cause despair.

Karen came to her mind often and she prayed for her, but felt ill equipped and very much a failure as a person, to say nothing of a mother. An emotional paralysis made her want to wrap in a tiny ball and hide forever.

It seemed ungrateful to even think this way, because, overall, her life had been blessed. But even as she had the thought, her eyes flooded with tears and she wept loudly, embarrassing herself. From a sunny spot on the floor, Friday watched unperturbed, as though female hysterics were an acceptable part of the daily routine.

Nineteen

At least her sheets smelled fresh and clean, she thought as she crawled between them at eight o'clock. She slept through until ten in the morning, then got up and washed her face. Her bruises were fading and her eye had lost its purple ring. Now it was only slightly yellowed and a little swollen. She noticed the scales sitting next to the commode and pulled them out. She had lost more weight. She had weighed one hundred thirty eight pounds when she moved to Kate's. The scale said she weighed one hundred eleven. She looked in the mirror, for the first time, noticing that her normally round face was gaunt and drawn. *Why didn't I notice before?*

And what had happened to those pounds? She couldn't remember dieting purposely, but knew she had lost the desire to eat. Anxiety had become a way of life, with all the commotion and threats.

Gordy had been right, and she hadn't even realized it. Actually, Gordy had been right about most things in her life. He was the best thing that had ever happened to her, holding her accountable and forcing her to deal with things before they overwhelmed her. And yet, even with his help, she had still been overwhelmed.

She wondered if she had had a breakdown. Never having had one before, she couldn't be sure.

The phone rang again, just then, wrangling her nerves. *No wonder people have heart attacks.*

The voice on the phone sounded familiar, but it took a moment to recognize the voice of Doctor Jeffries. He said, "Renn, I realize this might seem untoward, but you were supposed to return to my office for a follow-up visit. I made a note on my calendar, to call you if you hadn't returned by today."

She had no words.

He continued, "Why didn't you make an appointment before you left?"

She said, "Oh, it just slipped my mind."

He paused before saying, "You are on the edge, girl. If you lose any more weight, you'll be looking at major problems."

She felt embarrassed and cornered when she answered, "Oh, I'm actually doing much better since I saw you. Please don't give it another thought."

He said, "You don't have anorexia, but the results are the same. The heart muscle weakens. It's important that I see you again."

She said, "Honestly, I'm doing much better."

He was quiet for a second, before he added, "I guess it's your life and your body, but I hope you'll reconsider."

"Thanks for calling. Really," she said, before hanging up.

She shut his words out of her mind. *Just don't think about it. Everything's going to be all right.*

She phoned Mike, at her old office, just before noon, and he said, "I suppose you can return whenever you like, but…" After an awkward hesitation, he asked, "Renn, are you sure you want your job back?'

"Why wouldn't I?"

"I heard you were doing great at some new ministry in town and I assumed that's where the Lord wanted you."

When she didn't respond, he said, "Well, listen, I don't mean to sound like I'm prying, but you know I hope we're all in the center of God's will for us. I guess I'd just like you to consider that before asking to return. I don't want to encourage another 'Jonah in the belly of the whale' scenario. I hope you understand."

She hung up, feeling confused. How on earth was she supposed to deal with that cool reception? And what did he mean by another 'Jonah and the whale scenario'? *Lord, what do you want me to do?*

As she crawled back into bed, Friday cuddled up next to her and swished his tail in her face.

After a long nap, she rose and folded the last load of laundry, to the accompaniment of more Christmas music and found it comforting in her confusion.

Turning on her laptop, she saw that she had mail. She opened it and her heart skipped a beat to realize it was from Gordy. She read, "Renn, I know you didn't expect to hear from me, but I miss you. I want to see you. It's terribly lonely around here without you. We're all in a state of shock and grief. I thought you would want to know that Karen has gone into depression. I need you to respond to this message if you'll allow me to call. Please RSVP. Gord."

She smiled. He hated the name Gord, yet he signed his name that way for her benefit.

He missed her. They all missed her. She felt like she was full to running over and wept tears of joy for the first time in months.

She typed in: "Gordy, I'm a mess. I don't know who I am, or where I belong, but I miss you guys, too. Please tell Karen I love her and I'm sorry. I'm so sorry for disappointing you all.

But I'm just in such bad shape right now that I'd be no good to any of you. I'd love to talk to you if you want to call. If I looked a hundred years, I could never find another friend as faithful as you. I just don't know why it took me so long to see it. Love, Renn.

She pushed send, after only a brief hesitation. Not five minutes later the phone rang and Gordy said quietly, "Thanks for saying yes. I miss you."

She could hear him stifling sobs. "Gordy, are you crying?"

"If you must know, I am. Why did you run away like that?"

"I am so out of it, I don't know which way is up and I needed to be alone to figure out who I am."

"We could've helped you deal with this, babe."

"No, Gordy. I couldn't dump all this in your lap. You have enough to deal with, with the girls and the CPC. I am sorry. I feel like the girls there are more emotionally stable than I am right now."

"That's not true. You're just going through a rough patch. We've weathered those before, Renn."

"You're right, and I appreciate all you've done, but I feel like I need a little time."

"How long are we talking here, girl?"

"I'm not sure."

"Well, is it okay if I keep in touch?"

"Sure, I'd be grateful for a friend, right now, who doesn't need anything from me."

His voice was soft. "What does that mean?"

"It means that I have nothing to give right now. I'm like an empty bucket."

"I can live with that."

"Thank you, Gordy. I promise I'm not shutting you out, and I do want to come back. I do. Thanks for your kind words about how much they miss me. I feel so worthless, that I can't imagine why y'all would love me, but I'm awfully glad you do."

"Renn," he said, his voice quivering, "I'm going to be praying that you get past this in a big hurry."

She giggled, as her mind changed course. "Gordy, I got a cat."

He laughed before he said, "You did? Tell me about him."

"Well, he's three years old. His name is Friday and he's huge. He's peach and white, with long hair and a smushed-in nose. He likes to snuggle in the bottom end of a paper bag. He likes green beans and popcorn, too. Oh, and he sucks his thumb when he's happy."

"He sounds wonderful."

"Oh, he is. He makes me laugh, Gordy, and he snuggles with me and slaps his tail in my face when we're close."

"I'm glad you found a friend that makes you so happy."

She said, "He's only pinch-hitting for you while I'm away."

He sounded sad when he said, "Please, Renn, come back soon. I don't know how to get through each day without you."

"Gordy, I asked for my old job back."

He sounded distant when he said, "I have to hang up now. Bye."

She stared at the phone for a long time after he hung up. She felt so alone without him.

She fell asleep early and slept, but the faces of those she loved kept appearing in her sleep. Karen's depressed countenance, in particular, kept intruding into her rest.

In her quiet time the next morning, she asked, "Lord, am I supposed to ask for my old job back? I need to know what to do. The terrified child in me longs for peace and quiet, security and predictability. I'm practically willing to throw away the greatest loves of my life in exchange for it. Is that the wrong thing to want? Help me, Lord. I need wisdom. I don't want to hurt anyone any more than I already have. And please help me figure out how to live with myself after killing someone. Help me to know, to feel, in my heart—that I'm forgiven."

She opened her Bible for direction. Psalm 102:1-6 ministered life words to her spirit as she read: "Bless the Lord, O my soul; and all that is within me, bless His holy name. Bless the Lord, O forget not all His benefits: Who forgiveth all Thine iniquities; who healeth all Thy diseases; Who redeemeth Thy life from destruction; Who crowneth Thee with lovingkindness, and tender mercies."

Isaiah twelve, verses 1-4 also spoke clearly to her heart. "Then will you say on that day, I will give thanks to Thee, O Lord; for although Thou wast angry with me, Thine anger is turned away, and Thou dost comfort me. Behold God is my salvation. Therefore you will joyously draw water from the springs of salvation and in that day you will say, Give thanks to the Lord, call on His name. Make known His deeds among the peoples; Make them remember that His name is exalted."

All of a sudden *she knew*. She was not to hide and cower in fear, feeling unforgiven. She didn't need to insulate herself from pain anymore. That was God's job and she had usurped His position. The Word said it as plain as day. She was not to fear, but to trust. As the revelation seeped into the depths of her heart, she laid her head on her arms and wept with joy and relief.

She found Gordy's beeper number listed in her address book, and dialed the number. When he called her back a few minutes later, she said, "Gordy, may I come home?"

After a brief hesitation, he said evenly, "What made you change your mind?"

"Please, Gordy. The Lord just gave me Isaiah twelve, and it says I'm not to isolate myself in fear, but to trust and rejoice in the Lord. I have been usurping God's place in my life and I've asked Him to forgive me. Do you think you can you forgive me, Gordy? Can you all forgive me?"

He was silent for a minute. She prayed in the spirit and bit her lip. She felt pain deep in her chest, waiting for him to speak.

After what seemed an interminable length of time, he said, "Here, talk to Karen. I'll be right there."

Renn heard Karen sobbing and had to swallow tears of her own.

She said, "Karen, I'm sorry. I'm so sorry for everything. I hope we can start over. After I get settled, I want us to go visit your Mom, and see what we can do to get her some help. Would that be all right with you?"

"Oh, Renn. I have so much to tell you."

"Good, I can't wait to catch up on all the news. I'll see you in a bit, sweetie."

She started throwing her things in her duffel and knocked at Mr. Daley's neighboring apartment door. The cheerful gray haired gentleman seemed surprised to see her. She said, "Listen, Mr. Daley, I need to be gone and I wondered, could you do me a favor and take some groceries off my hands?"

"Of course, dear, I'd be glad to," he said. She loaded the food into a box and a few minutes later, set it on his kitchen table. "Thanks for helping me out," she said, hugging him and hurrying through his door.

Not ten minutes later, Gordy ran up the stairs, caught her into his arms and held her, weeping into her hair.

"Aw, babe, I've missed you so. You'll never know the huge hole you left behind."

He kissed her tenderly and she knew God had shown her the way to go. She put her arms around his waist and laid her head on his chest. After a few minutes, he settled her on the sofa. "Your face looks better."

She smiled through tears. "Gordy, God showed me something I've never understood before. He showed me that I feel safe with you. You're the first person to whom I can honestly say that." He burst into tears and threw his arms around her, holding her like he would never let her go.

Then Gordy did something odd; he sank to one knee and took her hand in his. His eyes were moist when he said, "Do you remember that day I was going to take you out to eat and twice things blew up in our faces? Well, that day I wanted to tell you something. Do you recall me mentioning that?"

She felt a knot of fear in her chest.

"Gordy, are you okay? You're scaring me."

He pulled her down onto his knee, and kissed her hand.

"Shh... listen to me, babe. I was planning to ask you to marry me."

He put his hand in his pocket and fished out a small navy velvet box, opened it and slipped a beautiful diamond ring on her fourth finger, left hand. "Please, Renn, say yes. I'm crazy about you. I thought I'd die when you left."

She gazed at him tenderly, with tears of joy overflowing from somewhere deep inside. "I don't know how you could, but I'm so glad you do. I love you with all my heart."

He dropped his head to his chest and let the tears fall. She took his chin in her hands and gently kissed his lips.

She nestled into his arms, letting her tears mix with his, as he said, "When you came into my life, I felt like the sun came out for the first time. I was crazy about you from the minute we met. I'm surprised you didn't see it written all over my face. Then when you left, I felt like something died inside. I can't tell you how glad I am that you've come back to me."

Her tears fell on his sleeve and he dried them with his kisses.

He finally said, "So what are we waiting for? I want to meet this cat of yours. What's his name?"

"Friday." She picked up the cat and laid him in Gordy's arms.

He laughed and murmured, "He looks exactly like your cat should look."

She made a face. "What does that mean?"

"He's so laid back, he's a scream."

As if to prove a point, Friday stretched to twice his length and yawned right in Gordy's arms.

They both burst out laughing. He said, "The girls are going to love him."

Renn said, "Gordy, I need to know, will you let me keep Karen?"

He gave her a wide-eyed grin. "You know what we did while you were gone? She and I got together and prayed for you and cried about you ten ways from Sunday. We have knitted our hearts together over you."

She threw her arms around his neck. "Oh Gordy," she said. "I can't believe any of this. I just don't know how you could love me after all I put you through."

He kissed her, brushing her cheek with his lips. "I'd walk through fire to get to you, Renn. Now let's go home."

She wept for joy. He tipped her head up and kissed her tears and finally he reached for his handkerchief. He dried her eyes, and said, "Those tears are precious, babe. Every one of them."

She laid her head on his chest, whispering, "You know, Gordy, I feel like God is putting Humpty Dumpty back together again inside of me. I feel like all the things that were wrong— are being healed. Can you believe it?"

"I've been claiming it for weeks now. You were in such terrible emotional pain that you couldn't feel or receive love from anyone. It just about killed me to watch it."

He paused. "Did you ever weigh yourself?"

She smiled, feeling shy. "I did."

"And?"

"I've lost twenty-seven pounds since moving to Kate's."

He looked shocked, "And why do you suppose it happened?"

"I think I was just so stressed all the time that I stopped eating, although I didn't intend to. I never even knew I was doing it. I just didn't care about food, never got hungry."

"I've heard about anxious people losing their appetites, but this is ridiculous. You eat like a regular person now, okay?"

She felt the old independent spirit rising up inside, but he read her expression, and immediately put up his index finger. "I know you feel like I'm trying to control you when I say these things, but you need to understand something very important."

He tipped her chin, to look into her eyes. "I'm not trying to control you. Exactly the opposite, in fact. I want to set you free to soar. I want to protect you and care for you. I want to encourage you and make you laugh for the next hundred years, or however long the Lord gives us. Can't you get that through that sweet, stubborn head of yours?"

His tender words cracked the remaining brittle shell around her heart. As it fell away, she could feel her anger dissipate. As she nestled deeper into his arms, she smiled and said, "Listen, do you think we could get something to eat on the way home? I'm starved."

Meet Nancy Arant Williams

Nancy Arant Williams lives in Missouri, with her husband. They own and operate the Nestle Down Inn (Christian) Bed & Breakfast in the heart of the beautiful Missouri Ozarks. She has two children, and three precious granddaughters.